---- ★ ----

"They're going to have trouble getting medics down there if the fire isn't completely out," Lillian said. The flames along the boardwalk spurted skyward again.

The crowd was quiet, the only sounds coming from distant car horns. We could see Duck Jarvis moving on the riprap. Slowly he sat up, holding his arm. Another firefighter yelled something, but Duck shook his head and began gingerly climbing from stone to stone, finding toeholds, testing them, inching forward in the near dark. Occasionally, shooting sparks fell and went out. Suddenly he lost his balance and slipped again, sliding down the riprap before catching himself. The crowd inhaled. Next to Duck, the seated figure toppled forward onto the sharp white stones.

---- ★ ----

Previously published Worldwide Mystery title by
BARBARA LEE

FINAL CLOSING

Dead Man's Fingers

Barbara Lee

WORLDWIDE®

TORONTO • NEW YORK • LONDON
AMSTERDAM • PARIS • SYDNEY • HAMBURG
STOCKHOLM • ATHENS • TOKYO • MILAN
MADRID • WARSAW • BUDAPEST • AUCKLAND

To Steve Bloom,
Without whom I'd still be using a typewriter

DEAD MAN'S FINGERS

A Worldwide Mystery/December 2000

First published by St. Martin's Press, Incorporated.

ISBN 0-373-26369-4

Acknowledgments

I am grateful to the many people who contributed their time and expertise as I researched this book. Special thanks to Lois Villemaire, Anne Arundel County Permit Application Center, who patiently answered my endless questions, and to Officer Carol Frye, Anne Arundel County Police Department; Battalion Chief Ronald C. Fleischmann, Anne Arundel County EMS/Fire/Rescue; Stephanie Cooke, Child Protective Services, Anne Arundel County Department of Social Services; Michael Bartlinski, Associated Psychotherapists of Maryland; Jennifer Purcell, University of Maryland Center for Environmental Science, Horn Point Laboratory; Richard Lego, Maryland Department of the Environment, Oil Control Program; Jeffrey Thompson, Maryland Department of Natural Resources, Non-Tidal Wetlands Division; Steve Szymanski, Scardina Plumbing; Barbara Feaga, Howard County Board of Elections; real estate agents Carol Cross and Fran Haines, and Joan Machinchick, who helped me more than she knows. Finally, my love and thanks to my husband, Bob, for his faith that books can be finished.

ONE

IF THE TRUE PURPOSE of marriage is to create a functioning social unit, my clients were making an awful mess of it. Toxic, corrosive words—his—hung in the hot air. The wife turned her face away from me, then slid into the passenger seat of their luxury car and stared straight ahead. Vincent Darner bent down to view his wife at eye level through the driver's side window.

"Can't let things be, can you, Charlotte? Always have to get your two cents in."

Go ahead, I dared him silently, say something else. Just one more thing. Call your wife a moron again. He stared at his wife a bit longer, and when she didn't move, he straightened up, collected a sheaf of legal papers spread out on the roof of his car, and shoved them at me.

"Sooner than later," he said. "And you can tell Lillian I said so."

I took the signed contract from him. Behind us, sunlight swept through the high, dense woods, tracing lacy patterns on the parched ground. The whine of a boat's motor sliced through the stillness. He waited for a few seconds, watching me, then got in the car beside his wife, turned over the engine, and backed up the pitted road. A tiny stone flew up under the tires, pinging against the trunk of my car.

Which is how a few minutes later I came to find myself standing on the public beach at Knapp's Point, looking out over the Magothy River. My former life in the New York advertising world had had its stresses, but none compared to a real estate agent's involuntary glimpse into clients' personal lives. I took another deep breath, my speeding thoughts ebbing a little. Charlotte Darner's stricken face retreated.

The watery horizon rippled with waves of afternoon heat. Below me, H. L. Mencken's fish factory teemed with more than fish. Thousands of sea nettles, large and small, had blown into obscure corners of the Magothy in their brainless search for water more saline. Transparent umbrellas pulsed below the surface, floating streamers of limpid slime like smoky ruffled arms. Around the circumference of each medusa, writhing hairlike tentacles held tiny loaded harpoons of toxin. I watched, absorbed, the Darners temporarily forgotten, as the jellyfish drifted and pulsed, colliding, spearing each other for lunch. Eat your grandson. Devour your mother. Darwin reigns.

Sea nettles are to Marylanders what cockroaches are to New Yorkers. Nasty but not fatal. And like cockroaches you can't kill them off. You can only fight back. But even that was tougher than usual this July. Local stores were running out of queen-size pantyhose and Vaseline, the first lines of defense against the stings. If you were unlucky enough to be stung, you'd better have vinegar or meat tenderizer on hand to keep stray harpoons from firing again. And baking soda to soothe the burning pain. All Marylanders, even newcomers like me, knew the drill.

Despite the heat, or maybe because of it, I found I was shivering. After a mild, short and dry winter, the weather had turned wickedly hot and dry. The level of the Magothy was low. Behind me, beyond the strip of crummy beach, underneath a picnic table, a miserable dog lay tied to a stake, panting, his mouth black with dirt. A young teenage boy rode a fat-wheeled mountain bicycle up and down the beach, yelling at the dog, sending up waves of dirty sand. From the water came the vexing drone of Jet Skis, waterborne motorbikes, one after the other, chasing, jumping wakes amid churning foam, their riders oblivious to the beating sun. Somewhere, a child wailed.

I roused myself. Vince Darner invaded my thoughts again. He was running for a seat in the Maryland senate, a fact I found astonishing, given his ugly manners. I pondered my options. I could tear up the property listing the Darners had just signed. Or I could find a buyer for the valuable waterfront acres. Reason triumphed, of course. Why lose a sale because I didn't like the Darners' relationship? Besides, you can just never tell about other people's marriages. Stay out of it, I told myself.

Undoubtedly, that was what my aunt, Lillian Weber, would

have advised. And after nearly forty years selling real estate, she was usually right. Besides, the Darners were more her clients than mine. My still-new real estate license entitled me to help her list and sell houses, not choose our clients. It had been at her request—and in her stead—that I had agreed to meet Vincent and Charlotte Darner at Knapp's Point this hot Sunday afternoon. Lillian wasn't much given to doing business in the woods on the roof of a car but Vincent Darner had been in a big hurry to get the property listed. And so my aunt, as always, obliged when she could.

I looked around Knapp's Point. It wasn't much different from all the other old beach communities that lined the irregular western shore of the Chesapeake Bay. Tucked away from the main roads, the beach was strewn with litter from teenage drinking parties. Nearby, people lived out their lives—like their parents and grandparents before them—in an eccentric collection of small houses. Some were mere feet from the seawall, others fronted rectangles of tired grass leading to long docks that repeated in parallel lines along the shore.

Nearest the beach, a row of small ranch houses—set sideways like mobile homes in a trailer park—gave each homeowner his precious feet of waterfront. Fences, mostly chain link and obscuring nothing, enclosed concrete patios covered with prickly, fading AstroTurf. This Sunday afternoon, homeowners tinkered with boats and clucked over their dying lawns.

Knapp's Point was in the awkward stage of gentrification. And it was going to get worse before it got better. Behind the row of waterfront ranchers were more nondescript homes, arranged helter skelter across narrow rutted lanes. But farther from the water lay a development of new houses: popular four-bedroom, two-car garage colonials built too close together on open farmland, their wide pale driveways the first and last thing you noticed. A few were still under construction. Just last summer it had all been dirt, with bulldozers dispatching any trees that dared to impede their progress.

To my right, beyond the public beach and small waterfront houses, was the Darners' property, a stretch of cool woods and adjacent farmlands that bordered the deep water of the Magothy. Soon executive homes would spring from the forest. A wise developer would keep the trees and add careful landscaping. Still, it wouldn't change the fact that for years to come, the new owners would confront old Knapp's Point every time they looked out their windows.

I wondered if I'd spend half a million to live here. No, probably not. Besides, the point was moot. Luck had smiled, and in a matter of days I would own a bungalow near a lovely secluded cove on nearby Weller's Creek.

Movement from the end house of the row of ranchers nearest the beach interrupted my drifting thoughts. As I watched, a woman dressed in a halter and torn cutoffs, her long and lightened hair held back by a kerchief, opened the screen door with her hip. In her hands, a plate of dark meat and a fork. The door banged behind her. With the expertise of long practice, she slid the glistening slab onto an outdoor grill. Blood splattered over the coals. The air filled with the maddening smell of seared meat. On the beach, the dog clamored to his feet.

The screen door opened silently a second time. Behind the woman, her husband, his body showing only a hint of fat to come, took a deep last drag on his cigarette and flicked it onto the concrete patio. He slid behind her, and in a quick silent move, grabbed her around her bare middle and playfully drew her back to him. Reaching under her halter for her breasts, he seized one in each hand.

"Get off of me, Duck Jarvis." The woman wiggled, then jerked away to face him, still holding the fork and bloody plate. On the beach, the boy on the bicycle stopped and watched. "You know I don't like you doing that when the kids can see."

He spat, moved toward her a second time, then thought better of it. "The kids ain't got nothing to do with it and you know it." He slammed off, down the concrete patio, turning back once before reaching the chain link gate. "Things need to fucking change around here or..."

His thought hovered unfinished as he headed across the browning grass to a Jet Ski waiting near the water. The chain-link gate banged and was quiet.

The woman had not followed him with her eyes, staring instead at the spitting meat on the grill. She turned it over once, then wiped her forehead on a glistening upper arm. A girl, a young version of her mother, her posture uneasy, came out of the house. The woman flipped the dripping steak onto the plate and handed it to her. "Your father's doesn't want it." She went into the house. The girl looked at the plate as if she didn't know how it came to be in her hand, then put it down on a small table and disappeared around the side of the house.

I looked away, toward the quivering horizon. My pulse had resumed its heart-sickening tilt. Everywhere the same corrosive ties, people lashed together in marriage, chafing and wounding each other. Were the Darners even now playing out the same scene? Well, not exactly the same, perhaps, but similar enough.

With one last glance at the water, I began the long trudge to my car. Ahead of me, the Jarvis girl darted across the road and headed for a cottage tucked serenely among the trees. I hadn't noticed it before. A bungalow, with an enclosed porch and rows of half-open jalousie windows, it looked trim and well kept. A long dock trailed from a scruffy patch of sand through swaying sea grasses to deeper water. The girl glanced once over her shoulder.

Suddenly, behind me, came the drone of a Jet Ski. As I turned, Duck Jarvis drew near—nearer the shore, nearer the long dock—then quickly retreated, fleeing a trail of glittering foam. The cottage porch door opened. A young woman in casually perfect clothes, her dark hair cropped close, ran down the path to the dock. She carried a cell phone in her hands. She yelled words I couldn't understand, but her anger was unmistakable in the blistering afternoon air. For a second time, the boy on the beach stopped his monotonous back and forth bicycling to watch and listen. His sister had disappeared.

And for a second time, Duck Jarvis buzzed the shore, veering at the last second to miss the dock. A second retreat, then back again, closer. Suddenly the motor gunned and he was over, swallowed by the moving water. The Jet Ski was on its own now, almost upon the dock. The woman with the phone leaped back several yards. The engine died, but it was too late. A crashing sound as cruising fiberglass splintered half-rotted wood. I glanced as the woman punched three short jabs on the phone, put it to her ear, then smiled.

Duck Jarvis thrashed. Yelping and slapping at the burning stings along his legs, on his arms, chest, and face, he tore himself from the water. Then he collapsed to roll on the beach, trying to smother the stings in hot sand. Beyond him, the dog, glad for the diversion perhaps, barked a few times, then fell back into the dirt, silent. The teenage boy dropped his bike and ran over to where his father writhed.

"Don't just stand there. Get your mother." The boy stood motionless. "Are you fucking deaf? Get your mother." The boy turned and ran lightly to the end house. From the corner of my eye, I saw his sister dart back across the furrowed road, then vanish behind the narrow houses.

The Jet Ski had gone aground in a stretch of tall grasses that filled the far cove. Time hovered, the sun pounded, the hot air scorched my throat. Duck Jarvis's yells hovered in the motionless air. Neighbors, I saw, had opened their screen doors, taking in the scene from decks and patios. Others looked up from their boats. The girl wandered down between two houses and stood near me, watching. Her toe kicked again and again at the sand. I looked at her face. She didn't even know she was doing it. I moved closer.

"Is your dad going to be okay?" She looked up, surprised, then she nodded. I guessed her age at about eight or nine. "Can I do anything to help?"

"Nah. My mom will get baking soda. For the stings." My turn to nod. "He and her"—she pointed toward the woman with the cordless phone—"they fight all the time."

In the distance, a siren blared, then grew louder. In a couple of minutes, a police cruiser pulled up. Then another. Behind them a lumbering EMS vehicle tore down the beach to where Duck Jarvis lay flailing in the dirty sand, howling obscenities. His wife in halter and shorts had disappeared.

"What do they fight about?"

"His Jet Ski. Lauren—that's her name—she don't like the noise it makes. And that makes my dad mad. Then he does it more to make her even madder."

The words were noncommittal, uninvolved. I looked again at her, her blond hair sprayed over her shoulders, her little girl's short shorts barely covering the tops of her legs. And your parents? I wanted to ask. Do they also fight all the time? But she had turned away and was walking along the water toward the Darners' woods, her back turned from the unhappy scene.

Disgusted by my own curiosity, I tried to turn away, too, and found I couldn't. All these people bound by awful ties to one another. Some by blood and some by marriage. Some just by geography.

On the beach, Duck Jarvis had pushed away the medics and was smearing on the paste his wife offered. The young woman with the phone conferred with a uniformed cop. Another cop, his sunglasses secured behind his head with a tight sports band, inspected the damage to her dock and wrote something in a small notebook. The Jet Ski lay silent, floating in the shore grasses. Neighbors began to speak to each other in low tones, shaking their heads. One woman said something to the girl, but she turned her head and kept walking.

Hot and depressed, I trudged back to my car in the woods and opened the trunk to remove a For Sale sign. Green and white for Weber Realty. The dry soil made planting it at the edge of the Darners' property harder than usual. Finally, sweating but satisfied that it would stay upright, I attached the narrow nameplate that hung below: Eve Elliott or Lillian Weber, our phone number. Getting in my car, I was aware that the dust that had accumulated on the BMW's burgundy paint had filtered over me. I turned up the drive, not looking back.

TWO

I FOUND MY AUNT uncharacteristically deep in thought. Behind her, across her deck and beyond the scorched lawn, the Magothy shimmered. I pulled up a sturdy Adirondack chair. Above us a wide green striped awning shaded the deck from the baking afternoon sun. I handed her the Darners' contract.

"That was fun."

"What happened?"

"Vincent Darner happened. I don't see how he'll ever get elected. Too mean."

Lillian was fiddling with the thick sheaf of legal papers I'd handed her, expertly flipping through them to make sure everything was in order. She looked up, satisfied. "He can be a little abrupt, I suppose."

"Abrupt? Good Lord, Lillian, every time his poor wife so much as opened her mouth to say something, he was all over her. Real nastiness for no reason. She finally shut up." I had a picture of Charlotte Darner sitting silently in the car, facing the windshield, watching nothing, thinking God knows what. "And she sort of hinted that the property was originally hers."

My aunt nodded. "Her grandfather and uncle used to farm it and run a small general store and marina. When they died, that was the end of that." Lillian was now stacking the pile of papers, first one way, then the other, on the wide arm of her chair. "I've always wondered when she and Vince would do something with it. But they never did. Smart move, probably. It's worth a lot more now. I don't expect any trouble selling it."

"So what's their big hurry to sell?"

"He didn't say and I didn't ask." I watched my aunt struggle with some thoughts, her mouth pursed. "I've known Vince a long time. He grew up poor, but he's done okay for himself. Built that chain of lumber stores." She looked over at me. "To answer your question, I would guess he needs campaign money.''

"But why not just get a loan and put the land up as collateral? It's certainly easier and faster.''

Lillian shrugged. "I don't know and it's none of my business.'' She straightened the already straight pile of paper. "Not that Vince's money pressures are any excuse for his being rude to Charlotte.'' She squinted into the sun. "Let's just get it sold quick. I suspect a fair amount of interest. With so few parcels left.''

"What about the environmental stuff?''

"We'll have a perc test done, but the area around Knapp's Point always tests just fine. And the soil is certainly dry enough this summer to swallow a few buckets of water.''

Selling waterfront real estate anywhere these days meant exacting attention to environmental matters. But in Anne Arundel County, Maryland, on the western edge of the Chesapeake Bay, the environmental spotlight shone with another level of wattage altogether. To further complicate things, Pines on Magothy and many of the surrounding communities had no public water or sewers. That meant wells and septic tanks. And sometimes trouble.

A perc test, I'd discovered, was a remarkably low-tech affair. Using a backhoe to dig a hole ten feet deep and four feet on either side, a plumbing contractor would dump in ten gallons of water, then time how long it took for the water to disappear. If the water was absorbed in three or four minutes, you were home free. If twenty minutes later you were still looking at a puddle, there were going to be problems. Big, expensive problems, often deal-breaker problems. And if as the backhoe dug, water rose in the dark hole, you might as well just give your land away. If you could.

"I'll call Mitch,'' Lillian was saying.

I wasn't surprised. Mitch Gaylin, with his infuriating good looks and charm to match, was Weber Realty's biggest competitor, having expanded Gaylin Realty from a single office in Annapolis to a well-managed chain of offices both north and south of Maryland's capital city. He was now buying up tracts of waterfront property in order to develop and build lavish new homes. He was also fair and respected by those who did business with him. Which didn't quiet the jumble of emotions that rose to the surface every time I heard his name.

"I thought he was doing custom houses. Not subdivisions."

Lillian shook her head. "Both. But he hires good architects and builders—the ones who do the least harm to the environment." I was amazed all over again at how completely my aunt had been won over by this ambitious and attractive man. "And he'd be sensitive to the Knapp's Point community. Though he can do a deal."

I looked over at Lillian. This last point was exactly why my aunt still went to work every day. At seventy-four, she was no more ready to retire than Mitch Gaylin—thirty years her junior—was. As for Weber Realty, there had been good times and bad times since my uncle Max had died two years ago. His death had been unexpected, in the middle of a prolonged recession that had hit the real estate market hard. It had been about the same time that Mitch, sensing a lull before opportunities to come, had quietly opened his first office in Annapolis.

At first, after my uncle's death, Lillian had floundered. Pressed for cash, with business stagnant, Weber Realty's solitary office on Mountain Road had come under Mitch's hungry gaze. But when the economy had improved, she'd also rallied. And he'd backed off. Lillian had found that his uncompromising ethics matched her own. They became friendly rivals and fast friends.

As had I. But intense personal interest on his part had begun to make me a little uneasy, then exasperated. Sometimes I even had the distinct feeling I was not unlike a prized hunk of waterfront Mitch Gaylin wanted. Whatever its cost.

"Speaking of development," Lillian was saying, "did you see that piece in the *Leader* this morning? About that young woman who…" My aunt was leaning over, rummaging around in a pile of newspapers on the deck beside her chair. "Who…oh, you know. The one who's going to do that documentary about overdevelopment ruining the Magothy. Lauren Somebody."

Lauren Somebody. The Jet Ski incident at Knapp's Point washed across my mind and I wondered if I had enough energy to tell Lillian.

"Here it is. Lauren DeWitt." My aunt had righted herself and was studying the paper. "She's so young. But she's making a lot of people very nervous. Me included. Since she'll probably have something to say about the Darner land."

I scanned the interview, looking closely at the photograph accompanying the article, then took a deep breath. "Lillian, when I was there an hour ago I watched some guy on a Jet Ski take out her dock. She called the cops." I described the scene to Lillian, who shook her head.

I put the paper down. "Though, you know, she's right. This whole area's already way overdeveloped."

"Sure, she's right. Of course we need to slow down. I'm sure this whole thing is going to explode in the next election. The schools and roads can't keep up. And Mountain Road..." She stopped, threw up her hands.

With just two lanes, Mountain Road was the only way in and out of the Magothy area. I didn't want to think about the back-ups and traffic jams. Nor, apparently, did the State Highway Administration, though there were persistent reports of studies and bypasses.

"If people around here know development has to be slowed, why are they so nervous about what Lauren DeWitt has to say?" I asked.

Lillian fiddled with her empty iced-tea glass. "It's the way she's going about it, I think. And her inflexibility. Everything's so black and white. She wants absolutely *no* more development. And she's not just documenting the development, or overde-velopment, she's also trying to change things."

"And the outsider thing." I knew all about being an outsider in Maryland.

"Of course. Plus—and we both know this is the real rea-son—there's just so much money involved," said Lillian. "Way too much."

My aunt fidgeted in the enormous chair, trying to make herself more comfortable. The empty plastic glass fell, rolling off the deck. I started to get up.

"Later," she said, her eyes following it onto the grass below. "You know..." I waited. "I ran into Florence this morning in Lyle's."

Florence Rainey was Lillian's longtime next-door neighbor, a recent widow with one grown son who lived with her. Their neat rambler was hidden in the dense trees, across a small stream and the irregular terrain that lay beyond the public right-of-way bordering Lillian's property.

"Something she said sort of bothered me."

I waited some more. Then impatience took over. "And?"

My aunt cleared her throat. "Well, for some reason she didn't tell the truth."

"She lied? About what?"

"Not lied, I don't think. No."

I couldn't think of a word that meant lie and not lie. "What then? What did she not exactly lie about?"

"About the number of trees they'll have to take down in order for Carl to have his house. And about the number of feet of variance he'll need," Lillian said. "Still, I really don't think Florence is lying exactly. It's more like she's putting the best face on things."

My aunt was staring at the water, sparkling in the distance. When she turned back to look at me, she was shaking her head. I was aware, as I had been a lot lately, that the ratio of scalp to hair was increasing. And the blue circles under her eyes seemed to be dug deeper into thinning skin.

"That house scares me, Eve. It's not just that it's too big. It's where it's going to go. And all the concrete for the driveway." She turned and pointed across her lawn. The occasional oak or sycamore eased the starkness of her water view. "You see that big old white oak? Over there. On the other side of the right-of-way?" I nodded. "Well that's where it begins. That whole line of trees will have to go in order for the bulldozers to get down there."

"Can he do that? Take down all those old trees?"

"Maybe. I'm sure his plan calls for planting replacement

trees but it's never the same. It'll depend on what happens at the hearing tomorrow.'' My mind wandered as Lillian launched into a discussion of real estate principles and environmental law. The thousand and one legal terms I'd memorized to pass the state licensing exam had fled to some dark corner of my memory. Where most of them belonged. With one exception: If it related to waterfront property or water rights, Anne Arundel County's meandering shoreline with estuaries and wetlands made it relevant.

"I suppose it also depends on Dick Hubbard," Lillian was saying.

"Who is he?"

"Annapolis attorney. Specializes in environmental issues. Carl's hired him to see that he gets his building permit. You'll like him," she said. "Which may be a problem. Everybody in Anne Arundel County likes him. So, he usually gets what..." She stopped herself. "We'll just have to see tomorrow."

"Lillian, where did Carl Rainey get the money to build a new house? And pay an attorney?" I thought about the modest rambler. "He and his mother don't seem to have the kind of money that it takes."

Lillian shrugged. "I gather when Florence's husband, Leon, died about a year ago, there was a life insurance policy."

"What did he die from?"

"Heart disease." She looked over at me. "Don't get any funny ideas. Leon had the policy forever. Before his heart was so bad. I know that for a fact. You hear me?"

"I hear."

She recrossed her legs. "You know, I feel as if I've been gossiping for the last hour. First the Darners. Now Florence and Carl."

"It's me, remember? I don't know enough people in Anne Arundel County to be a security risk. But I've got another question. Why would Florence not tell you the truth about the number of trees that need to be cut to build a new house? Surely she knows that Carl's plans are open for the public to see? And the hearing... You'll be there. And with that big Public Notice sign right out front, so will everyone else in the Pines."

"Yes, yes, but somehow..." I knew what my aunt was thinking: that a friend and neighbor of forty years was trying to smooth things over before they grew disagreeable. No wonder Lillian was bothered. If Florence Rainey felt compelled to bend the truth now, she must be worried that there was trouble ahead. That her son's plans had gone too far.

Lillian and I sat in silence. With her long iced-tea spoon she traced the jagged line the awning's shadow made across her outstretched legs. Then, even as I watched, she shook off her negative thoughts.

"I'm getting way ahead of myself. I'm sure we can work something out tomorrow at the hearing."

"Weller going to be there?"

She nodded. Weller Church was Lillian's longtime friend and arguably Annapolis's best attorney, one with deep roots in Anne Arundel County and a habit of getting what he wanted. He'd been named for Weller's Creek, which had been named generations earlier for his mother's family.

"So what did he suggest you do? Other than go to the hearing tomorrow morning and voice your concerns?"

"Just that. He plans to ask that the final ruling be postponed so we can gather our own information." She turned to look at me. "You know, I don't oppose Carl's house. I would never do that. I just think it needs to be modified so it fits in better with the site. And not so much driveway. I tried to tell Florence that."

"Want me to come with you tomorrow?"

"Sure. If you like."

Lillian, I'd learned long ago, worked hard to keep her deepest fears to herself, hidden under her it-will-all-work-out-for-the-best philosophy. Still, this time, she was worried. I followed her glance to the water. If Carl Rainey had his way, the tantalizing glimpses of the Magothy shimmering through tall trees would be gone. To be replaced by a view-impeding monster of a house. A classic example of what happened when people with no taste had too much money.

I learned over and squeezed her hand. Then I got up to retrieve the plastic tumbler. The deck railing was surprisingly hot and dry to the touch.

THREE

LILLIAN WAS fishing her briefcase out of her Cadillac when I pulled into a parking place behind her the next morning in Annapolis. Despite the ferocious early morning heat—already 90 degrees if the radio announcer could be believed—she was dressed in a full-skirted lime green suit. I caught up with her halfway across Calvert Street as she headed for the Arundel Center.

"Lillian?" She turned, a movement that had less flexibility than in past years. "Morning. Where's Weller?"

"Good morning. He called earlier to say he'd be a little late. Had some kind of plumbing emergency. Septic tank, I think. He'll be here in a bit. But no matter. You're here and I'm glad. We'll just get started without him if necessary."

"You feel comfortable with that?"

She stopped in the middle of the street in order to look directly at me. "Of course I feel comfortable with that. These are my neighbors and my friends."

Neighbors, yes. Friends, I wasn't so sure. When it came to waterfront property in Maryland all bets were off. Well, if she wasn't going to worry, neither was I.

Others were arriving now, people I knew by sight. Their morning faces were somber and sleepy and shiny from the heat. Lillian was soon surrounded and chatting with her neighbors. An elderly man she greeted by name held the courthouse door for her, then made the mistake of trying to guide her by the elbow.

"Step lively now," he said.

Lillian smiled stiffly, pulling free of him as soon as she decently could.

I recognized Marian Beall from the Lido Beach Inn. If Pines on Magothy had an unofficial mayor, it would have to be the

smart, gossipy owner of its only bar. To her credit, she did try
to get her information right.

The lobby was cool. People relaxed, laughing a little, as if
surprised to be comfortable. On the surface, it was just another
sweltering day under the air-conditioning. But beneath the
laughter, I could feel a nervous undercurrent. And despite Lillian's confident words, there was tension around her mouth.

Through the milling crowd, I got glimpses of Florence Rainey and her son, Carl, seated on a bench against the wall. There
was a kind of mutual grimness about them, echoing what I was
feeling. Carl Rainey stood up. A few from the community
greeted him. Others drifted in the opposite direction, checking
with the guard about the whereabouts of the hearing room.

Florence Rainey tested a smile, but it wasn't very convincing.
I glanced at my watch. Twenty after nine. The hearing was set
for nine-thirty. No Weller Church.

A sleek, good-looking man in a tan summer suit, the jacket
slung over his shoulder and his shirt collar open and minus a
tie, strode up to the Raineys for a word. There was something
different, more purposeful about him. Carl turned to greet him,
visibly relieved.

"Dick Hubbard?" I asked Lillian, who nodded.

The lawyer and environmental consultant. I wondered about
the missing tie and decided it was artifice, a kind of casual look
to keep people off guard. This was just a relaxed gathering
among friends, it seemed to say. No way Weller Church would
show up not wearing his usual bow tie and summer suit. Seer-
sucker it would be, and sweat he would, but it would mark the
old-fashioned respect he paid his clients and rivals alike.

The security guard said something I couldn't hear, then
pointed to a door to the left, past a reception desk and around
a corner. Nearby Dick Hubbard was greeting others, laughing
and chatting. The tension had dissipated somewhat. The crowd
filed in. I sorted through them one more time, looking for the
bow-tied lawyer.

"He'll be here." Lillian was at my elbow. "Let's just get
this over with."

The hearing room was wood paneled, with the seal of Mary-

land dominating the front wall. Pews formed a semicircle for
the gallery. An administrative hearing officer, a man in his early
sixties whose wife must have been responsible for his haircut,
was already seated on a raised platform under the seal. Between
him and the audience was a grouping of chairs and tables for
the parties involved. There was a podium with a mike and a
machine for the court stenographer.

"You know anything about this hearing officer?" I whispered.

Lillian frowned. "Will you just relax? His name is Earl Greg-
ory and he's been doing this forever. Weller knows him."

At Dick Hubbard's cue, the Raineys took seats on the far
right side. After greeting the hearing officer, he sat down with
his back to the audience. Lillian and I found chairs on the left,
leaving an empty one for Weller. Between the empty chair and
the environmental consultant sat a small man with the resigned
manner of one who lives in the shadow of people bigger than
he. He shuffled the papers on the table before him.

"Who's that?"

"I think he's the county's zoning analyst. With the Department of Planning and Code Enforcement," said Lillian. "It's
his job to look over Carl's plans and to go out to the property
to check things out."

The room was beginning to fill up. I glanced over at the
Raineys. Neither met my glance, but Dick Hubbard smiled
widely in my direction.

"Who is Ms. Weber?" asked the hearing officer. Lillian
raised her hand. He smiled. "I guess a few years ago I'd be
calling you Mrs. Weber, wouldn't I? But things have changed
and now you're Ms. Weber."

Lillian looked puzzled, then shrugged and nodded. The hearing officer glanced at the clock on the wall. The stenographer
found her seat, her back to us, her posture relaxed. The hearing
officer leaned in her direction. She looked around and shook
her head.

"Ms. Weber," he said, "am I to understand that your attorney is not yet here?" Lillian nodded again. "We'll wait for

another five minutes, then we have to start. There are others on the docket this morning."

"Why don't we just begin," said Lillian. "I'm sure he'll be along shortly." She looked across at the Raineys. Carl stared back. Florence, flushing as red as the flowers on her summer dress, looked down at her hands.

After administering the oath, the hearing officer announced the case number and the Rainey's address in the Pines. "Now," he said, looking up, "may I have the names of those expecting to testify this morning?" Starting on his left, he acknowledged the Raineys each by name, then Dick Hubbard and the zoning analyst, John Battles. Next came Lillian, then me. "And you are?"

"Eve Elliott. Mrs. Weber is my aunt."

"Oh, it's Mrs. Weber," he said, looking back at Lillian. "I guess some of us still like that Mrs. Hard to say Ms. Ms. Ms." He tried it a few more times. "Doesn't roll off the tongue, does it?" He looked out at the audience, over the half glasses that were attached to a rope around his neck. "Just a little humor, folks. We're not going to hang anyone here today." I glanced over at Lillian, who clearly couldn't believe her ears. Next there'd probably be Polish jokes. A latecomer in the back abruptly shut the courtroom door.

Florence Rainey testified that the hearing had been advertised by a sign in front of the property for more than fourteen days prior to this hearing. Then the hearing officer launched into a detailed description of the site where Carl hoped to build his house.

"The property," he said, "is zoned R-5 residential and has been classified as a Limited Development Area within the Chesapeake Bay Critical Area." The audience was soon coughing and fidgeting. The shine on their faces had been dried by the icy air-conditioning. Beside me, Lillian shivered in her suit jacket. "The Anne Arundel County Code requires a minimum one-hundred-foot buffer landward from any tributary stream. And Section 1A-105 (c) prohibits any development on steep slopes, that is, fifteen percent or greater. It's my understanding that in this case neither requirement can be met. And Mr. Rai-

ney''—here, the hearing officer looked up and nodded at Carl—
''is also petitioning to increase the number of feet of impervious
surface.'' This time his eyebrows went up and stayed up a bit,
then he looked over the half glasses directly at Dick Hubbard.
''Is that right, Mr. Hubbard? You are petitioning for almost ten
thousand square feet of impervious surface?''

''Yes, that is correct.''

''Seems like a lot of concrete. What are the dimensions of
the site again?''

Dick Hubbard told him. ''My client, as you can see from our
plan, will make every attempt to preserve the character of the
site. He will also take every reasonable step to ensure that run-
off and erosion during the construction stage will be kept to a
minimum. You will note,'' he said, ''that of the trees that of
necessity will be removed, all will be replaced on a two-to-one
ratio. I particularly want Mrs. Weber to know that.'' He looked
over at Lillian, who nodded.

''Noted, Mr. Hubbard.'' The hearing officer reviewed the
papers. ''Let me summarize for our many interested observers
this morning.'' He was smiling again, determined to keep things
cordial. ''The petitioner, Carl Rainey, is seeking three variances: eighteen feet instead of the one-hundred-foot minimum
buffer required for tributary streams. Secondly, he wants to develop some steep slopes. Thirdly, he has petitioned for a variance from the usual twenty-five percent of impervious surface
for a lot of one acre or less.'' He looked over his glasses at the
bored, squirming crowd. ''Impervious surface means that rain
can't get through it. Like concrete. Now, have I got that all
correct, Mr. Hubbard?'' Dick Hubbard nodded, smiled at Lillian, and sat down. The stenographer had been typing steadily
now, her fingers and shoulders relaxed. ''Okay, Mr. Battles,
your turn.''

The county's zoning analyst approached the podium. He
looked to be in his late forties, with his eyes dulled from too
many years in a government job. He testified that he'd reviewed
the Rainey's proposal along with the detailed site plan that Dick
Hubbard had filed in their behalf. ''On first blush,'' he said, ''it
would seem...''

There was a stir in the audience. Lauren DeWitt made her way along the left side of the courtroom and sat down in the chair beside Lillian, the one left empty for Weller Church. Dressed in navy linen, the pointed collar of her suit turned up to frame her face, she was more stunning up close than at a distance. She turned to Lillian, leaning in to whisper something into my aunt's ear.

"On first blush," the zoning analyst began again, "it would seem…"

"And you are?" the hearing officer interrupted.

"Lauren DeWitt. My apologies to the court for my lateness. I'm here to bring to your attention some irregularities with this site."

The audience murmured. Across the room, Carl Rainey's expression darkened and he ran his hand through his sandy hair. His mother looked worried. I couldn't see Dick Hubbard's face, since the zoning analyst was standing in front of him.

The hearing officer stared at Lauren. It was hard not to. The zoning analyst made a show of taking a big, annoyed breath.

"Do you represent Mrs. Weber?" the hearing officer asked her.

"In a way, yes," Lauren said. People in the room stirred, but it was nothing like Lillian's sudden and amazed turn of the head. "And all Maryland's citizens who are negatively impacted by excessive development. In this case, Mrs. Weber will be the most immediately impacted as she lives next door." She touched my aunt's shoulder. My aunt sat frozen, dumbstruck. "I've researched the documents and I have here a copy of the original recorded plat." She stood up and passed the document to the hearing officer.

Dick Hubbard was on his feet now, crowding the zoning analyst from his place at the podium. "You have only to review the plan and see…"

"A mistake has been made," Lauren DeWitt said, also rising from her seat. "You'll see that this lot was never recorded as a separate buildable lot. A legal plat was never recorded for it."

"Sit down, Ms. DeWitt." The hearing officer looked over at

Dick Hubbard. "You too, Mr. Hubbard. You'll both get your chance."

Next to me Lillian was shaking in distress, an unusual state for her. I had seen my aunt handle real estate settlements with all parties shrieking and muttering. But this was different somehow, more personal. She gathered herself and raised her hand. The hearing officer looked in her direction.

"Mrs. Weber, you will also have your chance to speak in a minute." He sat back, all business now. "Everyone will. Understood? First things first. Now, Mr. Battles?"

The zoning analyst resumed his place at the podium, then cleared his throat and droned his piece about inspecting the site. "It's clear," he said, "that this property, which is just over half of the original site, is burdened with several natural problems that will make construction difficult if not impossible without the variances requested by the petitioners. These hardships," he said, "are the result of essential characteristics of the land, and no fault of the petitioners."

Lauren DeWitt was on her feet again, addressing the hearing officer. "Sir, the site in question is not a separate lot. It was recorded as one parcel and must be handled that way. That"— she nodded at the document in his hand—"is a copy of the legal plat which shows that the date of 1933..."

"Sit down, Ms. DeWitt. This is the last time I will tell you."

I looked around. Where was Weller? Someone in the audience, a man I didn't know, suddenly stood up and looked directly at Lauren DeWitt.

"Why don't you go back to wherever the hell you come from," he said. "We don't need you here telling us our business." She sat quietly, looking at him, only her tapping fingers giving away any emotion. In the back of the courtroom, the security guard, his radio in his hand, stood waiting, tension in his face. The buzzing in the crowd increased.

"Order." It was a bellow. "Everyone sit down and be quiet. Or else you will be shown out."

The hearing officer motioned the zoning analyst to him. Together they conferred for a few minutes, shuffling the papers on the desk. The older man pointed at the document Lauren had passed up to him, studied it some more, then asked some questions. He then became agitated, looking first surprised, then annoyed, then anxious. The hearing officer yanked off his reading glasses and dismissed him. The crowd waited, quiet, hardly breathing. Lauren DeWitt stared. Dick Hubbard sat composed. The zoning analyst took his seat, his face flushed. The hearing officer looked up.

"Ms. DeWitt seems to be correct. It appears that there has been some sort of mistake made." He looked in the direction of the zoning analyst, who stared back. "The lot in question was never legally subdivided. The original legal lot encompasses it and predates the county zoning regulations written in 1952. The variances as requested this morning are hereby denied." He turned to Dick Hubbard. "Mr. Hubbard, if your client still wants a permit to build, he will need to submit plans that conform to zoning regulations for the entire parcel. We will then be happy to consider his plans in a timely manner." He then looked at the zoning analyst. "And you, Mr. Battles, you need to be a lot more careful. Given the number of years you have been at this, I find this mistake is very hard to understand."

He turned to the next case in front of him.

FOUR

SILENCE. The audience's buzzing had changed to dead, surprised quiet. Then it rose in an escalating mutter of disbelief and anger. I could see both emotions play out over Carl Rainey's face. Florence looked more fearful than angry. Dick Hubbard had moved quickly to place a calming hand on Carl's shoulder.

Beside me, Lillian stood up to gather the papers in front of her: notes for the compromise plan she never had the chance to suggest. A moderate plan, vintage Lillian, a plan in which everyone was a winner. If there was one abiding theme in my aunt's life, it was giving everyone a chance to win. It was what made her so good at selling houses, where emotions often ran high. Lillian radiated balance and trust, words not always used in the same sentence with the words *real estate agent*.

Oddly, it was these thoughts that raced through my mind as I watched my aunt's veined hands collect her notes, one by one, straightening and stacking them carefully. I had seen her do it a thousand times, yet this time it moved me deeply. Time floated, my feelings for her blocking out the surrounding agitation. I longed to put my arms around her.

Lauren DeWitt, to my surprise, beat me to it, engulfing my aunt in a big embrace. As always, Lillian's manners held her in good stead, but she looked spent, as if this gesture was more than she could be expected to handle. The younger woman glowed, all good health and confidence.

"Thanks, Lillian," she said. "I know we've never met before, but we've just won a big victory. An important one. Every new house that doesn't get built is a success." She launched into a brief rundown of the problems that lay ahead if development wasn't slowed down. Septic tanks overflowing into the Magothy. Bay grasses ravaged. Wetlands and wildlife habitats decimated.

Lillian nodded slightly, but she looked increasingly unhappy. I knew she might have supported Lauren, at least in part, but the young woman's guerrilla tactics didn't go down easily.

"You'll see," Lauren was saying. "This is only the beginning. And just the fact that people now know we're watching will slow down development. It makes all the difference when someone local gets involved."

With that, and a smile and a nod to me, she turned to go. Faces in the paneled courtroom suddenly came back in focus. People had been watching and listening.

Lillian turned to me. "All this talk of victory. This isn't how I wanted this to turn out. You at least know that, don't you?" I nodded, pulled a chair out of her way. "You know I wanted Carl to have his house?" She hesitated for a moment, then made up her mind about something. "I've got to go tell him that. And that I had no idea that that young woman was going to come in and sit down beside me and say all those things."

"I'm sure he'd appreciate your intentions, Lillian, but it looks like what happened didn't have anything to do with you. Lauren just called attention to a clerical mistake." I wasn't sure my aunt was listening. "Carl apparently can't build there because of zoning laws. Not because of anything you—or Lauren, for that matter—want."

I glanced toward the exit. The shocked and muttering crowd of Magothy homeowners was reaching the door in a moving lump. Suddenly, her lethargy gone, my aunt thrust her briefcase into my hands and made for the door. A young man, his blond hair in an overgrown crew cut, cut her off. She stepped back, puzzled. A skinny man I recognized from the local mini-mart hissed something, then turned his back on her, blocking her way. I could see people in the lobby crowding around the Raineys, comforting them with angry words. Lauren DeWitt was gone.

I smelled Weller Church before I saw him, his old man's aftershave reaching through the crowd and drawing my attention in his direction. People from the community made wide berth. There was an isolated catcall, I think from the young man who had suggested that Lauren leave town. The lawyer reached my aunt, offering his apology. She began telling him what had just happened.

"Then she sat down in your seat, as if she were representing me, though God knows I tried to say I hadn't invited her, but there she was. And now everybody thinks she was representing me. Which is exactly what she wanted, I guess."

My aunt stopped, lost in the irony of it and still astonished at how quickly the hearing had ended. Weller looked at me for clarification.

"She told the hearing officer that the Rainey's property was legally recorded as one lot, and so couldn't be subdivided," I said. "Something to do with that 1952 law. She had some document to prove that the zoning analyst had made a mistake."

Lillian was recovering. "Then the hearing officer called him up—the zoning analyst, I mean,—and they conferred and two minutes later, it was all over. The poor man looked mortified, like he wanted the earth to open up and swallow him. And Carl is furious."

I replayed the scene in my head, thinking that Lauren's success had to do with more than preparation and documents. It had to do with confidence. Like shoplifting. If you were going to steal something, better to make it a frozen turkey or a mattress, not a pack of gum. Confidence to the point of arrogance was never questioned. Something Mitch Gaylin knew a little about.

"And Hubbard? He say anything?" Weller asked.

Lillian shook her head. "The hearing officer didn't give him a chance. The whole thing was over in two seconds."

I glanced around. Dick Hubbard was still talking to the Raineys, calming, patting. "You know him?" I asked Weller.

"Yes, of course. Everybody does. We've locked horns a few times over the years. And though he skates a bit close to the edge perhaps, his clients usually seem to get their money's worth." He straightened his bow tie and looked at me. "Important, since his fees are not exactly on the low side."

"I'm not sure I really understand all this, Weller. What alternatives does Carl Rainey now have? Except to start all over again, this time planning a house that uses the whole parcel of land. Isn't that going to be a problem? Since it would mean two houses on one lot. You think Dick Hubbard will be able to find a legal way around that?''

Weller shook his head. ''I doubt it. My guess is that there will be two choices. Take down their rambler and build a new house in its place. Or get a permit to enlarge or improve what they've got. But it probably means just one house.'' He smiled at me. ''Unless Hubbard is better at this than even I give him credit for.''

Lillian was again looking around the lobby. The crowd had thinned out. ''Where are Carl and Florence? I need to talk with them.''

We found them outside. Carl was still talking with Dick Hubbard, lighting a cigarette with quick movements at the same time. After a few hard drags, he threw it to the ground, then crushed it to brown bits beneath his heel. The lawyer leaned in, talking fast. I wondered how much Carl was hearing. Florence Rainey, waiting near the door, looked small and lost. A few other neighbors milled about, probably worrying about their own property values. What would happen if their children should want to build a home next door? Or maybe a fence. Or a deck. Would they, too, find their plans thwarted?

Lillian went up to Florence. ''I'm so sorry this happened.'' The woman barely looked up. ''You must know I wanted Carl to have his house. That girl surprised me as much as she surprised you. I don't even know her.''

Carl noticed Lillian talking to his mother. Dick Hubbard shook his head, but Carl pulled away from him. Florence flinched a little.

''This whole thing worries me,'' Weller said to me. ''Since the land can't be subdivided, Rainey's inheritance is worth a whole lot less than he thought. I'm sure he intended to sell his mother's house and the land around it for a profit after she died.'' He clicked his teeth. ''And there are any number of others in the Pines who are in the same boat. Most wealth for old families around here is tied to their property values and so if they can't subdivide their lots... Well, I guess I better have a word.''

I watched as he lumbered in the direction of Dick Hubbard. Their conversation appeared to be cordial. Then Weller was back, shaking his head, watching as the other lawyer nodded a final time at the Raineys and then headed across the street to his car.

"Hubbard's playing this close to his vest, but I don't doubt for a minute he'll think of something."

Oddly, it sounded like a compliment. I suddenly wondered at the strange direction things had taken. Lauren DeWitt had saved the trees and my aunt's view, protecting her property values, and here they were—Weller and Lillian included—acting as if Carl Rainey was the injured party.

Beside me Weller took a rumbly, ominous breath. "Whatever happens, there are going to be big delays and it'll cost Rainey."

He mumbled something about the Magothy's water and sewer problems that I didn't catch. Ten feet away, Lillian was still talking with an intensity that I rarely heard, a kind of pleading for Florence's understanding. Carl was glowering at her. Suddenly, I was furious with him. How dare he make her feel any worse than she already felt? Or accuse her of something that wasn't her fault? Florence's eyes half closed as she listened to her son's angry ranting. Why, I wondered, wasn't he blaming the county for making a mistake? Or Dick Hubbard for letting things get this far along?

A few neighbors stood on the Arundel Center's steps, waiting to see what would happen next. The security guard hovered near the front door. Weller took my arm. "This has gone on long enough," he said. "There is absolutely no reason that Lil should have to defend herself. She isn't responsible for this. Young Mr. Rainey doesn't appear to understand that."

Carl Rainey didn't see Weller approaching. "I heard what that stupid girl said to you. Nobody expected anything else of her," he was saying to Lillian. "But you were different. We thought you were our friend and neighbor, not some sort of traitor." He lit another cigarette, took a deeply agitated drag. "You'll get what's coming to you. That girl, too," he said. "I'm not done here. You'll see. I'll take down all of the god-damned trees, every last one of them, and ruin your pretty view.

They can just try and stop me. Put me in jail if they like. But the damage'll be done. See how you like it to have no control over what you own." Mumbling something else I couldn't hear, he grabbed his mother and hurried down the steps to their car.

"That was totally uncalled for," said Weller. "He is a bully and not a very smart one at that. Are you all right, Lil?"

"No, Weller. I am not all right." But her tone had changed and I was glad for new the sound in her voice. The defeat was gone. And clean, good, curative anger had replaced it. "But one thing, I can tell you. This isn't going to go away. And it's going to get worse before it gets better."

Weller nodded. "Yes, you are probably right."

Lillian took back her briefcase. "Well, I'm not going to think about it anymore just now." She turned to me. "I'm going to the office. See if I can't interest someone in the Darner property. You willing to go out there in this heat? If someone wants to see it this afternoon? Just for a brief tour?"

I knew she wanted to make a few calls before putting the property in the Multiple List Service. Called a pocket listing, because the real estate agent metaphorically carried it in her pocket to show to special buyers, this listing worked only if the property was very desirable or had some other conditions.

"I've got a home inspection at eleven-thirty," I said. "I'll come back to the office for lunch."

She looked me over. "Go home and change your clothes first. I know these developers, and they like to tramp everywhere."

I took a deep breath. I knew these developers, too. And I had a bad feeling that I was going to spend the afternoon with a bunch of people I didn't much like.

Weller mopped his brow with the handkerchief, trying to keep up with the beads of sweat that popped on his forehead.

"That the Knapp's Point land, Lil?" My aunt nodded. "I wondered when the Darners were going to sell it. Worth something today, I imagine." My aunt agreed. "I can remember when it was mostly farmland," he said to me. "But there was also a marina and even a little store." He wiped his face once more, this time all over, then stuffed the square back in his pocket. "So little land left along the Magothy that's not developed. You used to be able to look across and see nothing but woods."

He shook off the memories, while for the umpteenth time I thought how paradoxical it was that everyone was so mad at Lauren DeWitt. After all, she was trying to save what *was* left.

Lillian kissed us both and headed across the street to her car. Weller turned to me. "I'll have the paperwork for Tilghman's estate ready for you to sign by late afternoon. Just let me know when you want to come by. Tomorrow or whenever is fine."

My stomach tightened only slightly. This was it. Ray Tilghman's wooded cove and bungalow would soon be mine. And for a very good price. In return, by the terms of the old man's will, I was obligated to care for his beloved dogs. I'd been doing exactly that for almost a year now, but buying his property made my choice to stay in Maryland final. I found I was calm about the whole thing, after months of waffling. A weight had lifted from my shoulders after I'd made the decision, and I hadn't looked back. Watching Lillian wave briskly as she maneuvered the Cadillac out of its parking spot, I knew why.

FIVE

HOME INSPECTOR Elias Claggett was waiting for me in front of a small waterfront property at Thom's Landing. It was, if I had my geography right, around the corner from Knapp's Point. The deep woods along the water between the two communities was the parcel of land owned by the Darners.

"You're late."

I wasn't, but it was too hot to argue. "Morning, Eli."

"Your buyers, they're late, too."

Eli, never easy, was in a mood today. Must be the heat. It had to be 105 degrees in the shade. Around us, small patches of scraggly lawn had browned until they resembled dirt. What began as dirt had turned to dust. It was hard to draw a breath without incinerating your lungs. Across the way, I noticed a small house had burned half to the ground. The fire looked recent.

"Well, some of us got better things to do than stand in the sun," Eli said. "So I'll just get started. If they decide to honor us with their presence, they do. If they don't, they don't."

"Five minutes, Eli. Give them five more minutes and if they aren't here, we'll go ahead."

He mumbled something I couldn't hear, then went to pull his ladder out of the back of his truck.

Thom's Landing was one of the Magothy's more unattractive communities, without a fraction of the pride of ownership found in Knapp's Point. The water views were bland and pleasant enough, but the neighborhood itself was treeless and shabby. There were far too many electric-blue tarps covering woodpiles and used appliances. Too many rusting boat trailers and oil tanks on weedy overgrown lawns. I'd passed a large new piece of plywood tacked to a tree. On it someone had painted in large, uneven kindergarten letters: "Trespassers will be shot."

I walked around the house. One story and more charming

than most, with a window box of geraniums someone had remembered to water. A sprawling bush, maybe fifteen yards from the water, probably marked the septic tank. Like Pines on Magothy and many other nearby communities, Thom's Landing had no public water or sewer. That meant wells and pumps and septic tanks, each house for itself. Occasionally, someone would suggest that it was time to build public utilities. But so far, the human inclination to put off until tomorrow what you didn't want to pay for today had prevailed.

My thoughts were interrupted by the sounds of hammering. A few houses down to the right, sweating workers in waist-high waders were installing a bulkhead. Fun work, with the blistering midday sun and the water churning with nettles. Occasionally, someone yelped.

Eli was still grumbling. Maybe it was all for the best the buyers weren't here. He might be the best home inspector around but given what Lillian referred to as his colorful personality, things sometimes got tricky. He lit a cigarette.

"Heard what happened this morning at that hearing."

I snapped around to face him. "Eli, that was just an hour ago. What did you hear?"

"Things." He shrugged. "If I was that Rainey boy, I wouldn't be losing any sleep. Dicky Hubbard's good. And he's got lots of all the right kind of friends."

I held up my hand. "Wait a minute. What kind of friends? Like political friends? Is that what you're saying, Eli?"

He grinned. "Nope, I'm not saying that. You're the one saying it."

"Okay, so why don't you just tell me exactly what you heard?"

He leaned close, still grinning. "You must have misunderstood. I didn't hear nothing."

Political friends? Like Vince Darner? Or the incumbent, Norma Sprague?

He smoked his cigarette down to the butt and tossed it on the driveway, where we watched it burn out.

"That's it," he said. "I'm starting." He picked up his ladder and clipboard and flashlight and looked at me. I shrugged, then unlocked the front door, holding it open for him. He was off in a rush of running water and slamming doors. The washing machine in the kitchen began a cycle, the toilet flushed, the kitchen faucet ran. He shoved back curtains, inspecting window sashes, lowering and raising and grunting. His stubby body fit neatly under the sink to inspect whatever there was under the sink to inspect. Through the whole process, he kept up a steady stream of derisive chatter. Intermittently, he stopped to make notes.

An hour and fifteen minutes later, as he was finishing up, the buyers arrived.

"How nice of you to join us," he said. He handed them his report. "You got some problems here. Septic's on its last legs and it's gonna be one expensive puppy when it blows. Windows all need to be replaced. Low water pressure. You can do one thing at a time in this house. Wash dishes or take a shower. Flush the can or brush your teeth." He grabbed the report back from them and turned the pages until he came to his complete list of woes. "Attic needs insulation. Tiles in bathroom are loose. Foundation needs repair on the south side. Electrical outlets outside aren't grounded." And on it went, the buyers looking increasingly disturbed. "Questions?" No one said anything. Another bellow from someone working in the water. "Well, kiddies, it's your money."

I turned to the buyers. "Why don't we go inside and look this over." They nodded. "Thanks, Eli. I'll be in touch." He harumped and picked up his ladder. I watched him, wondering for the millionth time how Lillian and he had become friends.

TWENTY MINUTES LATER, I was locking up and the buyers were on their way back to D.C., houseless and depressed. With a last glance at the geraniums, I got in the car and turned on the radio. No rain was forecast. Fires were banned in all state and local parks. No lawn watering or car washing. There was some tedious banter between deejays about how you could tell if someone hadn't showered for a week. Some smartass played a few phrases of Handel's "Water Music." I flipped it off.

Driving around the Arundel Marine van parked half in the road, I found myself thinking about Weller's words. About how little undeveloped waterfront there was left. I didn't like to think about it, but recently there had been signs of something happening across Weller's Creek in a uninhabited stretch of woods. Across from what would soon be my property. I hoped this didn't mean big houses and boats and noise. I hoped a year from now I'd still see woods when I stood on my dock.

The tacky houses of Thom's Point grew farther apart, and then they stopped altogether on the side of the road away from the water. Ahead of me, a road turned off to the left. Beside it was a sign, surrounded by careful landscaping: Thom's Landing Estates. I'd noticed it on my way to meet Eli, and now, curious, I turned in. I tried to tell myself this was professional interest, not driven by the fact that Charlotte and Vincent Darner lived here.

What I found was a manicured neighborhood of newish houses. But instead of the security fence and gate I'd expected, there were more begonias. No automated key card system to let residents and their guests in, while keeping everyone else out. I put the car in second and crept slowly past the large traditional homes. I'd have guessed the subdivision was built about five years ago. These were the bland, expensive, executive homes of successful, upper-middle-class couples with 2.2 children. Half-acre plots, nice landscaping, no waterfront but public boat access, some woods behind each house.

I pulled over and fished out a map of Anne Arundel County. A familiar car drew up behind me. Charlotte Darner stared over the steering wheel. To my surprise, she got out. Yesterday's modest dress had been replaced by tight jeans and an expensive cutoff top, a look more redneck Versace than I might have expected for Vince Darner's wife. Golden dangles hung from her ears.

"Hi," she said. "I thought that was your car. Is everything okay? With the listing and all? Did you come to see Vince? Because he's not here."

"Everything's fine. I confess to driving down here out of curiosity. A client asked me about this subdivision and so I wanted to take a look." Why was I lying? Well, not lying, just sort of padding the truth. What had I hoped to learn by driving down here in the first place?

Charlotte laughed nervously, then became shy. "I'm sorry about yesterday. Vince wasn't very nice. He's stressed, what with his political campaign and all. He always gets like this when he's stressed."

"I'm sure it's harder for you than for me."

Her smile faded, as she considered the truth in this. A thought occurred and the smile returned. "Would you like to come over for lunch? We live down there." She pointed to the next street, then searched a silly and expensive handbag for something. "Nobody much ever comes by. I could get us something. Or maybe Liz...she's the maid..." She stopped, aware of how this sounded. "Well, she only comes in once a week."

"Thanks, but I've got appointments this afternoon. To show your property." I wasn't sure she believed me. "Another time."

"Okay." She nodded and sighed. "Vince doesn't want me to work, you know. It's nice here, but not much to do. So it gets kinda lonely. Nobody much to joke around with or anything." She rallied. "Vince says I have to get involved with some volunteer work. The hospital or symphony or something."

Yes, that seemed about right. He'd want his wife to do volunteer work. Be good for his public image, particularly during a political campaign.

We both studied the banked semicircle of burgundy and white flowers surrounded by a larger circle of striped liriope. Someone had watered them, county restrictions or not.

"We used to live in Knapp's Point, you know," she said. "When we were first married. In a way, I was real sorry to leave." She fiddled with the fringe along the hem of her cropped top. "Promise you won't tell Vince I said that?"

I promised. "Charlotte, yesterday at Knapp's Point? What did you want to tell me?"

"Tell you?"

"Before Vince got, er, impatient and you went and sat in the car."

She worked her mouth, looked at the dusty ground. "I guess I was just wondering if maybe we could somehow not sell my land. It'll turn into another boring subdivision." She dragged out the boring part. "I thought maybe we could use it—the land I mean—to borrow money. You know, put it up as insurance."

"As collateral for a loan?" She nodded. "Does Vince know you feel this way?"

Another nod. "He says we have to sell."

"He needs the money for his campaign?"

Her eyes, darkly rimmed with black eyeliner, had grown a little worried, a little sad.

"I guess so. Vince doesn't talk to me much about money. And he wouldn't like me to talk." She stopped, embarrassed.

Behind us another car crept down the road, slowed. Charlotte waved at the woman in the driver's seat. With a whine the car backed up. A second whine and the window came down. A sleeker copy of Charlotte, with rich-woman hair, was driving. A manicured hand emerged from the car, flinging molecules of expensive perfume into the hot air, a bit of Rodeo Drive right here in Maryland. I saw that her mouth had been lined carefully in mahogany, then filled in with a rich red loam color.

"Hey, Dorrie," Charlotte said. "This is Eve."

"Doreen," she said. "I keep telling you, Charlotte."

"Sorry, Hon. I forgot," she said. "This is Eve. She's the real estate agent. For the Knapp's Point land."

Doreen looked me over. I felt sticky and ungroomed and plain. "You're the one buying Ray Tilghman's old place?" I nodded, hardly surprised any more that everyone in Anne Arundel County knew this. "Well, you got your work cut out for you. House is in terrible shape, I hear."

"It needs some work."

"You closed yet? On Ray's place?" She shook her hair, discharging another cloud of perfume.

"Not yet."

Her eyes glittered. She opened her mouth, then closed it. She

wanted to know the price. I wasn't surprised by this either.
What people paid for their homes wasn't just public knowledge
in Maryland, it was red meat in the take-no-prisoners world of
waterfront real estate. Owners and investors watched the post-
ings in local newspapers out of curiosity and self-interest. I
glanced at my watch, then turned to Charlotte.

"I'm afraid I'm going to be late if I don't go."

She nodded. But Doreen was in no hurry. Instead, she was
now studying me with frank interest, probably calculating what
was needed to turn me from a sweaty worm into a butterfly.
Then she abruptly announced she had an appointment. Her car
window whined up, and with a manicured wave she drove off.

"Don't mind Dorrie," Charlotte said. "She kinda puts on
airs since she married John and they bought in here." She
leaned close. "I think she's a little jealous of me, to tell you
the truth. Because Vince's made a lot of money and all."

"John who?"

"John Battles. He has some job with the county. Something
to do with the zoning laws."

I thanked her again for her lunch offer, then got back in the
car and thought about what she'd just told me. Odd match, the
zoning analyst and the vaporous Doreen. I wondered if she had
heard what a crummy morning he'd had. Still, she didn't seem
like the type to let herself get in a snit about a little job setback.

But Charlotte Darner was different. I watched her car disappear around the corner. She'd been pushed into a life she was
only half comfortable with. She didn't like her isolation. I tried
to picture her volunteering for a symphony fund-raiser and
couldn't. I'd have bet that under different circumstances, she'd
have been happy checking groceries or working in the farm
store. Clowning around with her co-workers. Having a few
beers after work.

I headed for home on Weller's Creek. In front of a vegetable
stand just outside of Pines on Magothy, two teenage girls were
trying to plant a sign in the parched soil. Re-elect Norma
Sprague for the Maryland Senate, it said. Vince Darner's opponent was a confident middle-aged woman wearing a big
smile. But a political poster? On July 2?

Charlotte Darner's words came back to me. I decided she wasn't just uncomfortable with her life, she had a secret. And it had something to do with why Vince Darner needed money. Of course, my brain was overheating and I was starved so it was perfectly possible that neither were true.

SIX

A LONG RUTTED ROAD to the left led to Weller's Cove. Will St. Claire's rusty pickup was suddenly just behind me. He waved, then pulled up at his two-room cottage. I would soon own it and the surrounding land, but it would continue to be his free of charge in return for whatever help I needed around the property. This arrangement—between Ray Tilghman and Will—had begun long before I arrived in Maryland. And we'd continued it. I slowed the BMW, watching him in my rearview mirror. He swung out of the truck in one smooth movement, his work shirt sweaty and stuck to his body. Grabbing a jug of water from the back of the truck, he unceremoniously emptied it over his head. I backed up.

"Hey, Will."

Grinning, his wet black hair sticking straight up, he came around to the passenger side and got in, dripping all over the BMW's expensive leather interior. I ignored the dripping, as my soon-to-be-former husband would never have been able to. Will himself was harder to ignore. He had removed his shirt and shoes and was working on the buckle of his pants.

"You going swimming?"

"I may be hot but I'm not crazy." He grinned some more. "Even the public beaches that have strung nets are having problems with the nettles this year. Actually, I was going to use your outdoor shower. Okay?" I nodded. The question had been a formality. We both knew full well that had I not been there, he'd have used the shower, then taken my dogs to run along the water or play in the woods. "What are you doing home?"

"I could ask you the same," I said.

"Siesta," he said. "Too hot to work." Will was a one-man landscape business, with the majority of his clients Anne Arundel County's rich and idle women. "So, you want to join me?"

he asked, mopping his face and body with his shirt. "For the siesta? Well, the shower, too, if you like?"

I laughed, suddenly a little uneasy. A few months ago, I actually might have. Our relationship had been a lot more than the friendship it was now. But that had changed earlier in the spring. And as the weeks and months had drifted by, Will had become lighter, more relaxed. Now he'd started a kind of playful sexual bantering. It was unsettling. I pulled up in front of my bungalow. Will got out.

"Here, Lance."

I now watched as Lancelot, Ray Tilghman's massive and good-natured Chesapeake Bay retriever, chased him through the pine needles in the clearing. The other dog, Zeke, a smaller black Lab mix, licked my hand briefly and lovingly, his eyes telling me how very hard he was trying not to join in the play. Then no longer able to stand it, he raced after the others running madly in the noonday heat.

I looked down the long dirt road—just wide enough for a car—that led to the protected cove on Weller's Creek. In the winter, I could see the water from my screened front porch. Suddenly, from somewhere, there came the ominous sound of a chain saw. I shivered. Unable to face the thought of eighty-foot oaks and loblollies and tulip poplars hitting the ground, I went inside.

The bungalow was cool, considering the heat and the lack of central air. I went upstairs. With the fan whirling overhead, I changed into a pair of thin cotton chinos and a baggy camp shirt. When I came down, Will was sitting soaking wet on the front steps, a soaking wet dog on either side of him. The garden hose was unwound near the side of the house. I sat down, trying to stay dry.

"Why are you in such a good mood?" I asked.

"Dunno. Just am. Must be the heat."

"Dogs are happy, too. The hose was a good idea." With the water full of nettles, they couldn't take their usual three-times-a-day dips in Weller's Creek. I patted Zeke, who leaned on me, soaking my pants and shirt. It felt good.

"I'd probably be busted if anyone knew I was wasting water like this." Will laughed. "Nice to have the rest of the day off."

"Speak for yourself. I've got to go to work." His eyebrows flew up. "Yes, dressed like this. Because I will probably have to spend the afternoon slogging around with some developer."

"Where?"

"Knapp's Point. Along the Magothy as far as Thom's Landing."

The news appeared to sober him up some. "Well, lucky you." He stood and glanced at my long pants. "You'll probably die of the heat, but at least the deer ticks aren't going to get you."

I got in the car. He came around to the driver's side window. "You'll put the dogs back in the house? After they dry off a bit?" I asked. He nodded. I turned over the engine, then turned it off. "Will, where are those chain saws working?"

His good humor melted. "Someone is apparently building a house across from you. On the other side of Weller's Creek."

"Who told you that?"

He leaned down to scratch Zeke's ears. "Woman I'm seeing."

I didn't ask for her name. I already knew it.

A VISIT TO the deli counter at Lyle's Market was not an uplifting experience. I was surprised, and not for the first time, how much I missed New York's wide variety of food. Far more than I missed the theater, the museums, or even the hoo-ha on the streets. It was an opinion I usually kept to myself, given the near-holy status of Maryland seafood. Any native, including Lillian, would be happy to tell you how blue crabs alone made up for any other deficiencies. I joined the checkout line.

"That it?"

"Yes." I scoured a side pocket of my handbag for some singles. No luck, so I fished out a twenty. I looked up, realizing that the checker was the woman I had seen yesterday arguing with her husband at Knapp's Point. Her cutoffs had been replaced by jeans, but like yesterday she looked hard and sexy. She was waiting expectantly, hand out.

"Hey, Jose?" She turned around, a smile flowing over her face as the checker in the next aisle teased her about something. Up close I saw that she was only about thirty-five, older looking than her years, probably from too much sun and too much strife. Makeup emphasized, rather than covered, the circles under her eyes. And as she bent to the cash register to make change, I could see a large bluish area on her neck. It was also covered with makeup and mostly hidden by her hair. Apparently the argument I'd seen yesterday with her husband was just the tip of the iceberg. I thought of the daughter, so matter-of-fact about her father's accident.

The woman handed me my change and thanked me cheerfully enough, her smile sincere if not long lasting. I hesitated. But what was there I could say? Get help? Get out? Take your children? Nothing really. Just thank you.

Grabbing the sandwiches, I headed for the car. A flyer was stuck facedown under my windshield wiper. If You Want Big Government Off Your Back, the headline read, Attend This Debate. Vincent Darner, looking a whole lot more pleasant than I remembered from yesterday, stared out at me. His platform was simple: less government and fewer taxes. Get rid of unnecessary and intrusive and expensive programs and regulations. He accused his opponent, incumbent Norma Sprague, of all of those things.

The debate was scheduled for this evening at the Pines on Magothy community center. It had all the makings of a nasty fight. And as I headed up Mountain Road, I found Eli Claggett's words about Dick Hubbard's political connections singing in my head.

AT THE OFFICE my aunt was listlessly chasing a large chunk of pale tomato around and around a square Styrofoam box with a plastic fork. She and her longtime assistant, Shirley Bodine, had given up waiting for me and ordered in salads. I deposited a roast beef sandwich on her desk. Abruptly, she snapped the Styrofoam lid shut and flung the container into the garbage can in the corner of her office. I settled in with a cup of fresh coffee and a swiss on ersatz rye.

Lillian took a couple of bites of her sandwich, then folded the plastic wrapper over it.

"I'll just save this for later, I think."

My aunt's appetite, never robust, hadn't returned after my uncle Max's death. Mostly she snacked a little here and there, sucking on glasses of iced tea in between. It worried me, but a hot summer day probably wasn't the time to address lost appetite.

I handed her the flyer from my windshield. "You know about this?"

She read, then nodded. "It's been scheduled for a while, but Vince sure hasn't lost any time trying to turn the fallout from this morning's hearing to his advantage. He may be our client, but I can't say that I like his politics much."

"Lillian?" She looked up. "Lillian, everybody in the Pines knows you support Norma Sprague. And Vince Darner must also. So why did he choose you to sell his Knapp's Point land? Surely there were other real estate agents?"

"Does this mean that you don't think he was attracted by my forty years of experience?" She wadded the flyer and lobbed it into the wastebasket. "Don't answer that. But think about it, Dearheart. Not only am I probably supporting the opposition, which proves how evenhanded he is, I am squeaky clean and he also knows that. And everyone else in Anne Arundel County knows it. Including my enemies."

"And the forty years."

"Yes, he may even think those are worth something." She smiled, then flipped through her Rolodex, punched some buttons on her phone, and after removing a large clip-on earring, put the receiver to ear. She frowned, redialed, this time adding the three digit area code. "This area code business is driving me crazy," she said.

I knew what she meant. Everyone in Maryland knew what she meant. We'd recently had to adjust to dialing the area code before every number, even if we were calling across the street. Bell Atlantic's farsighted executives found this a good solution to the problem of not enough phone numbers. Now they promised an overlay of two more area codes to muck up the system further.

Lillian drummed her fingers, waiting for the phone to be picked up.

"How are Vince Darner's chances in the election?"

"Good, I'm sorry to say. Norma Sprague has done a lot for this community. And she would do more if we'd re-elect her but people have this Dump Big Government attitude right now. They've completely forgotten that they benefit from it."

"Lillian," I began. "Eli..." My aunt held up her hand and pointed to the receiver.

"Norma, Lillian." There was a short wait, then some small talk. I ate my sandwich and finished my coffee as my aunt filled her friend in on what had happened this morning at the Arundel Center. "I just wanted to make sure you knew. He's going to use it, Norma." More silence, as Lillian listened. "You are joking," she said. "I certainly hope you are joking." A few more words and she hung up. "There's a rumor that Vince is going to trot out Carl Rainey tonight."

"How much difference can that make?"

"A lot. Get people more riled up than they already are. And Vince knows just how to take advantage of it." She pulled a pile of papers toward her. "Norma's asking supporters to show up. You willing?" She glanced up. "I'm assuming you are a supporter?"

"Sure. Yes."

"Ask Will, too, if you see him. Okay? I can't imagine that he agrees with Vince Darner. And Norma needs all the help she can get."

"Okay. Though, there's something you should know."

"What?"

I had been about to tell her that Will was dating Lauren DeWitt. But something stopped me. She'd find out soon enough. I again wondered what was going to happen when Lauren found out that the lovely waterfront woods near Knapp's Point was going to be developed? And that Lillian and I were the sales agents? Even more interesting was the question of where Will's loyalties would lie.

"Eve?"

"Sorry, I was daydreaming."

"It's the heat."

"Well, maybe. You know that little house in Thom's Landing?" Lillian nodded. "Eli found major stuff. Septic tank is about to go, he thinks. The buyers canceled the contract, but they aren't happy about it."

"Don't worry about them. He just saved their skin, whether they know it or not."

I nodded. "The house across the street half burned down sometime recently."

"The whole area's a tinderbox." As if to underline her words, there came the sound of a fire siren racing in the distance.

"Lillian?" She waited. "Uh, Eli said something this morning about Dick Hubbard having all the right kinds of friends. I gather he meant political friends. What do you think?"

A big laugh from my aunt. "Of course he has friends. Anyone who didn't just fall off the turnip truck knows he's got friends. Why?"

"Well, you suppose he's using those friends to get what he wants? Friends like..." I didn't like to say it. "Norma Sprague."

Lillian was rummaging around her desk looking for her reading glasses. They appeared under a pile of paper and she slipped them on and looked at me.

"Norma Sprague and Dick Hubbard are cordial, as far as I know. If that's what you mean."

"Well, what's his relationship with Vince Darner?"

"I have absolutely no idea. I'm sure that they know each other." She stared at me some more. "Where's this all going?"

I shrugged, then told her about my conversation with Charlotte in Thom's Landing Estates.

"So what?" she asked. I had to admit she had me there. "Well, speaking of the Darners, I've got some good news. Or maybe bad for you, but I've lined up three developers who want to see the property this afternoon." She consulted her notes. Two people I didn't know and Mitch Gaylin.

"Oh, great."

"Well, if you want me to call them back," she began.

We both knew she had no intention of doing any such thing. "When?"

The sound of a nasal male voice in the front office answered my question. We'd gotten used to air-conditioned silence the last week. No one was much interested in looking at anything in this heat.

"That'll probably be Hal Barnett's son. I've done business with Hal for years." I wadded up my lunch garbage, aimed it at Lillian's trash can, and missed. She gave me a look and stooped to put it in. "Look, Eve, this isn't a formal thing, it's just to let them see the property for the first time and get a feel for the lay of the land. See if they want to pursue it." She followed me into the front office.

SEVEN

IF I'D BEEN worried about tramping around all afternoon in the heat, I wasn't as soon as I saw Grey Barnett. He had taken off his suit jacket but he didn't look like he'd last ten minutes. I wondered if I should offer sunblock.

Instead, I introduced myself and we were soon on our way in a convoy of two, his big new BMW following my smaller older one. The others would catch up with me later by the Weber Realty sign. A half hour later we were standing in the wide clearing at the edge of the water, fanning ourselves and looking out over the Magothy. The woods were crackling dry.

"It's got potential," he said. I guessed him to be twenty-six or -seven, about Will's age, without the appeal but with a business degree from someplace with ivy on the walls. I knew this because he told me. Possibly more than once. "I'll call your aunt and talk with her when I get back to my office."

Instead of slapping the little creep senseless, I grated my teeth and ignored his small talk, mostly tales of past deals, all killers, if he were to be believed. Insects buzzed around my head and my mind wandered. My eyes kept returning to a large clump of drying brush between the woods and water. I could just make out part of a small shed or outbuilding. Vince Darner hadn't said anything about it yesterday. Maybe this was what remained of the general store that Weller had mentioned.

"Wait a second," I said. "I'd like to take a look at that."

He squinted, then shrugged, happy to let me fight my way through the undergrowth. The small structure was half gone but what remained was sagging badly on one side. There was a narrow window and a rotting windowsill. A thick layer of dirt and debris covered the floor and a faint odor permeated the place. I didn't stay to think about it since the heat was even more unbearable inside than out.

"What's in there?"

"Nothing. It needs to be taken down before it falls or burns down."

"Probably an old chicken coop or something," he said. If I'd had the energy to laugh, I would have. This guy wouldn't have known a chicken coop if it had chickens in it.

Ten minutes later, having retraced our path back along the edge of the woods that skirted the meadow, we parted. I drank some warm water from a bottle in my car and sat waiting with the motor and air conditioning running. With the windows up, things were just bearable. Except, of course, I was probably producing green house gasses. Was I morally obligated to turn off the engine and sweat? Yes, probably. I flipped off the engine and took another sip of water.

A big American car pulled up alongside of me in the dusty road. Red-faced and bathed in a greasy sweat, Julian Wachtel was a no-nonsense sort who saw dollar signs, not sunsets, when he looked across the sparkling water of the Magothy River. He left the motor running and the door open.

"Thought this was it," he said. "You got the plat?"

He took the oversize sheet I handed him, a copy of the original signed and recorded plat, and motioned me back to his car. He got in, spread it out over the steering wheel, letting the air conditioning hit him square in the face and neck, while I stood sweating outside. His chubby fingers traced the borders of the property. From time to time he glanced up at the woods and meadows in front of us, as if trying to imagine just what he was looking at.

"Okay, let's take a quick look," he said. "I'm not going to do a lot today but since I'm here, you can show me what you've got."

I went first, retracing my steps from half an hour earlier. He grunted as we made our way through the suffocating woods to the water. After about ten seconds in the sun, he'd seen enough and headed for his air-conditioned car, stopping only when he spied the brush I'd trampled to reveal the rotting shed. Muttering to himself, he slogged over. He was out in about two seconds, then after stomping around in more brush at the side, he returned.

"It may have been part of the old store," I said.

"That right?" He was breathing hard when we got back to the cars. "You tell Lil I'd be interested if the price's right." He was about to say something else when Mitch Gaylin pulled up in his Jeep.

"I see the price just got wrong," he said, loudly enough for Mitch to hear.

"Julie, you in on this?" Mitch turned to me. "Hi."

"Hi." I hadn't seen him for a month or so. I watched as he talked with the other man. For the first time, Julian Wachtel's beety face broke into a smile. Then he was gone, swearing he'd whip Mitch roundly if it came to a bidding war. I decided it was a tired show of male bravado. And undoubtedly for my benefit. Lillian might be okay to do business with if he had to do business with a woman, he was telling me, but I better know my place.

"First time you meet Julie?" Mitch asked. I nodded, then foraged in the BMW for another plat.

"Here. You'll want this."

"You look like you've been out here a while," he said. "You sure you want to do this today? It could wait. We could go someplace and get something cold to drink."

"Thanks. But I'm fine."

"Okay, whatever you say." Like Julian Wachtel, he studied the plat, looking at the boundaries, tipping it sideways once. He was in his mid-forties, with dark blond hair graying nicely. Brown eyes. Though at the moment I couldn't actually see his eyes since they were hidden behind sunglasses. As were mine, for which I was grateful. He looked over at me once, smiled, causing a half sunburst of wrinkles to explode past the sunglasses toward his temples. I'd forgotten about the sunburst. It changed his face. I took another gulp of water.

"Okay," he said. "Let's just go look briefly. Too hot for more."

We tramped in silence to the water, my third time this afternoon. The silence continued as we stood on the edge of the woods. Even from this distance, the houses at Knapp's Point looked shabby.

"Water's very low," he said. A couple of Jet Ski riders
bounded across the Magothy, playing leapfrog over each other's
wakes. I wondered if Duck Jarvis were at it again. But it was
three o'clock on a Monday afternoon. Not likely. We watched
their antics.

"Dangerous but fun. You can only steer when you're accel-
erating, so it takes a bit of getting used to. And people go too
fast," he said. "You ever been out on one?"

"No."

He turned to face me directly. "Can we call a truce here?
Look, I'm sorry about what happened, but if we're going to
work together..." Earlier in the spring, Mitch had made a bold
move to buy Ray Tilghman's bungalow out from under me. I'd
been furious. I watched as he pulled off his sunglasses. "Eve,"
he said, "I'm sorrier than you know."

I nodded, took a breath, realized I was, too. "Yes. I am too,
I guess. So, okay, let's forget it."

Oddly, that was that. We looked out over the water for a few
minutes more, watching the Jet Skiers, both of us a little embarrassed. I wondered if he'd heard about this morning's hearing at the Arundel Center but I was too sick of thinking and
talking about the whole thing to bring it up again. He turned to
go back and I followed in silence.

"I'd like to take a quick look at that," he said, pointing at
the partial shed now visible through the browning tangle of
brush. This time I waited in the woods out of the sun. But when
he didn't come back right away, I joined him, sure this sweltering afternoon would never be over. I found him poking
around in the dirt outside of the shed with the toe of his shoe.
Inside, a loose board fell to the floor.

"You see that?" he asked, pointing at what appeared to be
nothing more than dirt from where I stood.

"What? The ground?" He nodded. "I gather this shed must
have been part of the old general store when Charlotte Darner's
family owned the place."

"Julie Wachtel see this?" I nodded, puzzled. He scuffed a
little more at the ground. "He say anything?"

"No. Should he have?"

"Maybe. I'm not sure."

I moved a little closer. Together we looked at the dirt. A patch of new concrete was beginning to be visible where Mitch was scraping at the dirt. He unrolled the plat again.

"Look at that." A tiny square marked the shed. He studied the ground again, then with the toe of his shoe shoved aside more soil to reveal more concrete.

"What is it?"

"I don't think that this was the store. I think it was a small gas station. Probably had just one tank. For the marina and maybe the farm. I think the store was over there, though it doesn't look like anything remains of it." He pointed across the clearing. Then he pointed down at the concrete. "You see that?" I nodded. "I'll bet there's an oil tank under here. And since nobody's talking about it, and it's been recently covered over, it could be leaking."

We walked in silence along the edge of the parched woods. Environmental hazards had a way of slowing down development better than any number of leaflets or newspaper articles. I wondered what Lillian would say if Mitch were right about a buried and possibly leaking oil tank. I didn't wonder what she would do: pick up the phone and ask Vince Darner about it. Then, if she was still worried, she'd report it to the Department of the Environment. No sale could go forward until they gave the green light. And if there were a tank, and it was oozing something, that wasn't going to be any time soon. Particularly one this close to the water.

"You think Vince Darner knows about this?"

Mitch, lost in his own thoughts, rallied. "Probably. The concrete looks new. I hear he needs money. And he certainly wouldn't be the first one to try to slide by the environmental regulations." He stopped midpath. "I bet Julie Wachtel suspects something. He's been in this business too long not to have seen the signs and known about the possibilities. And he grew up here, probably even knew Charlotte Darner's family." The bugs were getting frenzied and Mitch absently swatted. "He would have known that that shed wasn't the old store."

"How did *you* know it wasn't?" Our earlier embarrassment with each other had evaporated.

"I spent half the winter studying old maps and local history."

"Why?"

"Looking for land to develop. In fact, if Vince Darner hadn't listed that property with Lillian, I might have gone to him directly to see if he and Charlotte wanted to sell."

We were both glistening with sweat by the time we reached our cars. I drank some tepid water and handed Mitch the bottle.

"Assuming there's a leaking tank," I said, "why wouldn't Darner just take down that shed and let the brush grow over the concrete? Who'd be the wiser?"

He shrugged. "Who knows? But the shed *is* shown on the plat. So maybe he thought that taking it down would call even more attention to the problem. Assuming there's a problem. Maybe there isn't." He didn't sound convinced. "He could have just hired someone a month or two ago to cover the tank with concrete, then let the dirt and dust settle over it and hope no one would notice. But the concrete's definitely new. And some of that brush looks dead, almost as if it had been placed there."

And that was that. Until he brought up the hearing this morning.

"Pretty nasty business," he said. "And now Dick Hubbard will try to do the right thing for the Raineys."

"But what can he do?"

"Not much. Except start the process all over again. Since the mistake appears to be the county's fault, maybe get them to expedite the next hearing or not repeat some of the environmental tests."

He moved a little toward me, to get out of the worst of the sun. Then he handed back the bottle of water. It was almost empty. I promised to let him know what Lillian was going to do about the Knapp's Point land.

A Jet Ski revved its engine somewhere nearby. A few large drops of rain exploded on the ground, creating small mushroom clouds of hot dust. Then the drops stopped.

EIGHT

HALF AN HOUR LATER I was sitting in my aunt's office, collapsed in a Queen Anne's chair in front of her desk, not much caring if I sweated up the Bargello upholstery. The air conditioner hummed. I explained about the rotting half shed and the new concrete and brush that covered it. She listened, then shook her head.

"Let me call Vince. He may not even know about it."

"Lillian, the concrete was white, brand new."

"Well, let's take things one step at a time. Vince is a client. I want to hear what he has to say first. Maybe there's a perfectly reasonable explanation." I shook my head. "If there isn't it'll have to be checked, of course," she said, "since the marina gas station was abandoned ages ago. But first let's find out all the facts." As she had earlier today, she flipped through her Rolodex, muttering to herself, then dialed. I waited and wondered what she really was thinking. As if afraid I might figure that out, she swiveled around in her chair until she was facing a credenza overloaded with piles of real estate forms. I got up and went into my cubicle. Five minutes passed. Lillian appeared at the door. She was shaking. And it wasn't from the air-conditioning.

"He knows about it," she said. "I'm just positive."

"He said so?"

"No. He denied everything. But I'm sure he's responsible for covering it up. He got very angry. Almost before I said anything. He knows exactly what a leaking oil tank can do to a sale."

"Lillian, if he denies everything, how can you be sure he knows?" There was silence. In the front office, the phone rang. After two rings, Shirley picked up. "Lillian? How?"

Her mouth was a narrow lipsticked line. "He suggested that we hadn't better mention this to anyone."

"Those were his words?" She nodded. "And if we do?" She shrugged. I let my breath out. "Does he know that Mitch and probably Julian Wachtel also know?"

She shook her head. "He hung up before I could mention them."

In the next room, Shirley was off the phone. The air conditioner now hummed in a different, higher key. My aunt took a deep breath.

"Before he hung up what exactly did he say?" Her hand was holding onto the edge of my desk, her nails carefully manicured, the veins on the back blue and ropey. "Lillian?"

"He suggested that I tear up his contract. And if I didn't do that, then, well…well, he didn't say." She slid into the chair in front of my desk. "Maybe, I'm fantasizing this."

After what I'd seen of Vince Darner, I didn't think so. "You agree to cancel the contract?"

"I did not." She shook her head. "I'm going to call the Department of the Environment. In fact, I'm going to do it right now. Just the fact that Vince made it clear that we shouldn't mention it means he knows about the tank and it's probably leaking." She leaned over the desk and pulled my phone around to her, then looked up and called for Shirley. "Can you get me my Rolodex, please?"

She was silently studying her nails when the secretary handed it to her. I watched my aunt find the number, then punch buttons with the eraser end of a pencil. Whatever familiar voice answered made her nod. I sat back down and listened as she explained about the tank in the broadest of terms, her voice nonchalant, as if to imply that this was all nothing more than a mere technicality. Just checking, she said. Then she listened to whomever was on the other line, asked a few questions, made some small talk, and hung up.

"That was Tom Weiss at the Department of the Environment. Underground tanks abandoned more than one hundred and eighty days ago need to be checked. They will first have to tear up the concrete to make sure that there is indeed a tank buried there."

"When?"

"Since tomorrow's the Fourth, it may be a couple of days before anyone from Oil Control will be able to get out there. Day after tomorrow soonest."

"What happens then?"

"If they find a tank, they have to make sure it's drained. Then take soil samples. Also water samples, since it's so close to the Magothy."

She took a deep breath, shoved my phone back in place, all the while looking at me.

"I thought I was already the least popular person in town," she said. "Wait until this gets around. Which it will. Well, too late to worry about it."

She returned to her office next door. I could hear her making calls. I gathered up my things and got ready to leave, my mind alive with the developments of the last two days.

"Eve?" I scudded back to earth and went into her office. "About tonight."

"You're still going to the debate? Vince Darner will probably go ballistic when he sees you. And after this morning..."

"All the more reason I have to go."

Later, getting into my car, I found I was worried. I also found I couldn't get Charlotte Darner out of my mind. If Vince were cornered, the Knapp's Point land tied up with an environmental investigation, what would he do? Was his wife going to bear the brunt of his frustration? She was already nervous about something. Or would he...I suppressed a shiver...take it out on Lillian? And just why did he need money so badly? And so fast? I shook off my thoughts, then headed home for a shower and a change of clothes.

THE PINES on Magothy Community Center was nothing so much as a large barracks. One story, with a full basement, built maybe thirty years ago, it sat at the edge of town where Lido Beach Road, the main drag, connected with Mountain Road. Landscaping, in the form of a few large bushes, had softened the utilitarian appearance. A large overhead sign announced tonight's meeting. Below that, in smaller letters, a food drive scheduled for later in the month asked for volunteers.

Lillian was standing near the front of the main meeting room talking with a woman I recognized as Norma Sprague. Since yesterday, her political posters had sprouted all over lawns and along the roads. Vince Darner's people had been busy, too. The result was campaign pollution in July.

The room was filling up, with people fanning themselves and finding seats. If there was air-conditioning, it wasn't doing much good. Norma Sprague's supporters filed to the left, Vince Darner's to the right, with his supporters soon spilling over. Carl Rainey stood to the side, clenching and unclenching his jaw. I had glimpsed Dick Hubbard when we entered, but I didn't see him now.

"Eve?" I turned to find Will standing behind me.

"Hi. I'm glad you got my message. Lauren with you?"

"No, but she's coming." He grinned. "She doesn't like to miss a good fight. By the way, she told me about the variance hearing this morning. She was pretty pleased that she could help Lillian."

I wondered what my aunt would say to that, but decided this wasn't the place to discuss it. "She mention that it got ugly? Lillian's worried that it's going to get a whole lot worse than it already has. Carl Rainey and some others were pretty nasty to her after the hearing. Maybe Lauren should be a little careful." My words sounded sanctimonious. I decided I'd think about my feelings about Will and Lauren later. A low rumble passed through the crowd.

"There she is," said Will. "I'm going to go rescue her from the mob with their pitchforks and blowguns." He touched my arm. "Which is no doubt unnecessary. And which she'll probably hate."

I watched him glide through the crowd, wondering if he understood just how angry many local people were at Lauren. Had he also forgotten that he, too, was an outsider?

I slipped into an empty seat by Lillian. "You run into Vince Darner?"

She shook her head. Up front, Norma Sprague had stepped off the platform and was talking to two women I didn't know.

I wondered if she appreciated what it had cost Lillian to be here.

The crowd quieted as Vince Darner took the small stage. He was in full campaign mode...sports jacket over crisp shirt, shoes freshly shined...standing prosperous and tall. A big-bodied man tapped the microphone and looked out to see audience reaction. Satisfied that we could hear, he stepped down.

"That guy checking the mike is the one whose Jet Ski destroyed Lauren DeWitt's dock. The one who got stung by the nettles." A flashback of him rolling in the hot sand, shrieking obscenities as his children and neighbors watched, came back to me. His face was still a little puffy.

"Donald Jarvis," Lillian said. "Everyone calls him Duck. And that's his wife, Josie." The supermarket cashier was herding her two kids in front of her, a teenage boy and the girl I'd already met. The girl stopped and said something to Lauren. Her mother abruptly grabbed her shoulders and shoved her toward the front of the room.

I also noticed Charlotte Darner in the back. Her jeans had been replaced by an expensive flowered sundress. Her husband took his seat on the stage. Norma Sprague followed.

I glanced once at Will and Lauren. To my surprise, Dorrie Battles...Doreen to me...was standing along the wall on the other side of Will, swaying on impossibly high-heeled sandals that made her tower over those nearby. But she looked less relaxed than she had in her air-conditioned car. I searched the crowd for her husband and found him walking toward her, paper cup in hand. She said something as he squeezed in beside her. He winced. But Doreen had lost interest, having noticed that Lauren was standing on the other side of Will. I heard Lillian breathe in and turned to see that she, too, was watching what would happen.

A terrible screeching sound suddenly came from the mike on the small stage, breaking the moment. The zoning analyst glanced up front, then back at his wife, maybe relieved that he was no longer in her crosshairs. Lauren said something to Will, who laughed. A rotund middle-aged man I didn't know had stepped to the mike.

"Who's he?" I asked Lillian. "The moderator?"

"Owns a local radio station."

The moderator set out the guidelines: Each side would make an opening statement. Then they would debate a series of issues including environmental regulations, child care and education, Mountain Road rush-hour traffic, and domestic violence. Vince Darner won the coin toss to go first.

"We are, my friends, in the hands of a government out of control. You know it and I know it. State troopers follow you on the highways. Folks in Washington and Annapolis want to take away your Second Amendment rights. The Environmental Protection Agency is busy reducing the value of your land. They already tell you when you can build a fence or take down a tree. And mostly they say you can't. Businesses are going bust because they can't make a decent profit with all of the new environmental laws. Which we have done just fine without for many years."

He hitched his middle. The crowd stirred.

"Wait now. It gets worse. There are those who want to prevent you from using your personal watercraft. Noise pollution, they call it. And they already tell you when you can fish and for what. How many crabs you can take as you sit on your dock. Now they want to tell you how many decibels your boat motor can make." A murmur from the audience, which had grown larger, crowding Norma Sprague's supporters into a small corner. "This morning we had another disturbing example of government intrusion. People's inheritances are being taken from them by big government."

He briefly described the morning's hearing and its outcome. The crowd buzzed, angered. Carl Rainey did everything but take a bow from the sidelines.

"God, Lillian, Vince Darner's such slime. I wish we weren't doing business with him."

"I don't think we'll have to worry about that ever again." She leaned closer as the noise grew. "You know, I've always tried to keep business issues separate from my personal feelings and from politics, but this time Vince is way out of line. Next he'll be saying that the FBI and CIA have infiltrated the audience. Ugh.'' She jerked forward.

"What happened?"

"Nothing. Someone just bumped my chair. An accident."

I wasn't so sure, but I decided not to look around. Had it come to that? People so angry with Lillian that they were literally shoving her?

Vince Darner sat down and Norma Sprague rose to speak. Carl Rainey, I wasn't surprised to see, was greeting people at the back of the room. Duck Jarvis slapped his shoulder. They were about the same age.

"Is Florence here?" Lillian shook her head. Norma Sprague began to speak, her voice turning to righteous anger as she outlined the consequences of what Vince Darner planned to do if he were elected.

Glancing around I could see Lauren DeWitt still standing with Will at the back of the room, her short hair wet and curling on her neck, her casual clothes flawless. I wondered what inspired her. What made her want to save not just the crabs and oysters but all the ugly, unpleasant creatures that lived in the boggy murk? And at some risk to herself? The *Leader*'s piece had quoted her as being in Maryland to research and write an educational film about the Magothy area. I'd have to ask Will who was putting up the money. Another thought occurred to me. Was the environment the real reason she was here? I decided I was getting as paranoid as Carl Rainey.

As I watched Lauren, Will leaned in and whispered something to her. She smiled back and nodded, black eyes intense, posture relaxed and confident. Suddenly, I was concerned not for her but for him. He was going to get hurt and there was absolutely nothing I could do about it.

NINE

If Vince Darner had mobilized the crowd, Norma Sprague rubbed salt into gaping wounds. Darner's supporters, most of them men, sunk into a swamp of ill-concealed malevolence and name-calling.

"This is just a debate, folks." The moderator didn't look optimistic.

"Not any more, it ain't," said someone from the back.

Vince Darner's side of the room began to swarm with people clambering to their feet. Most of them seemed to be yelling. Someone offered to put Lillian and Weber Realty out of business. A darker fate was in store for Lauren, if a stage whisper behind me could be believed. I looked over to where she was standing with Will and discovered that Doreen Battles and her husband had disappeared. In their place a familiar figure was leaning against the wall.

Patrick Simmons was an Anne Arundel County detective. We'd met when he was investigating another case earlier in the spring. Like me, a New Yorker and a newcomer to Maryland, he had nevertheless a way of making me very uncomfortable. That was when he wasn't making me angry. Just now, however, I was glad to see him. The clamor was growing louder. Another cop, this one in uniform, had materialized in the back of the hall.

Vince Darner left the dais. Norma Sprague looked around, concerned, then also stepped down. At the back of the room, Darner's volunteers passed a clipboard for the names and phone numbers of supporters. More than a few were signing. I saw wallets come out. Money changed hands. Some hovered around a table of pamphlets. Norma Sprague went back to the mike.

"Ladies and gentlemen, we need..."

She was loudly booed. The moderator again took the mike

and asked for order. The crowd ignored him. He grimaced, then said something nobody heard.

"I don't like the looks of this," I said to Lillian. "Let's get out of here."

She got up, causing a flurry of catcalls when Vince Darner's supporters noticed her. Oddly, the place quieted as we made our way to the exit. The hostile silence was in some strange way worse than the jeers. Will and Lauren had disappeared. I nodded at Simmons, who nodded back as if he'd never seen me before.

Carl Rainey stood by the door, staring with overt hostility at Lillian. "See," he said, "it's not over. Not by a long shot." I looked over to see if Simmons had heard. He had.

Norma Sprague caught up with us and put her arm around Lillian. "God, Lil, I'm so sorry. I had no idea what I was asking when I asked you to show up tonight."

Her words dribbled away as the clamor rose inside the hall.

"Come on," I said to Lillian. "Let's go before this gets any nastier."

I walked my aunt to her car. Her mouth, I noticed, was set. She was determined to face the hostility aimed her way. But I knew she was also desperately hurt by it. "Look, you're just the scapegoat here. If it wasn't you, it would be someone else."

She turned to face me directly. "Do you think that makes this any easier? These people are my neighbors. They used to be my friends. And they are wrong about me." She sighed deeply. "And there's probably nothing I can do to change their minds. Not as long as Vince and Carl are stirring things up." She got in her car and struggled with the seat belt. By the time it was hooked, she was composed again. "By the way, I forgot to tell you that after you left this afternoon, I called a friend at the Hall of Records to see if he could find an old map of Knapp's Point. He did and Mitch was right. That shed *was* a sort of one-pump gas station for the marina Charlotte's parents ran years ago. The store stood across the clearing."

"So what happens next?"

"The Oil Control people dig up the tank, drain it, then take water and soil samples."

"And if the tank's leaking?"

"It's going to be hard, if not impossible, to sell until everything's all nice and cleaned up. No developer will buy because no banker will lend money for land with environmental problems." My aunt briefly outlined the environmental procedures that would need to be followed before the land could be sold. The process was long and complicated and expensive.

Behind me, I could see that people were beginning to emerge from the community hall. Vince Darner wasn't among them. "The fact that Vince didn't disclose the tank doesn't look good," Lillian was saying. "It's even possible that if the Department of the Environment thinks he engaged in some sort of cover-up, they would act on it legally." She seemed suddenly to realize that this might not be the best place and time to discuss it. She turned over the Cadillac's engine. "I truly hope it doesn't come to that."

"Well, maybe it will help Norma Sprague's reelection chances."

"Don't count on it." Lillian looked grim. "Vince knows exactly how to turn this to his advantage. He'll say he's another victim of an overzealous government. Just like Carl was this morning." She put the car into gear. "About tomorrow night...what time?"

"You still want to go to the fireworks? Given all that has happened today?"

"I have to," she said. But I heard the fatigue in her voice. "If I don't, I look guilty and afraid."

I nodded, agreeing but not happy about it. "Lillian...uh...oh, never mind."

She frowned, knowing full well I had been about to tell her to be careful. I watched her leave, admiring her resolve and unhappy that she should have to endure this.

"Right in the middle of things, as usual."

I turned to find Detective Simmons standing behind me. A mist of red hair exploded over his wide forehead and near non-existent eyebrows. He took a long drag on a half-smoked cigarette, threw it on the ground, and looked at it with undisguised longing.

"I didn't know you smoked."

"I don't. But they're bigger and stronger than I am tonight," he said. "Pretty hateful, what went on in there. Your aunt needs to watch her step."

I nodded, wishing Lillian had been there to hear this bit of advice. "Did someone call the police?"

"If you mean is that why I'm here, the answer is no." He yanked me out of the way of a van that was backing out. "But someone must have. Otherwise, the uniform wouldn't have shown up."

I was surprised. "So you aren't here in any official capacity?" He shook his head. "Am I then to take your presence to mean that you believe that the government has its oppressive foot on your neck?"

He grinned, a curious thing in the fading light. "Well, yes and no. Actually, I'm gonna be your neighbor." I felt my eyebrows go up, apparently amusing him. "One of the guys in the Western District had a house for rent." He named an address. It wasn't more than a half mile from me. "That okay with you?"

Suddenly there were yells behind us, then scuffling. Through the crowd I saw Will leaning against his pickup, holding his shoulder, breathing hard, eyes filled more with surprise than pain. Lauren stood nearby, her posture giving away her anger. Carl Rainey, his face ruby with exertion and hate, was being hauled away by a bigger, older man who had him in a hammerlock.

"Just you wait," Carl said to Lauren. Then he spat.

She looked down at the glob of spittle oozing down her shirt. "You stupid fool," she said. I could feel her revulsion from where I stood. Or maybe what I felt was my own disgust.

"Nice," Simmons said, heading in her direction.

Behind me the air moved. I turned to find Vince Darner.

"I see that Lil has gone," he said. "Probably a good idea, given everybody's mood. Perhaps you would give her a message for me." He moved closer. "Tell your aunt that it would be a very good idea if she kept her fantasies about buried oil tanks to herself. And that goes for you, too."

"Fantasies? Is that a threat?"

"A threat?" He smiled widely. "Of course not."

I looked around to see Charlotte standing twenty feet away, watching us, her expensive dress out of place in the dust and heat. She didn't meet my eyes. Will and Lauren were gone.

Then from the scrubby pine woods behind the parking lot came the sound of a small explosion. Then another. The uniformed cop appeared from somewhere. I saw Simmons take off in the direction of the woods. From somewhere came a siren. A large car spun onto Lido Beach Road and disappeared into the night. Charlotte ran to her husband. The rest of the crowd was shouting and running. I stood rooted. Who was shooting? And who was the target? And how had tonight's debate become this ugly, this fast?

THE FOURTH OF JULY broke all records for heat and draught and hostility. Last night's scuffle was reported on the local news, but Carl Rainey hadn't been arrested for slugging Will. Or for spitting on Lauren. No one admitted to firing any shots. A police spokesman raised the possibility of illegal fireworks, possibility cherry bombs, and promised that they would continue investigating. Will and Lauren had declined to be interviewed by reporters. Vince Darner was less reluctant. He dutifully rejected all violence but warned that emotions were running high and that this was going to be a long hot summer. Things would get worse before they got better...Lillian's very words. Norma Sprague countered with a call for calm and reason.

I spent most of the day lying low, lingering first in bed, then on the couch under a portable fan. The dogs panted, then went belly up on the cool slate in front of the fireplace. Will called to report a bruised shoulder where Carl Rainey had hit him. For no particular reason, he said, except that he was angry at something he thought he'd heard Lauren say. And Will was with her and thus also guilty. And no, she hadn't said anything. Nevertheless they had declined to press charges. I hung up the phone, worried all over again that he didn't understand the full extent of the growing local animosity toward Lauren. And him.

I also worried about Lillian, but she was still stubbornly determined to attend the fireworks with everyone else. I pointed out that she could probably see them from her dock. She refused. I sighed and put the phone down. It rang.

"Hi," Mitch said.

"Hi."

"Just called to find out what you and Lillian found out about the oil tank." He paused. "Actually, that's a lie. I heard about the brawl last night and wondered how you were."

"I'm fine. Will has a sore shoulder. And Lauren is probably laundering her blouse." I explain about the spitting.

"I hadn't heard about that. Ugly."

"That's what Simmons said."

"Simmons? Interesting that he was there."

"He's moving to the Pines."

"You talk with him about what's going on?"

"Well, no, not really. Besides, what exactly *is* going on? There have been all these nasty little events. But are they related?"

"Who knows. Did Lillian confront Vince Darner with the oil tank problem?" I was quiet, wondering how much I should tell him. "Eve?"

"Yes. Okay. He warned her to keep quiet about it. He also wanted her to tear up his contract with us, but she refused. Then, he hung up on her." I could hear him breathing. Classical piano was playing in the background. "She was furious. Called the Maryland Department of the Environment right off. They're going to dig it up. Then he..."

"Darner?"

"Ummm. He, uh, cornered me in the parking lot last night, after Lillian had gone, and made this threat, which he swore wasn't a threat."

I was rambling and I wondered how much sense he was making about all of this. "Simmons know this?" asked Mitch.

"No, he was busy keeping the peace."

We were both silent. But it was companionable and I admitted to myself that I'd missed seeing him the last month.

"I had breakfast with Dick Hubbard this morning," he said.

"He's pretty unhappy with the county's zoning analyst for screwing up yesterday's hearing." The background music had stopped. "Wait a sec." I waited. Music again, this time violin. I heard him say something to someone, so maybe he was in the office.

We talked for a few more disjointed minutes, flitting back and forth between subjects, but he kept being interrupted. So when it got impossible, or maybe when neither of us had anything left to say, he told me he'd look for me at the fireworks.

"You are going, yes?"

"Yes."

I put the phone down, vaguely uneasy about everything. Then I ruminated and read and slept some more in the heat, waking late afternoon with a headache and the fervent hope that dusk would bring cooler temperatures.

TEN

IT DIDN'T. Instead, it brought cars to the Pines's narrow and dusty streets. Dozens and dozens, maybe hundreds, of cars. They were parked everywhere, on lawns and road shoulders, blocking driveways and the public right-of-ways to the water. I was forced to wedge my BMW in sideways between two vans and walk the last quarter mile to Lillian's house. A Ford Bronco, I noticed, had half crushed a bush near her driveway.

"The traffic is unbelievable. Why aren't the cops doing something?" We were standing in her kitchen, and still able to hear the car horns and occasional yells. "You couldn't get your car out of your garage if you wanted to."

"Well, I don't want to." She pointed to two folding lawn chairs leaning against the table. I picked them up. "You have to understand what a big deal the fireworks are here. And the carnival. The town spends most of its annual budget on it." She rummaged among some clutter on the counter, looking up when she found her keys. "Over the years the police have tended to look the other way about the illegal parking. So now that's a tradition of sorts, too."

"We could sit on your deck," I said again, without much hope. "Be more comfortable."

Lillian shook her head and locked the back door. She noticed my glance at her feet, encased in a pair of sneakers suitable for someone with aspirations for a career in the NBA. "If you know what's good for you, you'll keep your comments about my footwear to yourself."

I didn't say a word. But I did laugh. And for the first time in a couple of days, so did she.

Residents and visitors swarmed in the hot night, walking in the middle of streets, through gardens and fields, down the public-access routes. They cut through neighbors' yards to tramp along the edge of the Magothy to the dingy town beach. They carried coolers and lawn chairs and seat cushions and blankets. The fireworks would go up from a barge floating between the public beach and Arundel Island.

Dusk was falling fast as we joined the throng walking along the water. People had streamed down the right-of-way by Lillian's house and along the Raineys' wooded acreage. I saw my aunt allow herself one quick glance at the deep woods. Her face revealed no emotion, but I knew she was thinking about the tall oaks and loblolly pines that had been spared by yesterday's ruling. And was wondering how something so life-affirming as trees could have caused such a rift between neighbors.

Lillian's waterfront was easy to cross. There was a kind of wooden boardwalk—elevated in wet, marshy places—and a substantial dock that my uncle Max had designed the year before his death. Eight feet below the dock and running along the water was a seawall, a low, wide, and uneven hedge of large squarish quarry stones called riprap. Tonight a crowd of teenagers had assembled on the stones, jumping from one to another, pushing and shoving. There were shouts and laughter. The lighted end of a cigarette glowed, then was gone.

"I wish they wouldn't go down there," Lillian said. "They drink and leave garbage and beer cans and broken bottles, which I then have to have cleaned up."

We walked steadily, ignoring the hateful whispers flowing around us. The path that began when Lillian's boardwalk ran out was uneven and rocky. The heat seemed to grow in intensity, making me sneezy and shivery. Dusk fell around us. A stroke of heat lightning rent the blistering air over the water.

The parking lot between Lido Beach Road and the public beach was ringed with concession stands selling hot dogs and beer, fried dough and ice cream. In the center, a few rides—small but scary in their sorry state of disrepair—had materialized next to an arcade of booths. Carnies manned shooting ranges and offered darts to passersby.

"Sooo easy to win," one said. "Piece a cake."

Over his head dangled stuffed animals of pink and blue plush and framed pictures of Elvis. A small American flag stuck out of his shirt pocket.

"Three tries. One buck," he said, holding out the darts.

A couple of booths over, I could see Eli Claggett trying to ring milk bottles with little hoops. I wondered what color rabbit he'd choose if he won. Instead the man handed him a big inflatable yellow pencil and Eli said something, which if the man's expression was any indication, couldn't have been any too complimentary.

"Whatever would I do with a picture of Elvis?" Lillian was asking.

"You don't like the King?" the man in the booth asked.

"Let's go find a spot on the beach." Lillian nodded.

Kids were everywhere, chasing each other, spilling sticky drinks, screaming. I recognized the Jarvis children. A yellow lab panted hard and got underfoot. Norma Sprague, her blouse covered with red stripes and blue stars, was deep in conversation with a constituent. Her volunteers passed out pamphlets. I took one and stuffed it into the pocket of my shorts, then looked around. Smiles faded when people saw us. And they gave us wide berth, turning their backs. Murmurs dripped poison in the hot night. Lillian pretended not to notice.

If Norma was here, so was Vince Darner. Sure enough. Standing in a small circle of supporters, he was talking with Dick Hubbard. He gestured broadly, his movements jerky and irritated. Charlotte Darner stood a few yards away with Doreen Battles, who then turned and spotted Lillian. Her laughter froze and she glared. Beside me, I could almost feel my aunt recoil.

"Well," said Lillian, "I guess Dorrie's not very happy with me. But then, nobody else is either."

I glanced at my aunt but her face gave away nothing. "You know her?"

"Dorrie? Yes, of course. She grew up not too far from Knapp's Point. Up and surprised everyone when she married that zoning analyst a few years ago."

I looked around. Duck Jarvis was lounging a few yards away. His daughter ran up and said something. He shook his head, then scanned the crowd for someone. A frown drifted over his face. I followed his eyes. Josie Jarvis was standing near a concession stand talking to Lauren DeWitt. She was laughing.

Then, as if she sensed her husband's unhappy gaze, her smile wandered off to the edge of her mouth and was gone. I saw Lauren browse the crowd. Will. She was looking for Will. I was again surprised at the tiny prick of jealousy that floated up. Pushing it away, I watched the Jarvis girl find her mother. She shifted from foot to foot, talking a mile a minute to Lauren as Josie fished out some money. Lauren said something and the Jarvis girl nodded shyly. Then she faded back to the arcade. I still didn't see Will.

Lillian and I reached the edge of the tacky manmade beach. At the other end of the parking lot, by a stand selling ice cream, I got a glimpse of the Raineys. Florence looked slight and forlorn, sandwiched between Carl and the booth. Nearby, Charlotte Darner was now standing off by herself, eating an ice cream cone like a large solemn child.

A uniformed cop strolled by, looking around. After last night, the Anne Arundel police were apparently taking no chances. I wondered if Simmons would show up. A siren blared somewhere in the distance. I watched the cop talk into the radio pinned to his shirt, then head through the carnival crowd toward the main road.

"Evening, folks." Lillian and I turned to find Weller Church standing with a regal white-haired woman. He introduced me to his wife, then turned to Lillian. "Dixie and I are looking for a spot. Why don't you join us?" He pointed to an empty spot not far from the edge of the public beach and grabbed the lawn chairs from my hand.

"Lillian," I said, "I'll be right back." She nodded. I returned to the parking lot to find Will. Norma Sprague smiled at me. Josie Jarvis passed by. Duck caught up with her, grabbing her arm. She shook herself loose, clutching her elbow where he had grabbed her. There was a quick, whispered conversation, its venom almost tangible. Her face was panicked, stricken.

As I watched, the daughter ran to her mother. Duck Jarvis turned his attention to her. She looked at the ground, her toe kicking at the dirt. He grabbed her arm and she looked up finally, nodding. Satisfied, he headed off among the carnival booths and along the Magothy. I felt sick. It was the scene at Knapp's Point all over again. Josie absently patted her daughter's arm, then turned away, a sense of helplessness hovering around her. I didn't see the Jarvis boy, but the girl darted among the booths after her father. Charlotte Darner, ice cream gone, rejoined her husband, who scowled at her and pointed toward the beach.

ELEVEN

"EVE?" MITCH STOOD behind me. "I'd like you meet some-one." A girl, maybe seven or eight, with white-blond hair locked behind her ears and a blue giraffe in her arms, stood beside him. "This is my daughter, Laura," he said. "She's here on a vacation. Her mother is traveling in Italy."

"Daddy, she's not traveling," she said. "If she were trav-eling, I'd be with her."

"Well, okay, not traveling." Mitch turned to me. "My ex-wife just remarried. She's on her honeymoon."

The girl nodded. I fought back an impulse to ask how much the blue giraffe had cost him.

"Where are you sitting?" He held up a stadium blanket.

"Lillian is over there. With Weller Church and his wife." I pointed.

There was a short conversation between father and daughter concerning seating arrangements and ice cream. "You going to be here for a couple of minutes?" he asked. I nodded. Dusk was becoming darkness. A kind of land rush for prime beach real estate was soon on. Where was Will? "America the Beau-tiful" issued from a loudspeaker.

"We need some real music around here, not this canned stuff." I turned to find Marian Beall having abandoned her bar for the festivities. "Next year we gotta get one of the military groups. Lil here?" I nodded.

"Marian, you saw what happened at the Arundel Center yes-terday morning. It wasn't what Lillian wanted."

"Doesn't matter one fig what she wanted or intended. This is about money. Which makes folks emotional." She rooted through the pockets of her shorts, discovering a set of keys and a wadded tissue. Neither seemed to please her much. "Far too much emoting going on. And as usual, damned little thinking." I followed her glance around. A red-faced Carl Rainey was standing by the beer truck. "Ladies and gentlemen, exhibit number one."

"Have you seen Will?"

She shook her head. "Money and heat. Makes emotions run high," she said. "You tell Lillian to watch her step." Simmons's advice. What did they think was going to happen? Before I could ask, she had wandered off, her squat body lost in the crowd thronging the beach. I wondered whom she would vote for. I also wondered who was minding her bar. Maybe she'd closed it for the fireworks. I saw Eli Claggett near the beer truck. He approached Carl Rainey and said something.

Mitch came up behind me, carrying two beers in plastic cups. He handed me one. "There's apparently been some sort of accident on Lido Beach Road," he said. "Three or four cars involved. Just a fender bender but nobody can get through."

So that's what must have happened to Will. "Where's Laura?" I asked.

"I left her amusing Lillian and the Churches."

"She's a lovely child," I said, feeling like an idiot. He nodded. Fortunately, the first round of fireworks went skyward just then. It bloomed into a crackling flower of red darts floating over the water. We headed for the beach.

"Eve?" I stopped and turned to find Will behind us, his T-shirt soaked and breathing hard, as if he'd been running. "You haven't seen Lauren, have you?"

"Earlier."

"When?"

"A while ago. Maybe half an hour. Maybe longer."

Above us smaller fireworks were cascading downward, punctuated by an occasional tattoo of blood-pounding jolts or a golden fireball that detonated with a throbbing blast. The zoning analyst stood in line at the beer concession, fishing money from his wallet. Then he picked up two cups and looked around. A flashing jolt overhead made him jump. As it did me. Carl Rainey and Eli Claggett with his inflatable yellow pencil had both disappeared. Will moved closer, still half out of breath.

"You get caught behind that accident?" Mitch asked.

Will nodded. "At the intersection of Dwyer and Lido Beach

Road. I had to park about two miles away." His eyes scanned the crowd. "I was supposed to meet Lauren on Lillian's dock. But she's not there."

The fireworks were heating up, with volleys coming faster and louder and brighter. I could hear the audience on the beach taking up its part in the ceremony, with a Greek chorus of appreciation after each burst of color and noise.

"Maybe she gave up since you were late and thought she'd find you here."

Will said something I couldn't hear, and headed for the beach.

"Will?" He looked back. "Lillian is just to the left of the entrance way, by that little beach hut. Maybe she's seen Lauren." He nodded. I soon lost sight of him. Above us, a spray of white lights rained down over the water, the whistles followed by sharp reports. The Jarvis girl darted out from behind the beach shed, her hands over her ears, and ran into the crowd to find her mother. I didn't see anyone else I knew.

Somewhere a dog whimper turned into a long, high wail. I thought about Lance and Zeke, who were probably flattened under the bed. Mitch touched my shoulder and together we headed for the beach to try to catch the last five minutes of the fireworks. There were couples and families camped all around. Lillian and Laura and the Churches had already joined the approving chorus. Above us, the grand finale had begun. There were cascading crescendos of bursting flares, one after another, red after white after blue, the intensity rising to a heart-hurting close. Then it was over. People roared as the flares in the night sky faded, clapping and yelling their appreciation.

"Look," someone said. "Over there."

In the distance, from the opposite direction, I could see that a yellowish light, malevolent and glowing, had appeared in the night sky.

AN HOUR LATER I couldn't remember how Lillian and I and Mitch and Laura and the blue giraffe had found our way back to my aunt's house. Weller Church and his wife had been lost in the melee of barking dogs and screaming children.

The night sky was filled with flames darting from Lillian's long dock. We huddled on the far side of her house, away from the right-of-way. Behind us a growing crowd stood watching from the street and along the shrubbery, wherever they could fit in. There was the occasional chorus of oohs and ahhs as flames conquered dry timbers. But this time the sounds came not from happy children, but from the throats of nervous adults, all thinking that there but for the grace of God went their docks, their garages. Or their houses and woods and boats.

"Laura," Mitch said. "I want you to stay here with Eve and Lillian. Do you understand?" I held out my hand. The girl took it. Mitch turned to me. "The garden hose? Where is it?" I pointed. "I want to hose down the deck and nearby trees and bushes. In case the fire jumps to those trees and then..."

The rest of his sentence was lost. My throat tightened as a flaming plank fell through the darkness into the water. Lillian leaned against the side of the house, her hand to her mouth. This was Max's dock, designed over many winters and then built with loving care his final spring. Of course, at the time, no one had known it would be his last. Now his dock was one more thing taken from her. Laura let go of my hand and grabbed Lillian's.

"It's gone," Lillian said. "It's gone."

"Maybe they can save the boardwalk."

She shook her head. "Too dry."

We stood waiting with the crowd. The fire department was usually an effective alliance of volunteers and professionals. How they would get through tonight was anyone's guess.

There was movement around the corner as Mitch uncurled Lillian's hose and focused it on the deck and the corner of the house. Then he turned it on nearby trees and bushes. It was precious little, but it was something. Laura wiggled and watched. Lillian nodded her approval, all practicality now. The Raineys' woods weren't that far from the flames. A hard thought crept through my mind and I pushed it away. I had to believe that not even Carl, as furious as he was with Lillian, would purposely put her house, and even his mother's, in danger.

A section of the dock suddenly collapsed into the Magothy. Stray sparks ignited what was left. They fell in a shower of sparkling crystals. Someone was yelling now. A cop told people to move back. In the distance, a siren stirred the scalding air. There were more yells as someone directed traffic and someone else objected. Boozy voices mingled with children's screams. Someone had chosen to watch the fire from a perch on the riprap breakwater below the collapsing dock.

Lillian saw him, too. Her hand was on my arm. "Oh, Lord. One of those boys is still down there." She pointed at the figure sitting spellbound watching the flames against the night sky. "If that section of the dock falls, he is going to get hurt."

Within a couple of minutes a fire truck drove slowly down the right-of-way to within feet of the water. Dark figures jumped out and began stretching hoses.

Had a cigarette carelessly tossed set the fire? Or had the dock been ignited by a stray spark from the fireworks? It wouldn't have taken much. The darker thought about Carl Rainey's role again crossed my mind. The wind was picking up now, blowing hot dry air and whipping the flames. Suddenly, a billow of black smoke arose from where the dock had been.

"What's that? What's happened?"

"Tires, I think. Max had tires nailed partway under the dock. They were used as bumpers when boats docked. They must have caught fire."

I watched, fascinated, sickened, helpless. The stench of burning rubber intensified. The yelling and sirens became louder. A second fire truck crept to the water.

"What are they doing, Lillian?" asked Laura.

"Getting ready to pump water from the Magothy. This isn't like New York. We don't have fire hydrants here. It's why we have these narrow public right-of-ways between some of the houses."

"So that the fire engines can get to the water," Laura finished.

Lillian nodded. "But most of the time, it's just so everyone can use the waterfront. Even those people who don't live right on it."

I glanced at my aunt in her ridiculous shoes. How on earth could she calmly explain principles of land use to a child while her dock was burning and her house was in jeopardy? I looked back to the scene by the water. Carl Rainey stood close to where the fire truck was pumping and spraying water. He spoke to a solitary fireman standing by the water's edge, who turned and pointed.

"Thank God the breeze is blowing away from the land," someone in the crowd said. "Otherwise, the woods might catch."

"If those big trees go, then this house is a goner," someone else said. I turned to see the speakers, but it was too dark. With luck Lillian hadn't heard.

I wondered if Lauren and Will had found each other in the crowd. Probably not, or he'd have been here with her. Suddenly, I needed to know.

"Laura, stay here with Lillian. Your father will be back now that the fire department is here. I'm going to see if I can find someone."

I crept along the side of the house, scratching my leg on a holly bush, then moving toward my aunt's property line. It was edged with a long double row of tall, heavy evergreens that served as a privacy screen halfway to the water. People stood shoulder to shoulder along them, trying to see. I inched toward the road, trying to make out faces in the darkness. I recognized Josie Jarvis, her arms around her daughter, her son jumping up and down nearby. Will and Lauren weren't in sight. Nor did I find the Darners or Weller and Dixie Church or anybody else I knew. A third fire truck arrived.

A bellow went up from the crowd. I turned to see what was left of Lillian's dock fall blazing into the Magothy. The flames were mostly gone, though the fire department continued to spray water over the charred wood. Thick smoke still hovered, and the eye-watering smell of burned rubber permeated the air. Josie Jarvis's hand had gone to her mouth, her kids momentarily forgotten. Her daughter looked petrified.

I returned to Lillian. Mitch was back, standing with Laura. The girl had her arms around his waist and was gazing up at him. He looked over the top of her head at me and said something. It was drowned out by more yells.

I turned back to the scene by the water. To the left, along the raised boardwalk, firefighters still sprayed water on flames that spurted, died, then spurted again. Then the tire smoke was suddenly swept away, drawn off by a gust of wind and revealing the figure still watching from the quarry stones.

There was a small flurry of activity as a firefighter shed his gear, then scrambled, slid, and finally fell down where the smoldering dock had fallen. Glowing embers scattered. The crowd groaned. Behind him, the floodlights from a fire truck illuminated dark water with floating debris adding to the underwater hell of stinging nettles. Several other firefighters stood nearby. One shook his head. The crowd was silent now, collectively worried.

"That looks like Duck Jarvis who went down there," said Lillian.

I got a glimpse of Josie Jarvis, her kids at her side, the boy pushing to get a better look at the rescue efforts. The family approached where we stood, Lillian making way for them. Josie stumbled on something underfoot, caught herself.

"Are you all right?" I asked. She turned to me, about to say something, her eyes filled with anxiety, when the boy yelled and sprinted toward the water. She held her daughter back.

"Why did that fireman go down there, Daddy?" Laura asked Mitch.

"I guess he's going to try to rescue the person who is sitting on the riprap. Whoever it is may have inhaled smoke."

"They're going to have trouble getting medics down there if the fire isn't completely out," Lillian said. The flames along the boardwalk spurted skyward again.

The crowd was quiet, the only sounds coming from distant car horns. We could see Duck Jarvis moving on the riprap. Slowly, he sat up, holding his arm. Another firefighter yelled something but Duck shook his head and began gingerly climbing from stone to stone, finding toeholds, testing them, inching forward in the near dark. Occasionally, shooting sparks fell and went out. Suddenly he lost his balance and slipped again, sliding down the riprap before catching himself. The crowd inhaled. Next to Duck, the seated figure toppled forward onto the sharp white stones.

TWELVE

WITHIN MINUTES OF finding Lauren DeWitt's body, the flood-lights that had illuminated the scorched remains of the dock and boardwalk were trained on the riprap. Dark figures scrambled and crept, jumping sharp stones in the shocking light. Sirens echoed. As rescuers neared the prostrate figure, the crowd grew quieter, with whispers and rumors flying. Cops tried without much success to send people home. Wailing, overtired children did a better job. Parents reluctantly collected their coolers and kids and moved on, turning back to look one last time.

A crime lab van drove slowly down the right-of-way. Then I saw Simmons walking the large area enclosed by yellow police tape. Duck Jarvis stood to one side. A uniformed cop shooed two teenagers away. Carl Rainey had gone.

We now sat rooted and silent on Lillian's deck. Laura held Mitch's hand. My aunt said nothing, waiting only for the identification of the body. Someone in the crowd beneath the deck loudly offered to fetch binoculars from the trunk of his car.

"It's that environmentalist," the same voice said a few minutes later. "What's her name, Lauren Somebody." He looked again. "Oh, shit. You gotta see this. There's a gash in her head and blood all over her clothes and I think on the riprap." The onlookers processed this new information, launching more rumors.

"Can we go inside, Lillian?" Mitch was trying unsuccessfully to shield his daughter from the scene. My aunt looked for her key.

"I'm going to find Will," I said.

Mitch held the sliding deck door open for Laura and Lillian. "Wait a second." He went inside and returned with a flashlight. "I'll go with you."

"No." I grabbed the flashlight. "Thanks."

Word of Lauren's death had raced through the streets of the

Pines, not unlike the way the fire had demolished Lillian's dock. I could hear people speculating about the wound in Lauren's head and about the fire. Their voices were curious, excited, desperately interested. But something was missing: warmth, concern. Lauren Somebody, they called her. It wasn't just that she wasn't one of them. She had—at least to their way of thinking—wanted to interfere with the way they led their lives.

Two patrol cars guarded the right-of-way by Lillian's house, their lights spinning blue in the night. I turned in the direction of the public beach. Will was sitting on the front step of a house three doors down, his head buried in his arms.

"Will?" He looked up. "You know it's Lauren?" He turned to me, his face dry and empty. I sat, not touching him. "I'm so sorry."

He nodded. I could see his eyes in the porch light and they scared me. "Something is sick here," he said.

A few feet from us a stick with Vince Darner's campaign poster was wedged in the lawn. He promised to liberate us from big government, which stole our money and our freedoms.

The road in front of us was clearing rapidly. A few holdouts stood watching the distant crime scene but most were leaving in groups, walking two and three abreast down the middle of the street. A media truck—Fox News from Baltimore—crawled along, stopping when it came to the flashing patrol cars. The driver did a quick U-turn and wedged the truck between two of them. A cop told him to move on and after arguing a bit he did. One fire truck crept up the right-of-way and left, heaving around the tight corner with a loud sigh, off into the night.

I don't know how long we sat in the heat and dark, not speaking.

"She knew she'd made enemies," Will said, "but she wasn't ready to give in to them."

"Carl Rainey slugged you last night, for God's sake. And spit on her because he was so angry." Will looked sideways at me. "Sorry. I don't mean to blame Lauren."

"So don't then."

After a few more minutes, I persuaded him to return to Lillian's house. My aunt had shown Laura to a spare bedroom and the girl fell asleep clutching the giraffe. The four of us sat without talking, waiting for Simmons.

When the detective came, his eyes were shining. Did he actually like this? No, that wasn't fair. He didn't like murder, but rather the challenge of it, the game between hunter and hunted. Some day, now that he was to be my neighbor, maybe I'd ask him.

Lillian got up twice to answer the phone. The first call was from Weller, who offered any assistance he could. He reported a huge traffic jam, with people stuck in their cars for what seemed like hours. Norma Sprague called with essentially the same message. Mitch checked a couple of times on his sleeping daughter.

Compared to the rest of us, Simmons seemed oddly fresh. He thought about each answer before he asked the next question. He also seemed particularly interested in Will's whereabouts during the evening.

"So you never saw the victim tonight?"

Will shook his head. "We'd agreed to meet about nine at Lillian's dock, just before the fireworks were supposed to start. But I got hung up in that traffic jam and had to walk a couple of miles. And when I got there, she wasn't there. So I headed for the beach. I never found her."

"What time did you get there? At the dock?"

"It must have been close to nine-thirty. I waited for a couple of minutes, but it was very dark, so I went back up the right-of-way to the road, and then headed to the beach."

"And?"

He looked up. "And nothing. I thought she'd given up waiting for me since we were supposed to meet about nine. I found Eve and Mitch but no one had seen her in a while. It was before the grand finale."

"So you never found her," Simmons asked.

"I just told you five minutes..." Will took a deep breath. "That's right. I never found her."

"And at Mrs. Weber's dock? You see anyone?"

"No. It was dark, except when the fireworks went off, which lit up things for a couple of seconds."

"Anyone see you?"

"Well, if I didn't see them, how would I know if anyone saw me? Maybe whoever killed her saw me. I don't know." Lillian clucked. Will looked over at her. I saw her move her head slightly side to side. "Okay, yes. Lots of people saw me as I was walking from my car. It was like the *Night of the Living Dead* out there in the fields." There was a silence as we considered this. "Sorry. That didn't come out the way...oh, forget it."

A clock in Lillian's dining room chimed midnight. "So when and where was the last time you saw the victim?" Simmons asked.

"She has a name."

There was another exhausting silence, interrupted only by Simmons's breathing. "Yes, Mr. St. Claire, she does. Now when and where?"

"Last night. At that debate. After that cretin slimed her, she just wanted to go home. I don't know what time it was."

I heard the air-conditioning kick in. Will's angry, brooding answers to Simmons's questions receded. In fits and starts, the events of the last two days replayed in my mind. I could almost see the slumped figure wedged among the quarry stones. You don't like the King? someone asked.

"The King?" Simmons asked. "Ms. Elliott, you okay?"

"Sorry." I looked around the room. "My mind wandered. What did you ask me?"

"If you saw Lauren DeWitt earlier in the evening?"

"Just once, I think. She was talking with Josie Jarvis and her daughter. That was the last I saw her."

He made a note. "When and where was that?"

I racked my brain, trying to put things into chronological order. I thought about the crowded parking lot, the booths and bingo tent and unsteady rides, the vendors with their money aprons covering their shorts, making them look pantless. The colorful stuffed animals, the little American flags. Had the carnival packed and gone yet? Had anyone questioned the workers?

"It was before the fireworks started, I think. Were you

there?'' Simmons nodded and I wondered how I'd missed him. He waited, motionless. The others were listening closely. ''Lauren was near that fried dough booth, I think. She was talking to Josie.''

''Then what happened?'' Simmons asked.

''She must have gone to meet Will at Lillian's dock. I saw her look around. I thought she was looking for him. Later when I glanced over again, she wasn't there.'' Simmons was still waiting. ''I didn't see her after that. Or see her leave. Or think about her until Will showed up.''

We went on like that for some time, getting nowhere. Lillian looked exhausted. Mitch was oddly quiet. Will sat, head in hands, probably blaming himself for not taking Lauren's enemies more seriously. Simmons questioned him at length about Lauren's activities. He took phone numbers, then stood up. I walked him outside, leaving Mitch and my aunt to discuss whether to disturb Laura for what remained of the night.

The street in front of the house was finally clear of pedestrians. Behind us, we could see the water's edge, where dark silhouettes still prowled the crime scene. The fire trucks were gone. The media vans were gone. Stationed by the road, there were two patrol cars and a fire department vehicle. They would, Simmons told me, stay the night. We stood companionably in the dark.

''What about the fire?'' I asked.

''What about it?''

''Was it deliberately set?''

''The fire marshall will investigate.''

''Maybe the fire was set by whoever killed Lauren,'' I said. ''To cover up.''

Simmons looked at me. ''We don't yet know that the victim was killed. We don't even know how she died.''

I told him about the man with the binoculars and how he'd described for anyone who would listen—and that was everybody plus the media—what he saw. Simmons listened without apparent interest.

''We'll know after the autopsy.''

''And when will that be?''

"Probably tomorrow morning."

"That's fast."

"Yeah. Politics."

"Did you find a weapon? I mean something that killed Lauren? I mean...not a murder weapon since you don't know if it's a murder...oh, you know what I mean. What she died from?"

He shrugged. I gathered that meant no. But I also was sure there was something he wasn't telling me, something that told him Lauren had indeed been murdered. Nobody said anything for a few seconds, but neither of us was quite willing to break away.

"You get moved in?" I said, finally.

"Yeah."

"Not much fun, moving."

"Not much."

We stood a bit longer. My mind produced a lengthy flashback of the carnival, pictures returned to me in silence, figures moving in a soundless ballet. I saw people I knew come together and then move apart, then come together again. The sequence was dreamlike, bizarre, visual only—no smells, no sounds, no touching—like a silent film. I glanced over at Simmons, relieved he couldn't see into my head.

He folded his notebook and slipped it into his pocket. Why didn't I just tell him about the stupefying number of events, unrelated or not, that had taken place over the last few days? From Knapp's Point to the scene outside the Arundel Center in Annapolis? Maybe they had some bearing on the case. Or maybe not. It was Simmons's job to decide. Why not just tell him everything?

"You having company tonight?" he asked.

And that, I thought, was why not. A perfectly innocent question, given the grisly scene by the water, and yet he made it sound vaguely dirty. The muscles of my neck tightened. Will and Mitch were walking toward us. I glanced at Simmons and tried to believe his interest in my house guests was innocent. The trouble was that with Simmons nothing ever felt innocent.

"We're going to stay with Lillian tonight," Mitch said. "She was kind enough to offer and I didn't want to move Laura." I was glad. It would allow me to go home with a free conscience. I looked over at Will.

"You going home?" He nodded. "Want a lift to your truck?" He nodded for a second time. "Okay, give me a minute then. I want to say good night to Lillian."

I walked Mitch back into the house, leaving Will and Simmons standing uneasily in the dark, with nothing to say to each other that hadn't already been said.

"Simmons tell you anything interesting?" asked Mitch.

"Autopsy first thing tomorrow. And he didn't exactly say so, but I'm sure that he thinks she was killed. There's something he's not telling us. When I asked outright, he insisted it could have been an accident."

"He thinks he has to say that." He smiled, the crinkles a little deep at this hour. "But I'm sure they'll search tomorrow morning. Probably bring in divers to check the surrounding water in case some sort of weapon was used to kill her."

Lillian was sitting at her kitchen table, her eyes sunken from exhaustion. I looked over her shoulder. She was making a list of things to do tomorrow: notify the insurance agent, arrange for removal of the charred debris from the water's edge, get estimates for a new dock, buy groceries.

She looked up. "Life goes on." She added another item to the list. I looked down. It said Florence.

"I'm going now," I told her. "Be back tomorrow morning."

"Don't worry about getting here early. We all need to get some sleep." She pivoted a little in her chair to look at me. "You'll be okay?"

"Yes."

"Get Will to stay the night with you," she said.

I kissed her. "I'll be fine."

"It isn't you I'm worried about."

Mitch nodded slightly, then ran his hand through his hair. Outside, Will was waiting by himself. I didn't see Simmons. We walked to my car, now alone on the street. The blue swirling flashes caught in the glass of a nearby window and then rippled on to the next house. I turned back once. Simmons was leaning into a patrol car window to talk with the driver. An unhappy thought kept surfacing: Lauren DeWitt's death had horrified everyone, but how many had it surprised?

THIRTEEN

JULY FIFTH dawned dry and suffocating with still no rain in the forecast. I thought I could hear low-pitched and distant rumblings but maybe I was imagining it.

"Nothing's going to make it if we don't get some rain soon." Will stood on my porch, looking out at the dusty patch of ground in front of the cottage, shaking his head. "Two or three days of slow soaking. Otherwise, that's it."

He had spent the night on my couch, awakening in a state of eerie calm. In some ways I found it more unsettling than his outbursts last night. This morning he was composed, and like Lillian, oddly practical. I'd spent the night in an uneasy series of naps—awakening several times to the reek of burning rubber and the image of dark blood seeping among white stones.

The clock said eight-fifteen. Zeke struggled to his feet, shook himself, licked my hand, then clambered downstairs.

After coffee, Will attached his pager to his belt and headed off to look at what the drought had done to a client's landscaping. It appeared to be more in the line of a sympathy call than anything else. With the watering ban in place, there wasn't a lot he could do. Still, it would keep him busy, and he admitted the need to be busy while we waited for the medical examiner to tell us what had really happened to Lauren.

I clipped on my own pager. If Detective Simmons had wanted to stay in touch with any group of people, he couldn't do better than real estate agents. Like it or not, most of us were available round the clock.

The phone rang. Simmons. So much for the pager. He was on his way over. Fifteen minutes later the dogs announced him.

Saying that the detective looked hot would have been an understatement. He was mopping his face and neck with a large handkerchief as I opened the screen door. It was a losing battle, since the bubbles of sweat popped back immediately. A man given to working more comfortably after dark.

He followed me into the living room. Except for a small eat-in kitchen and the bathroom, the downstairs of my cottage was one large room divided into living areas. I pointed to the couch and took a tall chair next to the fireplace. The dogs behaved, but I suspected Zeke was thinking bad thoughts as he lowered himself to the floor, amber dog eyes never leaving Simmons's face.

"The autopsy?" I asked.

"All but the toxicology reports."

"And?" I stared hard at him but he just stared back, his pale eyebrows motionless. "Look, everyone in Maryland already knows that Lauren had a gash in her head and that there was blood all over. All the TV stations reported it this morning, quoting that guy with the binoculars. I told you about him last night."

"The victim was choked before she died," he said.

A hot whine had risen in the clearing in front of the cottage. Cicadas. Or rather, one cicada. Rubbing its legs together. Amazingly, no vocal cords were involved, no throats or insect speech. I calmed the buzzing in my head and focused.

"Choked? You mean someone tried to strangle her? She didn't bleed to death?"

"She died of brain injuries from the fall, her brain bumping against the side of her skull. And she cut her head on the... the..."

"Riprap."

"Yeah, riprap. We did find some blood and hair on the stones." Simmons had perched on the edge of what was a brand-new sofa. It was deep and soft and long and wide, with fat cushions. But he was clearly having trouble getting comfortable. He finally got up to wander about the room. Zeke stood up and the Chesapeake Bay retriever looked like he was thinking about it. I stayed put and waited. "She had marks on her neck where someone tried to cut off her air," he said. "Bruises that looked like they were made by thumbs."

"You knew last night, didn't you?" He nodded. "With all that blood."

"Her wound bled some because her heart hadn't yet stopped but it wasn't that much. The media reports of blood from here to there, spurting great fountains, spraying yards away over rocks, were—to put it mildly—exaggerated. Makes a better story that way."

We sat not talking for a few minutes. The radio was playing quietly in the kitchen. I'd forgotten to turn it off.

"What do you think happened?"

"I think she had a fight with someone on your aunt's dock. And that person pressed against her windpipe with his thumbs. They struggled and she must have fallen and landed on those quarry stones. She gashed her head. Then I'd guess she slid down and sort of got wedged there, like she was sitting and watching. Then she died of brain injuries."

"She was dead when we first noticed her?"

There was the sound of scrabbling dog nails on the floorboards as Lancelot moved to get more comfortable.

"Yeah, probably."

"When?"

"Can't know exactly. An hour, maybe more, before she was found."

Simmons' words seeped into my head: An hour, maybe more. I calculated backwards. If that were true...

"Do you mean that we were, uh, watching the fireworks? She died during the grand finale?"

"Possible," he said.

I didn't know why this seemed to make things worse, but it did. Maybe it was more like a war, with rockets and mortars overhead. I had a bad thought.

"You don't think Will had anything to do with this?"

"No. Luckily for your young friend Mr. St. Claire, there were a whole lot of people lurching through that potato field last night. Most of them appeared to have seen him there or later running along the road to the beach. After that he met up with you and then went to the beach to search for the victim. Your aunt and others saw him."

I nodded, then released my breath, causing Zeke to nudge my hand with his head. "So someone must have known that Lauren was going to meet him there?"

"Also possible. Or she may have been followed."

We considered the two scenarios. In the kitchen, the music ended and the radio was now chattering softly. Without hearing the words, I knew it was the weather report. Continued hot and dry, it would be saying. No end in sight.

I sat up straighter. Simmons was now tracing one of the bricks of the fireplace with his hand.

"Was the fire set or an accident?"

"Don't know yet. No report yet from the fire marshall's office. They're at the scene now."

Simmons had pulled out a notebook and I knew I was in for another round of questions. My mind was full of the events of the last few days. There were so *many* possibilities. He sat back down, this time at my desk.

"Has anyone notified Lauren's family?" I asked. "I noticed she wasn't mentioned by name on TV this morning."

"Her mother lives in San Francisco. We finally reached her."

Simmons must have gone through the little cottage in the woods in Knapp's Point to find the address and phone. I suddenly wondered if Will had had a key to Lauren's house. Is that how the cops got in? Had Will handed the key over at their request? Or had they just busted down the door?

"The landlord lives a few houses down. Elderly woman. We got the key from her," Simmons said.

"I didn't ask you that." He looked disconcerted for about five seconds, then proceeded to go over the events of the night before. He wanted me to go through it again, minute by excruciating minute.

Detail by detail I reported what I had seen. It was like a play, with actors coming onstage to say their lines, then exiting, only to return later with other cast members.

Simmons wrote from time to time. When there was nothing more to be said, I took a deep breath and hoped it was over.

But he merely changed the subject and asked me about Knapp's Point.

"What about it?"

"Mr. St. Claire said you were there when Duck Jarvis's Jet Ski rammed into the victim's dock on Sunday."

I nodded, then tried to remember. Did he think Duck Jarvis, who had found Lauren's body, had killed her? Duck had certainly hated her, but then so did Carl Rainey. And any number of others. They couldn't all be suspects.

"Hey, you plan on coming back anytime soon?"

"Sorry. I was just thinking."

He grunted, probably alarmed. "Okay, I'll bite. About what?"

"Just wondering who your suspects are. I mean Duck Jarvis and Carl Rainey are obvious because they both hated her. Are there others? Did you interview all those carnival people?"

Simmons made an exasperated little noise, then wrote something in his notebook. "Do you think we could just move on?"

I'd hoped that when I'd finished, he'd have had enough. No such luck. He now wanted to know about the variance hearing on Monday morning. I took a deep breath and told him what I could remember. Which apparently substantiated what he already knew since he didn't write anything down. He put his notebook away. The questions had, at least, confirmed that Duck and Carl were both in his sights. I decided to fish a little more.

"You know, when you start thinking about it, there are any number of people who had some reason to want Lauren dead," I said. "Duck and Carl are two. But a whole lot of people in the community were furious with her. I don't know how you are ever going..."

"By asking questions and by the process of elimination, for starters," he said. "Please just let us do our job." His voice was quiet. "One other thing."

"What?"

"What I told you about the bruises on the victim's windpipe is strictly between us. For now anyway. You aren't to tell Mr. St. Claire or your aunt or anyone else, for that matter. We are releasing to the media only that her death is being considered a homicide.''

I nodded. Not that I had any choice. The silence grew uncomfortable. Simmons broke it by leaving. I watched him walk across the clearing, crunching dried pine needles with each step. I caught up with him as he reached his car.

"Can I ask you a question?" He turned and rolled his eyes. Then he relented. "How come you told me about those bruises? On Lauren's throat?" The heat swirled around us. Then he unlocked his car door. Only another New Yorker would lock his car in the middle of the day in the middle of the Maryland woods.

"How come?"

He shrugged. "Probably a mistake." He was blushing, pink skin in a pitched battle with red hair.

"No," I said, "not a mistake." I turned back to the house, deciding not to push my luck. He was already sorry he'd told me.

He turned over the engine and backed around. When I could no longer hear his car, I let the dogs out to race around the yard. Watching them, I wondered if I should have mentioned Vince Darner's buried oil tank. And his acute interest in having Lillian and me keep it to ourselves. His half threats. Probably not related, but still, maybe Simmons should know. I went back inside and was fishing around my desk for his card, when the phone rang. Lillian wanted to know where on earth I was. And to tell me that if I wanted milk in my coffee, I'd better stop for some on the way.

FOURTEEN

LYLE'S PARKING LOT was largely empty this morning. I picked up half a dozen of what passed for bagels in Maryland. Clutching them, along with a package of cream cheese and a half gallon of milk, I again found myself in Josie Jarvis's checkout line. She was leaning against her register, staring at nothing, her blond hair ratty and her eyes hollow and bloodshot from a bad night's sleep. Or maybe from no sleep. After last night, I expected half the town looked this way, myself included. I noticed the bruise on her neck had faded. She fiddled with a pack of cigarettes stashed next to her register while I dumped my stuff on the counter.

"How's your husband?" I asked. "Is he okay after last night?"

"What? Why wouldn't he be?"

"Well, I don't know really. It just looked like he took a bad fall part of the way down the riprap."

"Yeah. Before finding Lauren." She didn't look up and so I studied her. Did she fear that Duck knew more about Lauren's death than he was admitting? "He's okay."

"I'm sorry about Lauren," I said, wondering what I hoped to accomplish by goading her. "I know she was your neighbor."

She looked up at that, handing me my change and the receipt and stuffing my groceries in a plastic bag without looking at them.

"I know you people—you and your aunt—you think nobody in Knapp's Point liked Lauren." She shook her head hard, dislodging a strand of yellow hair. "Well, nobody there wanted her to die like that. My husband included. And she was good to my daughter, Jenny. Spent a lot of time with her, helping her with her homework and giving her little gifts and all. And giving her..." She disappeared into her thoughts.

"Giving her what?"

"Dunno, dreams maybe."

"And you?"

"Nah. I ain't got no dreams." Her voice caught a little. She stuffed the hair behind her ear.

"I'm sorry," I said, taking my bag, aware of a line growing behind me. Josie didn't look at me any more, but her mouth was set hard to fight off emotion, her fingers again feeling for the pack of cigarettes. I *was* sorry I had meddled.

IT WAS well after eleven when I turned onto Lillian's driveway and let myself into the house. I found my aunt dressed in a pale pink knit suit with a floppy bow blouse. She was talking on the phone in her office, dangling a narrow shoe on one toe. After motioning to me to sit, she chatted a bit longer, then hung up.

"You see this? It was under everybody's door this morning."

She handed me a flyer. I turned it over to find a grainy black-and-white photo of my aunt, a head shot in a circle with a thick slash through it. Under the picture were printed words in large letters: "Put This Woman Out Of Business."

"Someone came in the dark and stuffed these under doors?" Even as the ashes from the dock fire filtered through the night air? And Lauren's death was on everybody's mind?

She nodded. "This is too much. Where did they get the picture of you?"

"No idea, but probably from some ad I placed. Pretty grainy. Looks like a copy of a copy." She leaned back in her swiveling chair, her legs now neatly crossed. "I've got a call in to Weller."

The phone rang and Lillian grabbed it, listened, then suggested politely that she had no comment and that the person need not call back. "WBAL News trying to make sure everyone in Maryland hears about these damn things. And they just happen to have a reporter parked outside in the unlikely event that I'd like to speculate on what Lauren's death had to do with me. If you want coffee, there are some dregs left. Or I can make new."

"Dregs are fine." I went into the kitchen to find the remains of a full breakfast on the counter. Trust Lillian to feed Mitch and his daughter waffles and eggs. It had always seemed odd to me that my aunt and uncle had never had children. But we'd never discussed it. Shoving a piece of cinnamon-raisin bagel in my mouth, I turned to find Lillian right behind me.

She pointed out the window, across the deck to the scene by the water. A couple of police cars and two fire department vehicles were camped at water's edge.

"Been people down there since dawn," she said. "Divers. A photographer and the crime lab people and the media. And about half the town apparently got up early to see what they could see. Young and old, they've all been here. Fire marshall's office has been running them off all morning. And it was a regular circus out front of the house."

Looking out, I could almost smell burning rubber. As for the dock and boardwalk itself, there wasn't much to see. Most of it had been reduced to a pile of blackened timbers or had disappeared into the water. Carl Rainey stood behind the yellow police tape, drinking from a Styrofoam cup. There were a few other neighbors I recognized by sight.

"Has anyone stopped by?"

"Somebody from the fire marshall's office came by to tell me they'd be down there for a while. Just a courtesy thing."

"He say what started the fire?"

"No. Very closemouthed. Said it was too early to tell but it could have been a stray spark from the fireworks or a lighted cigarette. You know how dry it is. And so on."

Yes. I knew. All the same, I allowed myself the luxury of wondering what neither one of us would say aloud: Had someone set the fire to punish Lillian for what many supposed she had done to Carl Rainey? Or even worse, had someone set the fire to cover up Lauren's murder?

"Your insurance agent show up?"

"He was here earlier but they wouldn't let him near the scene. Be back later or tomorrow, after the police and fire departments are done." She sat down at the kitchen table, out of place in her pink suit. "At least there wasn't any rain to spoil the crime scene." I sat down across from my aunt.

"Simmons came by this morning. The medical examiner has ruled Lauren's death a homicide. She died from the fall, apparently from brain injuries."

"He stopped by to tell you that?"

"He stopped by to question me all over again. That's why I was so late. We went through the whole scene last night. Plus the scene at Knapp's Point and also the hearing on Monday."

I had a thought. "He probably should be told about the flyers."

"Why? You think they are related?"

"Maybe. Don't tell me you think all of these things that have happened in the last few days are coincidences?"

"I don't think anything." She glanced up at me as I got another cup of coffee, finishing the pot. "Sorry. I didn't mean to snap. At least not at you. It's a fair question, I just don't plan to discuss it yet, either here in the kitchen or on television."

"I meant it seriously, Lillian."

"I know you did, but speculating about things isn't going to help."

And that was that. Lillian would reopen the subject when she was ready to and not a minute before. I'd been about to tell her about Vince Darner's threats in the parking lot of the community center, but now I changed my mind. It could wait. No use burdening her with one more problem. But I reminded myself to tell Simmons about them.

I turned to the front page of the *Baltimore Sun* and read the headline: "Environmentalist Perishes As Fire Destroys Dock." There was an eerie night photo of the scene on Lillian's waterfront. Lauren was just barely visible and barely recognizable as human, a small silhouetted shape against the sky, embraced by the quarry stones.

The phone rang again. My aunt answered it, mouthing "Weller" in my direction. After a couple of minutes, she thanked him and hung up. "The police are asking around about the flyers."

Simmons would know about them soon, if he didn't know already. I glanced at my aunt. Each new adversity appeared to make her more resolute.

I finished my bagel and coffee and was about to slide open

the glass door to the deck when the other line rang in her office and Lillian went to get it. There was a shout from the water's edge, but it was just someone from the fire marshall's office who had momentarily lost his footing and slipped an arm into the water to catch himself. He'd been stung by nettles. I could see him dancing about holding his arm. My thoughts returned to recent events. Lillian might not want to speculate, but she was going to have to acknowledge that there were coincidences here.

She returned. "Another TV station, one which had somehow found my unlisted number. Which is more than a little disturbing." She shook her head and sat down. "I think the only thing to do is to get on with things. Otherwise, we'll both go crazy. So, having said that, I've got tickets for the Andrew Lloyd Webber show at the Meyerhoff. You want to go?"

"Tonight?"

"I was supposed to go with Florence, but I don't think that's going to happen. I called her but Carl hung up on me when I mentioned it."

I glanced over at my aunt. She was now standing at the counter, dropping the rest of the bagels into a plastic bag and zipping it shut.

"Okay," I said. "I guess we aren't doing Lauren or ourselves any good by not going."

FIFTEEN

THE MEYERHOFF, Baltimore's symphony hall, squatted like a giant hat in what the city's economic development people referred to as the Culture Corridor. It formed a lopsided triangle with the Lyric Opera and the Maryland Institute. The art college had claimed an abandoned shoe factory and an old train station, turning the odd spaces into studios and galleries.

The three institutions sat encamped on the eastern flank of Bolton Hill, an elegant community of Victorian townhouses. The area was first renovated after the riots in the sixties, but the optimism of those early days of urban renewal was long gone and the community was now surrounded by blight on three sides. Residents were fleeing as fast as they could sign the sales contracts that would allow them to escape to the safety of the suburbs—well pleased that they got out with their lives, if not their bank accounts.

Lillian was explaining this as the Cadillac lumbered through the streets. We were early for the eight-fifteen curtain, so I was getting a tour and a history lesson. Lauren's death seemed far away, a bad dream that both of us were trying not to talk about. My aunt drove slowly, glancing around her, sighing at what she saw. Bolton Hill looked perfect, immaculate, with its three-story townhouses, white marble steps, and polished brass door fittings.

"Makes you wonder how it can look so good and be so dangerous, doesn't it?" My aunt drove down another exquisite street, slowing to let a car around us. It too slowed, apparently looking for a street address. "See that house, the pale green one?" Lillian asked. "F. Scott Fitzgerald lived there." We turned a couple of corners. "And that house," she said, pointing, "is where Woodrow Wilson lived when he was studying at Johns Hopkins." She glanced at the clock on the dash.

"Good heavens, we're going to be late." She headed east. The car was still behind us.

"How about there?" I pointed at a space on the street near a small empty lot sandwiched between two grubby office buildings. "Looks okay," I said. "And it's close. Grab it before that other car does."

The concert proved to be notable for its enthusiastic audience. For two hours the familiar Andrew Lloyd Webber melodies enveloped us. I surrendered to them, grateful to be far from the cynical comments of my New York friends about such productions. As the curtain came down on the final encore of "Music of the Night," we stood up and collected our possessions.

"Well, that was nice. I'm glad we came," Lillian said. "It made me forget the last couple of days." I glanced at her, a glance she saw. "Well, not completely."

The breeze had kicked up some since we'd abandoned real life in favor of a musical dream world. Hot night air swirled around us in the Meyerhoff's front plaza, kicking up bits of paper and dead leaves. Small vans waited to return gray-haired concert-goers to their safe suburban retirement communities. As always, I was amazed at how seriously most people in Maryland—my aunt included—took their concerts, dressing up in near evening clothes.

We walked around Symphony Hall, then crossed the street and headed for the car. I looked around. The Cadillac was gone. Maybe we'd come out a different door, but no, I was sure we hadn't.

"Lillian, speaking of forgetting, are we in the right place? Isn't this where we parked?"

My aunt nodded. Cars zipped past us and people walked arm-in-arm in the hot night, humming to themselves, oblivious to the heat. Had the car been stolen? I reached for my cell phone, then realized that I'd changed handbags, stuffing my wallet and credit cards in a smaller shoulder bag. When I looked up, Lillian was shaking her head. Without a word, she held up her tiny evening clutch.

"No phone?" She shook her head a second time. "Well, then let's go back to the Meyerhoff and call."

Fifteen minutes later a Baltimore city cop, his pale skin shiny under the street lights, listened as I explained the problem, then showed him where Lillian had parked and the sign.

He radioed someone and waited. His radio was pinned near the shoulder of his white short-sleeved shirt. We listened to an in comprehensible return squawk from the radio.

"You're in luck. It's been towed. Chesapeake Towing. The lot is in South Baltimore near the Anne Arundel County line." The cop wrote something. "Here's my name and badge number," he said. "And for what it's worth—if your car was parked on the street as you say—this doesn't seem right. Tow truck driver probably having a slow night. It wouldn't be the first time."

He looked sympathetic for a second, then his radio buzzed, and his features hardened. "You can take a taxi there." He turned and looked around for one. There weren't any. "All the cab drivers know where the lot is."

His radio squawked a second time and he was gone before I could ask any more questions.

"We don't seem to have a lot of choices," I said. "Let's go call a cab." A lumpy shape shuffled toward us in the dim light. We hurried across the street as a cab pulled up, driven by a middle-aged black man. I flagged it.

The cab driver was silent during the ride to South Baltimore. We passed Oriole Park at Camden Yards and the Ravens' football stadium, which was reassuring, then turned left down some narrow dark road a few miles further along, which wasn't. The neighborhood was half-industrial, half-residential. It was also poor and black and getting worse. In the dark, music pounded from radios and people sat outside on the crumbling stoops of the remaining sections of two-story rowhouses, drinking malt liquor out of paper bags. Boarded buildings were everywhere. Kids ran screaming in the street. A fire hydrant spewed cooling water. I thought I heard a shot.

And still the driver drove. The streetscape grew poorer, if that were possible, and now suddenly, the shells of industrial buildings long abandoned loomed hollow and toothless on the night horizon. There had probably never been any brave urban pioneers here, no Maryland Institute to reclaim the shuttered factories. It had probably been misery in the 1960s and it was misery today.

"It's down there," the driver said. He turned first right, then left, then right again, past a small sign, down a rutted, unpaved road. Lillian grabbed my arm in the dark. On either side of us, wrecks lay abandoned, enclosed and protected, oddly, by rolls of razor wire strung in winding layers on top of a chain-link fence. The menacing silhouette of a tow truck loomed ahead. The taxi crept along, stopping finally beside a one-story building on our right. There was no exterior light. The driver turned around. "In there." He pointed.

Lillian leaned forward to get a better look. In the darkness, the office light shone yellow and dim. I paid the driver and helped my aunt out of the car. Something ran under the car into the dust on the other side.

"Well, this is one godforsaken place," said Lillian.

The taxi was gone as if it had never been there, backing up the drive in a high-pitched squeal of relief. Somewhere nearby a siren rose, gained altitude, then faded just as quickly.

The office was staffed by a woman to whom life hadn't been kind. Her genes weren't helping her much either. Aggressively overweight, with rolls of fat visible at the top of her stretch pants, it was hard to judge her age. What money and effort she could manage had gone in the service of a tight, yellowish perm. She stood behind a counter with a sliding tray window bisecting the glass partition. At her feet I could see a large and filthy German shepherd. The dog trailed a length of heavy chain, its lot in life to protect whatever the tow truck dragged back. A fan blew hot air and overhead a fly tape flapped back and forth.

The whole office was perhaps ten by ten, cinder block, the size and ambiance of a jail cell. A small color television stood on a counter behind the clerk. The eleven o'clock news came on.

"You mistakenly towed our car. A gray Cadillac," I said.

The attendant listened impassively, sorting at the same time through a flat box of paper. It was all the same to her. I gave her the tag number.

"One hundred forty-five dollars." Grating my teeth, I pulled out a credit card. "Nope. Cash. Only cash."

"Cash?" I checked quickly. I had ten bucks and change. I glanced over at Lillian, who was searching her evening purse. She looked up, shaking her head.

"We don't have enough."

The attendant shrugged. "Guess you'll have to come back tomorrow."

On television, a blond anchor announced breaking news: a double shooting on North Avenue, including a sixteen-year-old girl, outside a nightclub. Lillian and I stood waiting and watching, not quite sure what to do next.

"The death of a young environmental activist and documentary filmmaker in Anne Arundel County is being considered suspicious," the anchor said, launching into the next story. There was some curious, eerie footage from last night. "Police are asking anyone who was at the fireworks display in Pines on Magothy last night who might know anything about Lauren DeWitt's death to call them." We waited, but after a phone number flashed on the screen, that was it. Lillian took a deep breath and looked around. There were no chairs.

"You have your checkbook?" I asked Lillian. She shook her head.

"Don't matter. We don't take no checks. It's rules." The attendant pointed to a sign on the wall.

"I wish I'd used the lavatory before we left the Meyerhoff," Lillian said in a low voice.

On TV, the weatherman appeared with more dire news: All over the state, crops were dying. Farmers were using next winter's hay to feed their livestock. Lillian fished a tissue from her bag and patted her face. Behind the safety glass, the woman drank impassively from a can of Coke.

"Rats," said the anchor, distastefully. "They are a big problem in Baltimore." She described the problem, then the city's Rat Rub Out Program. The screen was filled with images of thin-faced vermin rummaging in the overflowing garbage piled high in some dark alley. An expert from some university spoke of disease and gave advice on eradication. "But," said the anchor, "some folks may have found another way to get rid of the rats. And help a good cause at the same time. Our Marcy Tippett has the story."

The camera zoomed in on a young reporter standing in another alley, this one partially lit. People milled about the piles of debris and broken furniture.

"With the sudden increase in rats, an east side bar has decided to hold their Rat Fishing Contest a bit early this year," began the reporter.

The camera zoomed in on a beefy young man sitting on a broken chair, a fishing pole in his hand. Standing by him was a friend, wearing a backwards baseball cap and holding a baseball bat. The reporter, looking repulsed and careful about where she was stepping, inched over to this unlikely tableau.

"Catching anything?"

"Three so far. Got a twelve incher, not including the tail. On ice." He grinned provocatively at her.

"What are you using for bait?"

"Chicken parts."

"Oh."

"They take the bait and then Bill, here," he motioned with his elbow toward his friend with the bat, "he finishes them off. Smack, smack, and they're done. Rat pie for everybody."

The reporter shivered and in an incredulous voice turned back to the camera and explained to the audience that fishing licenses could be had for three dollars and that the money collected would be donated to a foundation for pediatric AIDS. It went on this way for a bit more, with an interview with the owner of the bar and a shout of victory from the alley. Quickly, the producer cut back to the studio.

"Unbelievable," said the anchor.

The woman behind the counter turned to us. "You should see some them rats 'round here."

Somewhere a siren wailed as the city braced for a deadly night.

SIXTEEN

LILLIAN GLANCED at her watch. The woman finished her Coke. On TV, the news was wrapping up. The familiar music of the *Tonight Show* played, then Jay Leno appeared and did some clowning with the studio audience. I was watching Lillian. She was trying not to let on how much her ankle was bothering her.

I knocked on the sliding window. "Excuse me. Could we please use your phone?"

The woman shook her head. "Public phone's outside." She pointed, a movement that suggested not so much indifference as helplessness. Her eyes returned to the television. Something pulled up outside.

I went to the door in time to see a tow truck drag a battered van up the rutted driveway, then turn left through an opening between two shapes. The darkness was almost complete. "Wait here," I told Lillian. "I'll be right back."

Once outside, I was surprised at how stationary the air was. The front had gone through, delivering no rain. The breeze from an hour earlier had died, leaving only stillness. Walking gingerly in the dark, I headed toward the lights on the tow truck. A silhouetted figure hopped out and was unhitching the van. I could hear the crackle of a radio. The driver returned to the cab, his head down, his face hidden by a baseball cap. He appeared to fiddle with something.

"Hello. Excuse me."

The driver reached over to pull the door shut. What light there had been inside died. He put the truck in gear and swung it around, nearly grazing me in the dark. Seconds later I was alone, standing in solid dark, only the glow from the office's yellow light beckoning. The adrenaline kicked in. I took a deep breath, trying not to think what could have happened.

The dog barked from the office. The tow truck's brake lights winked briefly as it stopped before turning left out of the drive.

Dust glimmered, then settled. I sneezed. The darkness was disorienting, making me feel lightheaded. The dog barked a second time. I heard a sharp command, then the low familiar rumble of the television. Following the sound and the pale light that vanished feet from the office door, I crept back, looking for the public phone. If there was one, I didn't see it. Maybe around the other side of the building. It was even darker here. I tripped over a stunted bush, cursed, then felt my way back around front. I opened the door. Lillian wasn't there.

"My aunt," I asked the woman. "Where's my aunt?"

"Restroom." Her phone rang. She pulled her stool with her to the back counter, turning away from me. But I saw her face melt with pleasure when she discovered who it was. The call went on for a bit. I wondered what was keeping Lillian. "Park...Friday. I says to Gordie, you drive us and..." She coughed then and after a bad spell, picked up where she left off. "Crabs...okay...small wood." There was something more about travel arrangements I didn't catch. She hung up, still animated by the call.

"I didn't see a phone outside."

Her face had morphed back to indifference. "It's there. Maybe light's out. 'Nother cab be along sooner or later."

What was taking Lillian so long? "Where's the restroom?"

She pointed to a door on the left wall a few feet from the front entrance. It opened onto a short corridor lined with fake pine paneling. I passed a dusty office, nearly filled by two old metal desks. There were also a couple of chairs, which like the woman and the dog, had seen hard use. The one window was completely blocked with a small air conditioner. From somewhere came the sound of running water.

"Lillian?"

"In here. Just a minute." I heard the toilet flush a second time. Then rustling from behind the door. It opened.

"Well, that was about as nasty as it gets," she said. I peered in. What was wrong with these people? How could you have so little self-respect that you were willing to work under these conditions? That you didn't even bother to clean the toilet? Lillian held onto the wall.

"Look, Lillian. We have to get out of here. We'll get your car tomorrow."

"You find a telephone?"

"No. Maybe it's there, but it's pitch black all around the building. But another cab has got to be along sooner or later. Or maybe there's a phone back here."

I ducked into the wretched office, Lillian behind me. Suddenly the woman was beside us, blocking the way out.

"What do you think you're doing in there?" The dog stood beside her, suffering from the heat and from his dysplasia, but on the job nonetheless. "You ain't allowed in there. I was just being nice to her," she nodded toward Lillian, "about the toilet."

"Please," said Lillian. "If I might just take the chair into the waiting area while we figure out what to do. I have a bad ankle and it's bothering me quite a lot."

I knew what this cost my aunt to admit. But the attendant's features eased a bit, as if she too had a bad ankle. "Yeah, okay."

I started to help wheel the chair out, then realized that a car was coming down the stony road. The attendant went back to her cell behind the plastic sliding window, taking the dog with her. I looked down. On the desk was a pile of what looked to be invoices. I grabbed the top one and stuffed it into my handbag without looking at it.

"Lillian, stay here." I ran through the front office, past two drunk and giggling teenagers. Outside, a taxi driver, another middle-aged black man, was looking down, counting his money and figuring his tip. By the looks of his face, it couldn't have been any too good. "We need a cab."

He looked up, nodded, his features composed in the face of this clear evidence that God was indeed in his kingdom.

"Wait a second. I have to get my aunt." The attendant had her hands full with the drunk kids, their giggles turning to surprise, then anger, when they found that they were going to need a wad of cash to retrieve their van.

I didn't wait to see how this new scene would play out.

Instead, I half grabbed, half pushed Lillian out the door before the taxi driver could change his mind.

"We want to go to Anne Arundel County," I said. "Mountain Road, near the Magothy." He turned around, looking startled, then slowly shook his head. "Baltimore. I go to Baltimore." He sounded as if his roots were somewhere else, somewhere with a slower pace. "I take you if you go to Baltimore."

I took a deep breath, wondering what came next. But Lillian had recovered. She leaned forward. Together, she and the driver agreed on an all-night diner where we could wait for someone to pick us up or get another cab.

"You think you could call Will?" Lillian asked. "I don't think we're going to have enough money for another cab."

I nodded, then sneaked a sideways glance at her. Something was very wrong here, and we both knew it. I didn't want to worry her more by discussing it. A tow truck hauling something passed us. I saw the name on the side and leaned forward.

"You know anything about Chesapeake Towing?" I asked the driver. He looked into the rearview mirror and grinned widely.

"I know without them I go out a business in a week."

"How's that?"

"I take six, seven fare most every night. Good business for me," he said.

"From near the Meyerhoff?"

He nodded slowly. "People, they think they park okay if they see the empty lot. But the tow truck get them."

"We'll probably laugh about this later," said Lillian. With memories of the razor wire and abandoned buildings, I wasn't so sure.

TWENTY MINUTES LATER we were sitting in a booth at the Sip and Bite. It was the only free booth, the others being filled with members of Baltimore's late-night variety show. A few looked to be students. A couple of hookers. Sleepless neighbors and all-night workers chatted with the waitresses and short order cook. A well-dressed middle-aged couple scarfed down scrambled eggs and pancakes. The air-conditioning was cold, the grill hot.

"Believe it or not, this place is kind of famous," my aunt said. It was a Greek diner, decorated with paintings of the mother country. Empty spaces on the wall had been filled with framed reviews, one included a mention from the *New York Times*. Across from the seven or eight booths that ringed the windows on two sides were a few bar stools along the counter, all taken, and a glass-fronted grocery case filled with big lumps of raw meat.

"Ready, Hon?" a waitress asked Lillian. She had cheerfully cleaned our table and deposited red plastic tumblers of water and flatware and napkins in one fluid movement.

We pooled our money and pondered breakfast. I left Lillian to order and went to the public phone just outside.

Will didn't answer. When his answering machine came on, I left a message telling him where we were and leaving the phone number if he got home in the next few minutes. I didn't have much hope, either that he'd get the message, or once back inside the diner, I'd hear the phone ring. The receiver in my hand made a loud squawk. I hung up.

Across the street there was construction, with dirt piles and heavy equipment fronting the water. We appeared to be on some part of Baltimore's Inner Harbor. Catercorner was another restaurant, this one shaped like a ship, complete with portholes and decks. I fished in my bag for more change. The invoice I'd taken from the office fluttered to the ground. Retrieving it, I turned the sheet to catch the light and saw what appeared to be an invoice from an Amoco station in South Baltimore. It was machine-addressed to the owner of Chesapeake Towing.

I folded the paper and with my fingers shaking, dropped another quarter in the phone. We needed more than a taxi.

SEVENTEEN

LILLIAN WAS SIPPING hot tea and contemplating a big plate of scrambled eggs when I slid in across from her.

"Will didn't answer so I just left a message saying I'd talk to him tomorrow." I took a sip of water. "I called Mitch. He thought he could make it here in about forty-five minutes."

My aunt had been carefully arranging a paper napkin in her lap. Now she looked up in surprise. "You called Mitch? To come all the way from Annapolis?"

"I had to call someone. After paying for this, we haven't got enough cash for another cab. Actually, Lillian, I think that maybe I should have called the cops." My aunt picked up her fork, then put it down and stared at me across the Formica. "Look, I know this sounds crazy, but I think what happened tonight wasn't a mistake. Someone purposely towed your car. Probably just to harass you."

My aunt snorted in disbelief. I suddenly wondered what would have happened if we'd parked in one of the garages or lots near the Meyerhoff. But it would have been all too easy for someone to park there as well, then disable Lillian's car. A few sharp slashes to each tire would have done it and no one would have seen.

"Okay, then," I said. "You want proof? Guess who owns Chesapeake Towing?" I pulled out the invoice and handed it to her.

"Vince Darner? Vince owns that towing company?" She looked up, her eyes reflecting a jumble of emotions. "But so what? That doesn't prove anything."

I suddenly wanted to reach across the booth and grab her by the collar of her silk dress and tell her to cut it out, to stop being so willing to give him the benefit of the doubt. Instead I took a deep breath and carefully considered my words. "Look, Lillian, think about what just happened: We were towed ille-

gally—even the cop thought so—then the attendant tells us to
use the public phone outside. Which may or may not exist, but
I couldn't find it.'' Lillian arranged her flatware in a neat line.
''Now, I'm not saying that anything terrible would have happened to us if we hadn't gotten in that cab, but it's after midnight and here we are eating eggs in some diner in Baltimore
waiting for Mitch to come fetch us.''

The waitress—pencil behind her ear, also a habit of Lillian's
and one I had long found endearing—filled my coffee cup and
deposited a plate of pancakes and eggs over easy in front of
me. ''Get you anything else?'' I shook my head. She turned to
my aunt, noticing her untouched plate. ''Something wrong,
Hon?''

''No. Everything's fine.''

The waitress nodded and moved on with her coffee pot, chatting easily about the drought and heat and resulting crime wave.
Last night I heard her tell the people in the booth behind me
there were three shootings. One of them fatal. Predictable,
somebody said. Crime always gets worse when it gets really
hot. Don't forget Christmas, another voice said. That's always
bad, too. The others agreed.

''Lillian, for whatever reason, Vince Darner needs the money
from the sale of Charlotte's land. And he's furious that you
refused to cancel his contract. He probably also knows you
already called the Department of the Environment. So now,
maybe he's getting you back.''

''Do you do know how insane that sounds?'' My aunt was,
I could see, making plans to eat, but then she dropped the fork,
causing all progress to stop. ''This is Vince we're talking about.
I've known him forever.''

''You can't deny what happened tonight.''

The waitress delivered a clean fork. Around us, the Sip and
Bite's clients came and went: the poor and the rich, the hungry,
the hot, and the friendless. To a person, they appeared grateful
for an air-conditioned oasis in the sweltering night, grateful for
the comfort of midnight food and for the cheery waitress and
calm man cooking behind the counter. At the moment, he stood
at the grill with his back to us. Then, wiping his hands on his

apron, he turned to make change and small talk at the cash register.

Through the window, I saw Mitch parking his Jeep on a side street. He looked younger than usual, awakened from sleep less than an hour ago and hurriedly dressed in jeans and an open-necked short-sleeved knit shirt. I felt guilty. Two hours ago I should have asked the first taxi driver to take us home.

"Hi." Mitch slid beside me in the booth, having said hello to the waitress.

"You know her?"

"Sure. I come here sometimes when I'm in Baltimore."

He ordered coffee, then smiled at me. The man had been rescuing me from bad situations since I'd moved to Maryland. But this time I really was in his debt, not a position I particularly relished. Still, I could see Lillian was comforted by his presence and I decided it had been the right decision. Besides, with Will not answering his phone, who could I have called? Weller Church? Simmons? The list was sobering and short after the events of the last few days. Mitch drank off his first cup of coffee, then motioned the waitress for more. I remembered his daughter.

"I forgot all about Laura. Who's staying with her?"

"She's at camp. Horseback riding and computers. Been planned for ages. She was a little spooked by the similarity of Lauren's name and hers. As if there was some hidden meaning in it. We had a talk about coincidences before she left." Mitch turned to Lillian.

"I have enough cash if you want to get your car tonight."

My aunt shook her head. "Thank you, but heavens no. It's far too late." She looked all in. "And it's a nasty place in the dark. Tomorrow's fine."

HALF AN HOUR LATER, the dark streets of Pines on Magothy rolled out in front of us. All traces of last night's circus were gone, all but the faintest odor of burning rubber, and maybe I was dreaming that.

Within thirty seconds, and before anyone could lend a hand, Lillian had half tumbled out of the back seat of the Jeep. She went inside trailing a thank-you and a wave. The clock on the dash said almost one-thirty. Unlike my aunt, I was more awake than I'd been earlier.

A near full moon rose above my BMW parked in Lillian's driveway. I searched my handbag for my car keys. The Amoco station invoice addressed to Chesapeake Towing fluttered to the floor of the Jeep and slid under Mitch's feet. He retrieved it, studying it in the dim light from the dashboard. Then he handed it back.

"What do you really think happened tonight?"

I looked over at him. He killed the engine.

"I don't know what to think," I said. "But too much has happened these past few days for it to be all coincidence. Though Lillian doesn't want to admit that. I suppose you heard about the flyers someone stuffed under doors in the Pines this morning?" He nodded. "And there's the whole mess with Vince Darner and the oil tank. And now we find out he owns the towing company." I waggled the invoice. Mitch had slouched deep into the Jeep's leather. "It's also pretty hard to believe that her dock just happened to burn down. Though there were kids down on the riprap smoking when Lillian and I walked to the beach." I paused, stuffing the invoice back in my handbag.

"And Lauren DeWitt?"

"What about her?" I glanced sideways at him, then shook my head emphatically. "Oh no. I'm not going to stick my nose in any of it. Let Simmons do his job."

"He know everything that's happened?"

"Except tonight. And about Vince Darner's threats."

The town was quiet. No cars, no distant music. Just the tattoo of a million crickets pulsing in high gear. I turned to stare into the deep woods that ran along the right-of-way next to Lillian's property. Carl Rainey's woods, at least momentarily spared.

"Mitch, you know anything about a house going up across Weller's Creek from me?" If he was surprised by the change of subject, he didn't let on. "I've heard chainsaws working over there recently. Couple of times, actually. Not on the water, but definitely not too far from it."

"Vince Darner's building a house somewhere along Weller's Creek. Bought the land last year. That's probably it."

"Vince Darner? But that makes no sense. Why wouldn't he just build on the Knapp's Point property he and Charlotte already own?"

Mitch didn't answer right away. "I can think of two reasons," he said, finally. "First, Knapp's Point is better suited for a subdivision, not just one big house. It'll bring in more money that way. And..."

"Let me guess. He doesn't want to be surrounded by the riffraff who already live at Knapp's Point." Mitch nodded. "The guy's slime. How can he get elected? Are people that blind?"

Mitch shrugged. "I think people have had it with government. Particularly all the environmental regulations. Sometimes just to take down a tree, you have to call in the EPA or the Army Corps of Engineers. And that's in addition to satisfying all the state agencies and the county agencies. Then there are the local covenants. That's why what happened to Carl Rainey struck such a chord. People are afraid the government can just move in and arbitrarily reduce their property value."

"Which it can." He nodded. "Well, okay, so I understand that, even if the greater good is supposed to be served." I sat thinking, trying to put myself in Carl Rainey's place. His property *was* worth less today than he'd thought it was a week ago. "Then how is it, with all of those hurdles, that Vince Darner gets to take out a hundred-and-fifty-year-old stand of trees and bulldoze what are probably tidal wetlands so he can build a house on the water? With no one around to mess up his view with their nasty little redneck houses?"

"He's smart. I'm sure he was very careful when he bought that land. Made sure that it was buildable."

I had a flash of the carnival on July Fourth, of Dick Hubbard talking steadily and seriously in Vince Darner's ear.

"Is Dick Hubbard involved?"

"Maybe, I don't know."

"Well, I don't like it," I said. Then I realized that in some

ways I was no better than Vince Darner. I wanted my view,
too. Mitch fortunately didn't point this out.

It was hard to remember it was the middle of the night. Nobody moved. Slowly, half against my will, a bond was devel-
oping between us. I sensed more than saw him. For a few
minutes we sat in companionable silence. Then we talked about
the drought. We talked about the fish kills affecting the water-
sheds and rivers on Maryland's Eastern Shore—thousands of
fish found with lesions and now some watermen and water-
skiers similarly afflicted. The culprit was thought to be a mysterious microorganism called pfisteria. We also talked about
Anne Arundel County politics and real estate.

As always, Mitch was a first-rate source of information. I
had to hand it to him. Annapolis was a small, gossipy, insular
Southern town, but somehow within just a couple of years of
opening his first office, he'd managed to gain the trust of those
with influence and money. I sat up in my seat.

"Mitch, what's going on here? Who is behind all these things
that are happening around Lillian? I'm not saying that they are
all happening to *her*. Though some certainly are." He listened.
"I'd like to know why her car was towed tonight. And why
Vince Darner needs to sell his property so quickly." I waited,
hoping he'd volunteer some information. He didn't. "And the
relationships between all these people. I'd like to know more
about them."

"Which people?"

"Duck Jarvis and Carl Rainey, for starters." I looked over
at him. "And Darner."

He brushed something off his jeans. "Also Dick Hubbard,"
I said. "I'd like to know what his part is in all of this."

"Hubbard?" Mitch was shaking his head. "You think he's
harassing Lillian? Or involved in Lauren's death?"

"Did I say that?"

"But you're wondering about it."

I shrugged. He could write people off if he liked, but I wasn't
so sure. People lied and cheated and did whatever they had to
do in their own best interest. Here I was all of a sudden burn-

ingly interested in Vince Darner's house across Weller's Creek.
And why? Because my own view was imperiled.

"Eve?"

"Yes, yes. I *am* letting Simmons handle the investigation into
Lauren's murder, but you think he's going to chase down whoever illegally towed Lillian's car?" I fingered my keys. "I need
to get home and let the dogs out." I leaned over and touched
his arm. "Thanks for fetching us. I know I ruined your night's
sleep. But with Will not home and...anyway, I'm grateful."

"You're welcome to ruin my sleep any time you want."

I couldn't see him very well, but I could guess about the
smiling eyes.

"I didn't mean that the way it sounded." He sat up. "Actually, that's not true. I meant it exactly how it sounded."

EIGHTEEN

MY WATCH SAID seven-thirty. I was standing in the bathroom peering into the mirror, unhappy with what I saw: deep blue circles and yesterday's makeup. And in serious need of a haircut. My skin felt tight, stretched over bones. From now on I vowed to leave late-night conversations for teenagers and students or anyone else whose need to discuss the meaning of life couldn't wait for daybreak. Zeke, standing in the doorway, yawned widely, then licked his chops and yawned again.

I'd awakened a few minutes ago to the dogs barking and Will letting himself in the front door. Wrapping myself in an old terry robe, I'd accepted the cup of instant coffee he'd handed me. He looked about as good as I did, his dark hair spiky and stubble up and running along his jaw.

I collapsed into a wicker chair on the front porch. The shrieking chorus of heat-induced cicada clamor, my favorite sound of summer, rose from the trees. Oddly, this morning it didn't sound so reassuring—rather more like sirens in the Baltimore night, the pitch escalating, then dropping off. I drank coffee. Will sat down, put his mug on the table, and his head in his hands. After a moment, he looked up.

"Flaming headache," he said. "Booze just makes me want to lie down and die the next day."

"Aspirin. Bathroom."

By the time he got back with more coffee, I could talk in sentences.

"What happened last night?"

I gave him the abbreviated version of our adventures, hitting the high points. Retold in the light of day it was a little hard to call up the fear that had inspired me amid the rusting wrecks and razor wire.

"I think towing Lillian's car wasn't meant to harm her so much as inconvenience and harass her."

"And you think the same person who did that is responsible for the flyers."

"Well, it certainly looks that way, doesn't it?" I retied my robe. "By the way, I need to go back to that tow place and get Lillian's car sometime today. You got time to drive me?"

"Look out there," he ordered, pointing to the dusty clearing in front of the cottage. "The only thing I need to do is water. And it's the one thing I can't do. So yes, I've got time."

Unspoken was the thought that Lauren was gone and that he needed to be busy. "Simmons call you again?" I asked.

"He showed up last night to ask about a million more questions."

"About what?"

"Lauren's relationship with her neighbors."

"Because of last Sunday. Simmons was here for a couple of hours yesterday morning after you left. He said you told him about the Jet Ski accident. He wanted my version."

"I'm not surprised," he said. "He apparently thinks that Duck Jarvis had a motive for wanting Lauren dead."

Sweating from the coffee, Will suddenly ripped his T-shirt out of his jeans and wiped his face with it, sticking it back in when he was done.

"Will, did you and Lauren ever talk about Duck Jarvis?"

"Sure. She thought he was a toad. Hated everything he stood for." He scratched Zeke's chest. The black Lab swooned with pleasure, slumping onto the floor. "I saw them get into it good a couple of times. Lauren was a lot smarter, so she always got the best of the arguments. Sometimes it was pretty subtle, but even when he didn't get it, he knew she was provoking him. She scared me a little, the way she needled him. Particularly when he was drinking. And I know that..." He stopped.

"What?"

"Well, uh, just that despite her arguments with Duck—or maybe because of them—I think the women in the neighborhood secretly admired her."

Josie Jarvis's words in Lyle's Market the day after Lauren's death drifted back to me. Words about how whatever the rest of us thought, people in Knapp's Point—and she'd included her husband here—hadn't wished Lauren harm. "Will, I'm sorry about Lauren."

He was absently scratching the dog's ears. Then he looked over at me. "Yeah. I liked her. And I was attracted to her. But I didn't love her."

"Why are you telling me this?"

He thought a bit before answering. "Because I guess I'm afraid that you will...because I care still, uh, what you think."

He reddened at this last. On the other side of the porch the Chesapeake Bay retriever struggled to his feet, then padded over and sat down next to him. It was hard for me to get the picture of Will and Lauren out of my mind. They had looked complete together, almost identical in some ways: nearly the same age, both with dark hair and fair skin. Will with his luminous blue eyes, Lauren with her biting brown ones.

The awkwardness passed.

"She was just so focused," he said. "Intent on letting everyone know what overdevelopment was doing to the Magothy." The dogs wandered off to try to sleep through the mounting heat. "You know how most of us only want to save the crabs and oysters or the rockfish? Or deer or rabbits? Anything fuzzy and cute or edible? Well, not Lauren. She believed that mudworms also had their place."

"Why was she so interested in the environment?"

"She grew up green. Her father was the executive director of some foundation to protect the Hudson River."

"I thought her family was from San Francisco."

He shook his head. "Her mother lives there now. But her parents divorced when she was in high school and she continued to live with her father so she could finish her last two years at the same school in upstate New York."

"She have brothers or sisters?"

He shook his head. "And her father died in an ice-fishing accident a year ago." Getting up, he flipped on an overhead fan, which did us no good. "After she graduated from college, she went back upstate to work with him. I think it was some public relations job. That lasted for a couple of years. Then she went to New York to do graduate work in film. And then somehow—I don't know how exactly, but her father's connections probably didn't hurt—she persuaded some organization to bankroll a documentary about what overdevelopment was doing to the Chesapeake.''

I was getting exhausted listening, and I didn't think it was from lack of sleep. Lauren appeared to have accomplished more in her few years than most people did in twice that number.

"She could be fun, too," Will said. I looked over at him. "Really. She wasn't always serious."

He didn't seem inclined to explain and I didn't ask. The phone rang, getting us both off the hook. It was Lillian, who sounded more rested than she had any business being. I offered to get her Cadillac with Will's help and we agreed I'd drop by as soon as I could.

"Lillian," I said, sitting back down. "I told her I'd be there in half an hour to take her to her office, then we'd go get the car. That okay with you?"

He nodded. "I talked with Lauren's mother."

"Is she coming east for the funeral?"

"Maybe." He stirred in the wicker chair. "She's having Lauren's remains cremated and sent to be buried next to her father in New York."

"And the service will be there?"

"Yeah. Some of her father's friends are making arrangements."

"You going?"

He nodded. "I got the impression that her mother isn't all that well. I also thought you and Lillian could help with her stuff—you know, selling Lauren's furniture and cleaning out the house—so I gave her your number."

"Okay. Sure." Something was bothering me. "Will, why did Lauren come here? Why the Chesapeake? Why not New York, maybe the Hudson or the Adirondacks? Where she had ties."

He shrugged. "I think she just wanted to do a documentary, so she looked for a timely and colorful subject." He leaned over to tie his sneaker. "And it wasn't the whole bay. She'd narrowed her focus to the Magothy area, just a few communities." I didn't say anything. "You have to understand," he said, "that Lauren was pretty calculating. Not in a bad way but she knew what she wanted and went for it."

Unlike the rest of us mere mortals. All those of us who lurched along through our lives. I wished I liked Lauren better knowing all this, but somehow I didn't and that was that.

Will was staring out through the screened windows. "She thought that the Chesapeake had all the elements for drama: character and scenery and history and tradition. And best of all, from the perspective of making a documentary, it had problems." He looked over at me, his eyes telling me that he well understood the irony: that the very environmental issues that gave Lauren fits also gave her work.

"The oyster thing?" In recent years, two microscopic diseases had nearly wiped out the oyster beds in the Chesapeake, reducing the harvest to nothing and eliminating the natural filtering necessary to a healthy bay. Somewhere in a new building shaped like a crab on Baltimore's Inner Harbor, scientists hunkered down in their labs, trying to find science fiction-type solutions.

"Yes, oysters. And now pfisteria," he said. "But she was most concerned with overbuilding. She thought the Magothy was about to have big problems with leakage from aging septic tanks."

"A regular paradise for an environmental activist."

That sounded snotty and we both knew it, but he ignored it and I decided I'd better have a look at my feelings about Lauren DeWitt sometime very soon.

"In her mind, the fights were so black and white," he said. "The white hats wanted to stop development and pollution of all kinds. And the black hats—developers and people like Duck Jarvis on his Jet Ski making noise—didn't."

I got up to put a couple of frozen muffins in the microwave, then plopped them on plates and returned. There wasn't any butter. Will inhaled his anyway, but I found I was still under the influence of last night's pancakes. So I gave him most of mine, then divided the rest into two bites and handed them over to grateful dogs.

"Did you know that during the 1920s and 1930s they harvested caviar from the Chesapeake?'' I shook my head. ''But no one's seen a giant sturgeon in decades.''

''Will, about Lauren. What else was she interested in?'' I didn't exactly know what I was going for here.

''Usual stuff, I suppose. Film and books. And not surprising, outdoor stuff. Hiking and kayaking and camping.'' He thought some more. ''But also clothes and how she looked. Her vain, shallow side.'' I raised my eyebrows. ''Don't look at me like that. Those are her words, not mine.''

''And?''

''And social issues—equal pay for equal work, abortion rights, affirmative action. That sort of thing.''

More causes. Including some scary feminist ones that worried people like Duck Jarvis, even as they secretly attracted wives and daughters. I stared outside. The clearing under the pine trees was beginning to shimmer with heat.

''Can we get Lillian's car soon?''

He nodded. I went to shower and dress, hoping I owned enough makeup to cover the blue caves under my eyes.

NINETEEN

EVEN IN THE GLARE OF morning light, Lillian's neighborhood had recovered. And the odor of burned rubber no longer hung in the air.

The Rainey house came into view. The large sign advertising their variance hearing was gone and on this hot morning, the small rambler looked forlorn. Backed with hundred foot oaks, it was dominated by cars, two in the drive and another parked under the carport. Carl and Florence were apparently a three-car family. Florence was puttering around a cement patio, watering plants in pots, shaking her head over the rest. I stopped the car and got out.

"Florence?" She jumped, then looked around at me. "Sorry, I didn't mean to startle you. Can I talk to you?"

"Uh, Carl's inside. Just got home," she said. "I don't want him seeing me talking to you." But she pulled me aside, out of easy view of the kitchen window. "Tell Lillian I'm sorry this has all happened," she said. "I wanted to talk with her the other day when she called, but Carl answered the phone and..." Her voice was so low, I had to lean nearer. She glanced at the house. "He's still real mad with Lillian. It's all he can talk about. Sleeps, eats, breathes it. Takes it to work, brings it home again."

"But it wasn't her fault that the variance was denied."

"No. But it seems unfair though, don't it?"

"Yes, in many ways it does. But it's a legal thing, the way the land was recorded, nothing to do with Lillian. She wanted Carl to be able to build a house."

Florence's soft features, clobbered by age and gravity, softened further. She looked defenseless, bewildered by recent events. I wondered if Simmons had questioned her. But he must have, since Carl had publically blamed Lauren for preventing him from building the house he wanted. I hoped that Simmons had been a little kind.

"Florence..."

"Ma?" Carl was suddenly standing in the carport, sizing up the situation, an Orioles cap in his hand. He stuck it on his head. "Ma, go in the house."

She did. Without looking back. He turned to me.

"What do you want?"

"I want to talk to you about my aunt. I think you did those flyers." He said nothing, but his eyes flickered. "Lillian isn't responsible for what happened at your hearing. She wanted some modifications of your house plans, but she wouldn't have prevented you from building."

The foolishness of this conversation struck me. What did I expect him to say? Did I think he was going to break into smiles and hold out his hand, agreeing that it had all been a terrible misunderstanding and since my aunt hadn't wanted to deny him his variances, he was very sorry and would personally pull all of the offending flyers from beneath front doors and print a retraction and apology in the local paper? The silence lengthened as I poked at my motives.

"You better go," he said. "And you can tell your aunt that I hold her responsible. I saw what happened afterwards. That New York girl hugging her, like they planned it all along. Well she got hers, didn't she?"

This was useless. He was going to believe what he wanted to believe. Just as I'd hoped that Simmons had been nice to his mother, I hoped that the detective had spared nothing with this jerk.

"Carl, did you set Lillian's deck on fire?"

"You think I set that fire?"

"Maybe if you couldn't build your house, then maybe you didn't want Lillian to have a dock." I met his gaze.

"You really are fucking blessed crazy, you know that?"

"You had to have known that with all the people around, someone would see a fire quickly."

Something new flitted over his face, something that looked like anxiety. But it was gone quickly, replaced by a kind of trumped-up anger he didn't really feel. This was a man, I decided, who derived his courage from others. Not someone who came to it on his own. Thin, his head almost too big for his body, he was a commonplace bully. As Weller had said outside the Arundel Center a week ago. So who was giving him the courage to stick it to Lillian?

"Well, if you didn't set the fire, then you won't mind telling me where you were during the fireworks?" I had a picture of him standing by himself near the booth selling beer, nursing his grievances, his face flushed from booze and the rage that he had nurtured and fed.

"I don't have to tell you anything." He glanced toward the house. "You better leave."

I got in my car. In my rearview mirror, I could see him watching me. Thinking. He went inside.

LILLIAN WAS waiting for me. Before I could so much as turn off the engine, she was sitting in the passenger seat.

"What took you so long?" She rummaged in her briefcase. "Here are the keys and registration." She shoved them in my jacket pocket. "There's some cash in the safe at the office so you don't have to stop at an ATM." She fussed with her seat belt, finally getting it latched, then looked up. "Now before we go, look at me and tell me you aren't going to do anything stupid. Tell me you'll just pay the money and get my car back."

"Lillian, I'm going to get your car back. Nothing else." She threw me a look but didn't say anything more.

We drove by a yard displaying Vincent Darner's poster.

"You know," she said, "I've never seen business this slow. Even with the heat, it's unusual." She reconsidered. "Actually, we did get one call. A Mrs. Bristow—she's the woman who owns the house in Knapp's Point that Lauren was renting—wants us to sell it for her. She's 'through foolin' with renters.' Her words."

"Why us? Given the local hostility?"

"Don't know. Does it matter?" I shook my head. "She lives a few houses down from the cottage. Quite elderly and uses a walker." Lillian shoved a pile of paperwork into a big envelope and put it in my briefcase. "You'll have to go through the house by yourself." She thought of something else. "Oh, I forgot. I got a call from Lauren DeWitt's mother this morning."

"Will told me he gave her your number."

"This is just so terrible for her," Lillian said. "Worse, the poor woman was recently diagnosed with cancer. It all sort of all poured out, I'm afraid. She's arranged for a service for Lauren in upstate New York, where most of her friends are." Lillian sighed, then changed the subject. "I also called Eli. He'll meet you at Knapp's Point. I'd like to get the Bristow house listed as soon as possible. Though I understand the dock has to be rebuilt. And part of the seawall."

"What about Simmons?"

"I called the police department. They told me he was finished at the house. And Will has a set of keys apparently, since Mrs. Bristow gave hers to the detective." She pulled her arm back from the ledge of the open car window when it became too hot, then pointed to the air-conditioning. I turned it on. "I suppose it wouldn't hurt to check with Detective Simmons himself first."

I had another thought. "Lauren's clothes and furniture are one thing, but what about her work? The documentary she was working on. Does whoever bankrolled her get that?"

"I don't know. I suggested that her mother talk to Weller, who could advise her. She did think that Lauren might have had a will. She said her daughter was organized that way." Lillian took a deep breath. "Our job is just to take an inventory. There are only a few things of Lauren's that she wants. She'd like us to get rid of everything else. Once it's legally possible to do so."

"So what do I do? Other than meet with Mrs. Bristow and then Eli?"

"If you could make a list of what's in the cottage, that would be a good start." I pulled into one of the parking spaces in front of our office. Next door the bays of the body shop were wide open. I could see a dark figure moving around inside. I bet paint dried as fast as you could slap it on these days.

"By the way," Lillian began, "did you, uh, close on Ray Tilghman's house?"

"Thought I'd call Weller's office later," I said. "Why?"

"Just wondering." She looked away. "Actually, to tell you the truth, I suppose I'll be happier when you are signed, sealed, and delivered."

"Lillian, I'm not going back to New York. You know that."

"Yes, I know. I was just kidding." I wondered. "I'll be right out," she said. "Only take me a minute to get the cash from the safe."

I waited, for her and for Will, then turned on the radio. The Lovin' Spoonful sang about summer in the city, about how the back of your neck got hot and gritty. The sun glared through the windshield. Minutes ticked by, the song ended. A commercial for prefab sunrooms roused me enough to flip off the radio. Lillian came out to hand me a small envelope. Will's pickup pulled up beside us. She greeted him, then turned back to me as I was locking the BMW and hauling myself into the passenger seat of the truck.

"Just get the car," she said.

TWENTY

IF I THOUGHT I was going to learn anything at Chesapeake Towing this morning, I was mistaken. With the exception of the razor wire, the place looked innocent. The fat woman was gone and in her place, a man who was probably younger than he looked was running things. No sign of the dog. I found the public phone around the corner, not far from where I had stumbled into the bushes. The exterior light overhead the half booth must have burned out.

Maybe last night I'd seen adversity where there was only indifference. Hard, small lives lived the best they could. I pictured the woman crabbing off a pier. Friday, she'd told her friend on the phone, they'd go crabbing near a small woods. It was oddly poetic. Beside her would be a package of chicken parts rotting in the sun. She'd tie pieces of string to necks and backs, then attach the strings to the railing and lower them into the water. A lattice of thin vertical lines would soon run down the pier. Nearby would be her cooler, a bushel basket, and a long net to haul in the flailing blue crabs. She was a chicken-necker, in the local patois. The watermen who plied the Chesapeake for their living were indignant at the number of crabs these amateurs were allowed by law to take.

Outside the towing company office, Will's truck's idling motor climbed to a higher pitch. The attendant got around to waiting on me. I fished out the money, accepting a receipt in return. Our crime had been parking in the unattended lot between the two office buildings where we'd seen the sign. The cop was right. The tow truck driver had been having a slow night and we'd been caught in his net. One of many cars. Well, one way or the other Vince Darner was going to hear about it.

"Out there," the attendant said. "Caddy's parked over beyond that Buick." He pointed to a side door. Will was just behind me.

"What's taking so long?"

"Nothing. You see Lillian's car?"

"There." He pointed. Two minutes later, I was ready to back out, no easy task in my aunt's aircraft carrier. Will leaned in the window. A picture scuttled through my mind: Vince Darner glaring at his wife's profile in the overheated woods near Knapp's Point.

I looked up at Will. Although he'd changed his clothes, he hadn't shaved. Our drive to Baltimore had been silent, each of us lost in our own thoughts. Gone was the early-morning intimacy, nurtured on the porch by the tender eyes of dogs. He'd nodded when I told him Lauren's mother had called Lillian. And that Mrs. Bristow wanted to sell the Knapp's Point cottage.

The rest of the ride had been too hot even to think. Like the taxis last night, Will's truck had no air-conditioning. He didn't mind, but the heat still made me miserable. I had mopped and fanned myself with a small clipboard I found on the seat. Newcomers, bar owner Marian Beall had once told me, usually suffered hard during Maryland summers. But you'll get used to it, she'd promised. No sign of that yet.

Somewhere nearby a noon siren went off, wrenching me back to the present. Will was impatiently shifting his weight from one foot to the other.

"So you're going to Knapp's Point this afternoon?" he asked. "Eve?"

"Sorry," I said. "This heat has my brain fried. Yes. After dropping off the car." I glanced at the clock on the dash. It was a minute slow, if the noon whistle was correct. He started heading back to his truck. "Oh, Will, I almost forgot. I probably will need the keys to Lauren's house. You have a set?"

He returned, then nodded. "Not on me. I'll have to meet you there."

"You sure you want to do that? Go through Lauren's house with me?"

"Yeah. I'm okay with it."

"Thanks." If there was something interesting to be learned, I'd have a greater chance of learning it with Will there. We agreed to meet at Knapp's Point at two or a little later.

"You know how to find your way out of here?" His tanned arm swept in a wide arc to include the blight of the surrounding neighborhood. I nodded. He squeezed my shoulder. "Okay. See you later."

I maneuvered the Cadillac to the main road, past the wreckers and the wrecks, trying not to ruin Lillian's paint job. Near the road, I got a glimpse of the sorry German shepherd, half-dead from the heat, lying under the steps of a corrugated iron shed.

Once on the main road, with Chesapeake Towing and its disagreeable memories safely behind me, I began to realize that I was not only tired and hot, I was also starved.

A sign on a corner store offered Fried Lake Trout. Even the greasy whitefish—a mainstay of Baltimore's poorest black neighborhoods—sounded almost good right now. Driving with my left hand, I checked Lillian's glove compartment for something to munch. Then under the front seat. Nothing. Unlike my BMW, the interior of the Cadillac was tidy and spotless. I did find a map that was falling apart at the seams. But no snacks. The Lovin' Spoonful song looped through my brain, not doing a thing to distract my growling stomach.

Threading my way back to the highway south, I searched for landmarks. Like last night, the streets were a catalog of architectural and human suffering. But in between the grossest structural misfortunes, the occasional new building—mostly low-slung bunkers of low-tech manufacturing—broke the monotony. I knew why: tax credits. Savvy businessmen agreed to build businesses in this unhealthy inner city location in return for some very healthy tax relief.

Thoughts of businessmen set me to thinking about Vince Darner. Had he really made all his money from his chain of lumber stores? Or were there other companies? Like Chesapeake Towing? And why did he need a big infusion of cash right now? Given the way his supporters were shelling out at the community center the other night, could the election be the real reason? I also wondered just how much Charlotte knew—about what he did and why he needed money so urgently that he was selling her family property? I hadn't pressed the point with Mitch last night. Still, I bet he knew why Darner needed money. And if he didn't know, he could find out.

Coming to a stop at a red light, I checked the map, then prepared to turn left onto the highway that would take me south to the relative prosperity of Anne Arundel County. Will's pickup was still in front of me. When the light changed, he turned right to Baltimore. A little flutter of surprise swept down my back.

IT WAS ALMOST one-fifteen when I stopped at an Italian market on Mountain Road. I bought a colossus of provolone, two kinds of olives, roasted peppers, tomatoes, and shredded lettuce on a long roll. The filling had been drenched with good olive oil and the whole thing wrapped in waxed paper. I nearly grabbed it out of the shopkeeper's hand. And it took every ounce of will power I had not to devour half of it in the car, olive oil sluicing down my face as I drove.

Lillian had finished her lunch by the time I handed her the keys to the Cadillac.

"Oh, good, you're back," she said. "Car okay?"

"Seems to be fine."

"No trouble?" I shook my head, trying to unwrap my sandwich without destroying the carpet. "Okay. Did I tell you that someone from the Oil Control section went out to the Knapp's Point property this morning?" I was stuffing sandwich in my mouth. "Well, there *is* a tank, which has to be dug up and drained."

"Vince know they've been there?"

Lillian frowned. "I don't know. But it doesn't matter, does it? There's not much he can do about it."

No, he probably couldn't do anything to the Department of the Environment. But what he could do to Lillian, and maybe to me, made me nervous. I decided to keep my opinions to myself.

Lillian left and I finished the rest of the Italian sub in two bites. Every last olive. And since last night's lack of sleep had begun to nibble around the edges of my brain, I chased it with two cups of coffee. Feeling better, I phoned Simmons, who was not only in his office but apparently expecting my call.

Weller and Lillian, I found, had paved the way for me to inventory Lauren's possessions and get the house ready to sell. Though I gathered from the tightly controlled breathing on the other end of the phone, this had made Simmons none too happy. The detective even permitted himself an ostentatious groan when I mentioned that not only did I have a set of keys, I planned to use them this very afternoon. I heard someone in his office ask him a question.

"Hold on," he said.

Patrick Xavier Simmons was used to putting others on hold. An ex-New York homicide detective, I didn't doubt he'd seen every awful thing that man can think to do to his fellow man. My New York life, by comparison, must have seemed all sweetness and light. During the years he'd been standing over young men dead in the street and fishing corpses out of the Harlem River, I'd merely been persuading my fellow men to buy things they didn't want or need. Unrelated work. And unrelated worlds. Nonetheless, I sensed a narrow and unsteady bridge between us.

"Okay, now," he said. "You're going to the victim's house this afternoon?"

"The woman who owns the house wants it sold quickly." I could hear him breathing.

"Yeah. I know all that."

"Well, better to deal with me than with some real estate agent you don't even know. Right?" There was no answer. "Hello?"

"Yeah."

"You want to be there while I make my inventory?" A negative grunt. "Look, I'm sure you've removed everything that you need for your investigation. And gone through everything else. Right?"

"Yeah."

"Well, then, what possible harm can I do?"

"Just do what you have to do," he said, his voice weary.

"Fine. Thank you. By the way, what did you take from the house? I'll need a list for Lauren's mother."

"Computer. Work files. Other personal papers like her checkbook and letters. A..."

My brain unfogged. "A what?" Silence. What had he been about to say? I was too tired to be anything but merciless. So I said nothing.

Finally he spoke. "I gather the victim wasn't unaware that she was making a lot of locals very unhappy."

Somewhere, deep in my brain, a couple of intuitive cells rubbed together. "Lauren had a gun," I said. "That's it, isn't it?"

"There was no gun in the victim's house."

"What did you find then? Bullets? The box it came in? A receipt?"

"You said it, not me."

"What did I say?" No answer, but I could hear rustling. "There's no gun?"

"No."

"Well, where is it?"

A small, fried noise on his end of the phone was my answer: The police didn't have a clue. My thoughts were tumbling. Lauren had known that her life was in danger. She'd apparently been afraid enough to get a gun. And now it was missing.

"What about the water around the riprap? Maybe she had it with her when she went to meet Will." Suddenly, the obvious occurred to me. Maybe she'd planned to meet someone else that night, with Will as security if things got unpleasant. But who? And why? Besides, Simmons would have thought of this. I came to.

"Sorry. What?"

"Am I talking to myself here?"

"No, no, I'm listening." A pause. "Really. I am."

"Yeah. Yeah. Look, the divers didn't find anything."

There was something else. "What about those explosions Monday night? At the community center? You think that was a gun? Simmons, I have to tell you I don't think they sounded like gunshots." Silence except for some labored breathing.

"Simmons?" Oh, God, it was the name thing. We'd been through it before. "Look, I'm sorry. But I just can't call you Pat. I just can't. No reason really. So, Detective Simmons, were those explosions from a gun?"

A pause. "Simmons is okay, I guess." Another pause as if he realized that the sky might fall and he'd better pedal like crazy in the other direction. "Uh, as long as we're alone."

This time, as my sandal approached my mouth, I took notice and clamped my lips shut before I made this conversation any more awkward than it already was.

"So, okay," I said, "now what about those explosions?"

"Probably illegal fireworks."

We were both quiet. I wondered if Will knew that Lauren had a gun. Did anyone else know?

"Simmons?"

"What?"

"You're telling me things again. Things you aren't telling other people. Is this some sort of crafty police technique? Or are you telling me with the hope that I'll turn into a sieve?" A long silence. I again bit my lip and waited him out.

"I didn't tell you about a gun," he said.

"Whatever you want to think." An impatient grunt. I gave up. "By the way, when do you plan to return Lauren's computer and files and personal papers?"

"When we're done."

"And when would that be?" My voice was as neutral as I could make it.

"Hold on." I waited, stacking papers on my desk and thinking about Lauren's gun. "Ms. Elliott?"

"It's Eve," I said. Silence. Nuts. We were still mired in the name problem.

"Okay. Okay. Okay. Are we about done with what we're going to call each other for now?" I agreed. "To answer your question, I don't know when we'll be through." His voice was peevish, like he'd had his fill of personal conversation for one day. It was okay as long as he was asking the questions, but turn that around and...

"I told the victim's family attorney—your friend Mr.

Church, by the way, but then I expect that you already know that—that we'll provide his client with a list of what we have impounded for our investigation. You won't find anything, you know. In the house.''

"I don't expect to." I hoped my tone was professional. "I'm just going there to get the house ready to sell."

Someone again said something to him. Then he was back. "Er, Eve?"

"What?"

"This gun business also stays between us. Think whatever you want to think about my motives but no talking. You got that?"

I agreed and hung up. Why *did* he let me guess about the gun? It hadn't just sort of slipped out. It was like the marks on Lauren's throat. Well, whatever his reasons, I now knew these things. Trouble was I didn't have a clue what to do with them. And I was sworn to secrecy.

TWENTY-ONE

KNAPP'S POINT WAS baking in the afternoon sun, its residents suffering the heat behind closed doors, shunning the pleasures of waterfront living in favor of daytime television. I saw a flickering light from the Jarvis house as I inched down the road to a small bungalow.

"Dee's hard of hearing," yelled a woman next door, unloading groceries from her car. "You have to knock real hard."

I was thoroughly overheated up by the time Mrs. Bristow made it to the door, a walker helping her manage the ten steps. But she greeted me enthusiastically. As she made her way back to her chair, humped over from a paralyzing case of osteoporosis, I glanced about. It was a room to make your heart ache, filled with the past. A room to live in until you died, quietly, when your time came. A gray tabby jumped from a table to a chair, checked out his choices, then leaped to a highboy.

"That's Stan. Belongs to a friend of my daughter's. I'm just keeping him for now." When she smiled, her face cracked into a parched riverbed of lines. "I met your aunt once. Liked her. Nasty business with those flyers. And that poor girl." A recollection of some distant memory occupied her for a bit. I didn't like to disturb it.

"You knew Lauren?"

"Not really, but a bad thing, you know, her dying like that," she said. "But you've come to have me sign the contract. So, we better get to it before I wear out."

I handed over a pile of papers and we discussed prices and repairs and all the thousand other details real estate agents need to discuss with their clients. I found her agile of mind, smart and curious and quick. She listened, asked a few questions, then signed without fuss, wherever I pointed.

"That red-haired detective has my keys," she said. I told her about Will's set and she nodded, then sat back, exhausted by the effort. I stood up, promising to be in touch. The cat was washing.

My watch said two-fifteen. I parked in Lauren's drive and circled the cottage. It was well kept, smaller than mine and hidden deep in the trees. I walked down to where the dock had been. Someone—maybe Lauren herself—had neatly piled the rotten timbers at the edge of the water.

Far out in the Magothy, a couple of Jet Skis suddenly appeared, chasing one another like randy squirrels, cutting across wakes and jumping waves at reckless speeds. The buzz *was* annoying, but it also looked like fun—despite the increasing number of accidents waterbikes were causing. The Jet Skis disappeared, then returned, their drivers churning up foam and yelling.

What was keeping Will? Why had he gone to Baltimore? I suppressed a prick of worry and headed up the furrowed road. Behind the Jarvis house, an old Chevy was toasting in the sun. After a moment's indecision, I let myself in their chain-link fence and banged on the side door.

"Melody," said a disturbed and resonant male voice on the TV, "I don't know what you're talking about." The voice was deeply offended as a high-pitched female voice accused him of things he swore he didn't do. To no avail. The high-pitched voice didn't believe a word he said. Nor, frankly, did I. A commercial for dog food came on. I knocked on the door again. The sun beat hard on my neck. The door opened a crack.

The Jarvis girl peeked out from a dim room, the only light that of the flickering television.

"Hi," I said. "I'm a real estate agent and I'm going to sell the house next door. Where Lauren DeWitt used to live. I wanted to ask your mother some questions about Knapp's Point."

The girl was momentarily distracted by something inside. Then she returned.

"I saw a car out back."

"That's my dad's car," she said. "My mom's at work."

With that, the door closed. Was the girl afraid to talk because her father was home? What did I expect to learn? I couldn't

answer that, but I also was sure this girl—Jenny, her mother
had called her—was the eyes and ears of the neighborhood.
That she saw and heard things that others did not. Something
also told me that Simmons wouldn't have a prayer with her.
She'd clam up and that would be that. But did I have a right
to try to pry information from a child?

As I hesitated, the door opened again, as if she'd been waiting for my knock. And when I hadn't, she'd taken the initiative.
Now it was my turn.

"Maybe I could talk to you." Only her eyes moved. "I'm
going to the house now. If you decide to take a walk a little
later, I'll be there."

JENNY JARVIS turned out to be eight going on nine. We sat on
the steps of Lauren's house, waiting for Will to bring keys. The
unfortunate mutt I'd seen last Sunday panted hard in the dirt.
The mention of Will had seemed to relax her, but she still
glanced through the trees toward her house from time to time.

"Did you know Lauren very well?" I asked. She leaned over
to rub the dog's ears. "What was she like?"

To my surprise, my question unleashed an avalanche of
words. They had been friends. Lauren had helped Jenny with
her homework. She'd given her magazines and samples of
makeup to play with. She'd showed her how to tuck her long
hair in a ponytail, then braid it. The girl put a hand up to touch
the blond strands that splattered over her shoulders. It looked
hot and sticky.

"My dad won't let me cut it," she said. "I showed him a
model in a magazine who had hair just like Lauren. But he
won't let me."

"What about your mother?" I asked. "Would she let you?"

"She'd have let me but my dad doesn't like short hair." She
leaned closer. "My mother wanted her hair cut short, too."

"She did? Well, how come she didn't do it?"

"She said it wasn't worth it."

A picture of Duck and Josie and the Jarvis family life was
emerging. The girl stared, head tilted, telling me that it was my

turn in the conversation. Jet Skis whizzed by on the water, swooping in and out of each other's paths.

"Do you ever ride on your father's Jet Ski?"

"Sometimes. He lets Jimmy more. Sometimes even by himself."

"Jimmy is your brother?"

"He's thirteen," she said. "He gets to do a lot more than I do."

I wanted to tell her the sad news that age had nothing to do with it. That Duck Jarvis's boy would always get the better part of whatever Duck had to give. I glanced down at the girl, expecting it was a truth she, too, understood.

"Was that girl your daughter?" she asked, suddenly. "The one the night of the fireworks?"

"My what?" Then I understood. Laura, Mitch's daughter was about her age. "Oh, no. She's the daughter of a friend. She was visiting from New York where she lives with her mother."

"Oh." I stayed quiet, hoping she'd talk more. "My dad tried to rescue Lauren, but he didn't know it was her down there on the riprap," she said. "He had to go down there in the dark to get her."

"Did he get hurt when he fell?"

The girl shook her head. I remembered the scene: Josie, her arm around Jenny, the son racing for the water as Duck had slid, then stumbled and fallen onto the riprap. I remembered the anxiety that had eaten up Josie's eyes and face. The anxiety of a wife who has argued with her husband, but now that he was in danger, wished she could take it all back.

Jenny was drawing in the dust with a stick. What had she felt that night? Duck had been very angry with her, too.

"Jenny?" She looked up. "The night of the fireworks. Why was your father so mad at you and your mother?"

She dropped the stick, making the dog jump. "We were talking to Lauren and he didn't want us to. He hated her because she wanted him not to ride his Jet Ski. She said it was noise pollution. She called the cops on him."

"Last Sunday, I think she was afraid he was hurt."

"He was just stung by nettles." I saw her glance at me when she thought I wasn't looking, sizing me up to see which side I was on. It was something she understood—taking sides—taught well by her father. You were either for him or you were against him. If I wanted to know more about Lauren, I'd have to tread carefully.

"Did Lauren die on the riprap?" she asked, suddenly.

"The police are trying to find out. Detective Simmons."

"He asked my mom and dad a lot of questions."

"Did he talk with you?"

She shook her head. "Just them." Her voice had taken on a pinched quality. "He wasn't very nice to my dad. I would never ever talk to him. Ever. Even if he wanted to. He thinks my dad killed Lauren."

Her statement was matter-of-fact. I held my breath. But that was all. She got up. The woods screeched with brittle summer sounds. The heat burned the inside of my nose. What do you think, I wanted to ask her. Did he kill her? From the road came the sound of a car engine. "My dad's going back to work," she said.

"Why was he home?"

"To get baking soda." She sat back down. "For the nettles. He builds seawalls and stuff and he gets stung a lot." A hundred feet away, the pile of rotten timbers was baking in the sun. "He could build Lauren's dock up again."

It was almost companionable, this waiting. Had she and Lauren sat here like this? Maybe reading magazines or braiding hair. Or just hanging out, listening to the sound of the cicadas when the Jet Skis and motor boats ran to deep water. "I'm sorry about Lauren, Jenny."

The girl, I saw then, wasn't as close to tears as I was, oddly separated off in her own world. Again, the angry exchange between Duck and Josie at the carnival the night Lauren died came back to me. Then her father's sharp words. No wonder she had opted out of scary feelings, if someone you depended on was angry and yelling at you all the time.

I glanced at the Jarvis house, wondering if I should tell someone about the mark on Josie's neck. But what did I know?

Nothing really, just that two people locked in marriage had deeply disappointed one another and were thrashing hard, unable to make things right. A run-of-the-mill marriage gone bad.

The girl beside me set every nerve in my body to twanging. What wasn't clear was why. I ran through the possibilities. Because she deserved better than her family could give her? Because she'd had to learn how to fence off her feelings in order to survive? Or because she knew something she wasn't saying? That her father was tormenting her mother? Or perhaps something that she had seen or known because of her friendship with Lauren? Something she wasn't going to tell Simmons. Never. Ever.

I let my intuition have free rein. The girl knew something. I was sure of it. But I couldn't begin to say why I knew.

"Jenny, did Lauren ever talk to you about other things? I mean other than about hair and clothes or your homework?"

The girl nodded, engaged again. "Sometimes. She used to tell me about the film she was writing. I mean the documentary."

"About the Magothy."

"It was about the wetlands and what was going to happen to them if people keep building too many houses. We studied about the wetlands in school last year." What followed was a surprisingly concise presentation of what overdevelopment could do—maybe was already doing—to the ecology of the Bay. The girl had listened hard. Both at school and to Lauren.

"How come you're so interested in all this?"

"I'm going to be a marine biologist."

"What does your mother think of that?"

"She says it's pie in the sky."

"And Lauren? What did she say?"

"She said it was hard to do but that I could do it if I really wanted to."

"And what do you think?"

A wave of uncertainty washed over the girl's face, so acute that I wished I hadn't asked. She knew the deck was stacked against her. In more ways than one. Years from now she'd face a father who probably thought his daughter didn't need an education. There would be no money and, worse, no moral support.

Will's truck spun into a space by the cottage with practiced ease. Jenny ran when she saw him, the dog slouching along.

"Hi. Sorry. I'm late."

"You are at that," I said. "Jenny and I have been talking about all manner of things."

"I see."

Jenny had grown shy again. She looked back and forth between us, uncertain whether she was still welcome.

Suddenly, her brother, rounding a corner on his bike, spied us standing in the woods and headed in our direction. He came to a hard stop, spewing dirt and sand and pine needles in a wide arc.

"Jimmy," said the girl, brushing off her legs. "You jerk."

"Go home," he said. "Or I'll tell Dad. You're not supposed to be talking to strangers."

Will stared at the boy, his jaw muscles clenched. I glanced sideways to see how Jenny was taking this and found her indifference had been replaced with anger. This wasn't any kind of ordinary sibling spat. I'd bet this was a replica of what went on between Duck and Josie.

Eli Claggett's arrival broke the moment, his truck blowing away the silence.

"Need a new muffler, Eli?" I asked.

"Yeah. But if you keep me standing around here for much longer, I won't make enough money today to buy one."

"You got here three seconds ago."

"Yeah, well?"

Will started to laugh, his anger at the boy momentarily forgotten. Jenny looked baffled, unable to take in this new hurricane. Her brother grabbed her arm, then turned away, distracted by a Jet Ski nearing land.

On impulse, I pressed a business card into the girl's hand and mouthed the words: "Call me." She stuffed it into the pocket of her shorts but I didn't know if she understood. But by the time Jimmy had turned back, she was composed. I watched her yank her arm away from him.

TWENTY-TWO

LAUREN'S HOUSE showed all the signs of a police mugging. There were dirty surfaces in the bathroom and kitchen, furniture at unlivable angles, closet doors opened to expose her life. I glanced at Will. His beard seemed to have grown darker since this morning, making him appear at once forbidding and melancholy.

Outside I could hear Eli making his rounds, first clumping across the roof with an interesting curse, then tapping on this and that. Ten minutes later, coming through the front door, he banged the ladder on the top of the frame, unleashing a storm of paint particles.

"Hey," Will said. "Watch it."

"Keep your pants on. I didn't do it on purpose."

"Okay. Okay. We know that." Will scowled. I put my hand on his arm. "You really want to be here for this?"

"I'm fine. It's just that guy." He nodded in the direction of the stairs where Eli had disappeared.

"Yes, I know. But Lillian trusts him." I also wondered about Eli, but since my aunt never wavered I kept my mouth shut. Now I focused on the task at hand. "I need to make an inventory." Will was looking around. "You really don't have to do this."

"It's okay. I'll do the office."

I began in the kitchen, going through the cabinets and drawers. Lauren had been supremely tidy, with boxes of cereal and pasta and jars of olives and peanut butter arranged for easy access. Near the back of the food shelf, behind the tuna and hot sauce, I searched for the inevitable can of creamed corn. Not there. Which blew my theory that every kitchen had one for mealtime emergencies. You just had to look hard enough.

The small freezer was almost empty, but someone would need to empty the refrigerator itself. I pulled out a forgotten head of lettuce fast reverting to primordial black muck in its plastic bag, then opened the door under the sink to dispose of it. There were bags for recycling cans and bottles and paper, but no garbage can. I put the oozing plastic bag back in the refrigerator, hoping I'd remember to remove it before I left. Another time, another place, it might have been funny. Today the whole business was depressing.

Eli came downstairs. "Windows okay. Bathroom okay. Roof okay. Furnace okay." He started on the downstairs, checking more windows, kitchen appliances, pipes under the sink. I heard a painful grunt. Then he was standing beside me. "I'm getting too goddamn old for this."

"So when are you going to retire?"

"You'd love that, wouldn't you?"

"Of course not. I like our little meetings," I said. "They're so...so genial. Pleasant even."

He grinned widely. "House itself is in good shape. Though whoever the hell lived here has dirty hands and must be blind as a bat. Dock and seawall need replacing, but you don't need me to tell you that."

Will had joined us. "Whoever lives here? You don't know?" For once Eli could do nothing but shake his head. "This was Lauren DeWitt's house."

There was a small roar. "The woman who was killed? You mean she lived here? Her?"

"You really didn't know?" He shook his head. "Lillian didn't tell you?"

"People don't tell me shit." His brow furrowed. "Like the other night. That detective. The one from New York City." He carefully pronounced each syllable.

I grinned inwardly. Simmons interviewing Eli Claggett would have been good, very good. "So Eli? What did you and Simmons talk about?"

"Whaddayathink? Wanted me to tell him who killed this here girl." Eli's weathered face was that of an aging and spiteful troll. "Police always want you to do their work for them. And you know what?"

"What?"

"I don't know."

If that were true, it would probably be the first time in his life he'd ever admitted it.

"Eli?"

"What?"

"Oh, nothing. It's okay. Don't tell me what you talked about with Simmons." I took the report he handed me. He made a face and left.

Will handed me his list from the office. "Not much there. I'll go upstairs." He sprinted up two stairs at a time. I could hear him opening and closing drawers and closets.

Within an hour, we had finished. There hadn't been all that much. Lauren hadn't had time to collect all the small household items that ward off domestic anarchy. Picture wire and silver polish. Krazy Glue and paper bag holders. There were few tools and fewer bottles and cans of this and that, used once, then remaindered to the dank real estate under the sink. Even the medicine cabinet had been almost empty—free of interesting brown bottles and prescription pills. I pulled out remedies for poison ivy and sunburn plus bottles and tubes of makeup and eyeliner. Then I joined Will upstairs.

"Just clothes and some personal stuff," he said. "I made a list."

"Like what?"

"Pictures. Jewelry. Not much really."

The closet revealed neat shelves of sweaters and shirts, clothes carefully hung, thrift shop finds and Italian shoes. I touched a vintage jacket, a straw hat, a pile of white T-shirts. Her taste was eccentric and full of confidence. And her scent clung to everything. Will stirred behind me. I closed the closet. We went downstairs.

The house was also oddly paperless, except for a pile of recent magazines and some books, mostly thrillers. There were no letters, no checkbooks, no bills, none of the avalanche of paper that documents a life. I guessed it was all in custody, along with Lauren's computer and disks and work files, held somewhere in a police bin, waiting to tell Simmons why she had been killed. And therefore, by whom.

I went into her office and sat down at her empty desk. Above me was a large, detailed map of Anne Arundel County push-pinned to the wall. A rectangle encompassing the Magothy area had been ruled off in red. I studied the squiggles representing the miles of waterfront within the rectangle, then the lacework of highways and roads, big and small. There was a topograph-ical map of the same region on the side wall. Simmons hadn't wanted either.

Will went to the kitchen. I glanced at Eli's report, then stuck it in my handbag. We'd have the dock and seawall rebuilt, but otherwise Mrs. Bristow's house was in good shape. And when Weller decreed it, Lauren's personal stuff—the things her mother wanted—would be packed and shipped, the rest given to charity. Her furniture and car would be sold. Then someone would clean and paint. The house felt oppressive.

I also couldn't get Jenny out of my mind. What was hap-pening right now? Was her brother tormenting her? Was she in her room with a book, thinking about a future she already sus-pected might be denied her? Or was she making plans to wreak revenge on her brother? I wondered if she'd call me. But why would she? Unless she knew something about her father. After all, she *had* announced rather bloodlessly that Simmons sus-pected her father of killing Lauren and she hadn't gone to his defense. I suddenly remembered the blue smudges on Josie's neck.

Will returned from the kitchen with a bottle of imported beer, its neck surrounded by golden foil.

"Want one?"

"Not really. I don't suppose there's a bottle of water in there?" He went back to look. I heard the refrigerator door open and shut, then a drawer slide open. It jammed and he jiggled it back and forth. I got up.

"What? What did you find?"

"Oh, nothing, just this." I took the wadded paper he held out—one of the ubiquitous notices for missing children. On it were two small pictures. A carpet cleaner advertised on the flip side.

"Wedged in there." Will pointed to a flat utility drawer. I

peered into the offending and forgotten drawer. It held all the familiar clutter that nobody can quite bring themselves to throw away. A couple of months ago, I'd shown a house, empty except for the utility drawer. My buyers had eagerly rooted through it, anthropologists looking for clues to the previous owners. I glanced at Will. He was staring at the drawer.

"Are you looking for something?" I asked.

"Huh? What?"

"I have the feeling you are looking for something."

He sat down on a nearby chair. "There *is* something." I waited. He didn't look at me.

"Will?"

"Uh, okay, I'll tell you. I'm sure Lauren had a gun. I never saw it but she mentioned a few weeks ago that she was getting one. I tried to talk her out of it."

He drank. "After Carl Rainey slugged me and spit on her in the parking lot. The other night." I nodded. "After that, she mentioned it again. But this time, it was as if she already had one."

"Did you ask directly?"

"No, too much going on. And she was totally grossed out by the spit and just wanted to go home."

"Er, Will, maybe this isn't my business, but how come you didn't go home with her? Or how come she didn't go to your place? I mean you were hurt and she was possibly in danger."

"Yes. Simmons asked that," he said. "She just wanted to go home alone. I was worried about her, but she was stubborn. What could I do? Insist?"

"No. Of course not."

"But you see, it makes me think that she must have had a gun, since she felt safe alone."

"Did you talk with her on the Fourth of July?"

"Once. In the morning. She was writing and didn't want to be interrupted. So we agreed again that I'd meet her at nine on Lillian's dock."

"You are sure that the gun didn't come up?"

"Of course I'm sure. But I'm also sure she had one. And

now it's either gone or for some reason the police don't want people to know about it.''

"You didn't tell Simmons?''

"No.''

I didn't ask why. Outside, the Jet Skis romped and buzzed, the irritating noise penetrating the house, getting under my skin. No wonder Lauren hated them. They were soon joined by an outboard motor, its drone decreasing as it reached cruising speed and left Knapp's Point behind. Then it was quiet.

"It doesn't matter,'' Will said. "I went to a gun store in Baltimore earlier today. The police had already been there. So they know there's a gun.''

"Why Baltimore?''

"You think anyone around here would have sold her a gun?'' I thought that over. "More interesting is why your pal Simmons didn't say anything about it.''

I twisted the top off the bottle of water Will had found for me, growing increasingly uncomfortable. I looked over at him, wondering what to do.

"Oh, I see,'' he said. "He did.'' A statement, not a question. I shrugged. All of a sudden, his blue eyes sparked. "But they didn't find it, did they? I'll bet her gun is gone.''

"You said that, not me.'' I felt like Eli Claggett at Thom's Point a few days ago as he deflected inflammatory remarks about Dick Hubbard's snug ties to political figures with legal finesse.

Will stood up. "Well, that at least is settled.''

"What's settled? That Lauren had a gun?''

"Yeah, and that it's missing and the police know and aren't saying anything about it. And have made you promise not to, either. Right?''

I shrugged again. He nodded. We went back into the kitchen. I studied the pictures of two missing children on the narrow slip of paper. Again, a picture of Jenny in her skimpy shorts floated through my mind.

"Will, do you think Duck Jarvis hits his wife?'' He didn't register surprise. "Did Lauren ever say anything about it? Mention that she saw anything?''

He shook his head. "But he's a Neanderthal. And he drinks. You heard his kid this afternoon, trying to be like him. So it's possible, I guess. Did the girl tell you something?"

"No. But Josie had a bruise on her neck the other day." I then related my conversation with Jenny. He nodded, finished his beer, opened the door under the sink. I heard the bottle fall into the recycling bin. "It makes me crazy to think we can't do anything."

We stood for a few minutes in the small house in the woods. It would soon be empty and sparkly clean and I would fasten a lockbox on the outside and escort prospective buyers through. It was unlikely there would be a stigma, since Lauren hadn't been killed here. Her death would be a novelty, however. People would want to know the details. I could hear myself saying in a few cool words that she'd died on July Fourth under suspicious circumstances and that the police were investigating. And I'd leave it at that. I'd omit the moment her lifeless body, blood on her face, fell headlong onto the sharp white stones as everybody in town watched. If they wanted to know about that, they were on their own.

Will touched my shoulder. "Are you done here?"

"Yes." He held the door to the house for me. I took one last look around. Despite the furniture, the police grime, it already seemed empty.

"Here. You'll need these." He handed me the house keys.

We parted after a few minutes, my nerve endings twitchy and hot as I watched him back out of Lauren's drive. Where *was* the gun? I unlocked the BMW, then looked back at the house one more time, vaguely uneasy. Were we all missing something? But what? Oh, God. The garbage.

Two minutes later I was opening the refrigerator. Gingerly picking the lettuce up, I reached under the sink and brought out the paper bag and dumped it in with a brown splat. Lauren probably had a compost heap, but for today this would have to do. I quickly gathered up all of the trash: bottles and paper alike, and stuffed them together in the bag. There'd be no recycling this time. I'd just take all of it and find a Dumpster somewhere.

Picking up the bag, I headed for the door. Then I saw it. There was a penciled phone number on the edge of the paper bag. Had someone caught Lauren unpacking her groceries? Or had she called the information operator for a number, then found she had nothing to write on? Grabbing a pencil, had she written the number on the back of whatever was handy—in this case a supermarket bag?

I returned to the kitchen. Above the utility drawer, over the counter, was a wall phone. Smoothing out the bag and squinting at the number, I dialed.

"Permit Application Center. Tim Clayson speaking." The voice was young, alert, clear.

"Uh, Mr., uh, Mr. Clayson?"

"Yes? Who is this?"

"What department have I reached?"

"This is the Permit Application Center, but I asked you first."

"Mr. Clayson, do you answer the phone there all the time?"

"Sometimes. Not always. Why?"

"Did you talk with a woman named Lauren DeWitt sometime recently?"

"Uh, yes, a couple of times." His voice trailed off. "She's the woman who was killed, wasn't she? Who is this?"

"My name is Eve Elliott. Can you remember what she wanted?"

"She wanted to know if she could come in and research a building permit. What's this about?"

"And could she?"

"Sure. Anyone can. Is this official?"

"When did you talk with her?"

"A while ago. I couldn't swear to the date or anything. Are you with the police?"

Lauren had seen the sign outside the Rainey property, then done her homework before the hearing. And the document she had handed the hearing officer last Monday had convinced him to deny the variance.

"Hello?"

"Yes, sorry. I'm still here."

"I can tell you more," he said, casually, "but you have to tell me who you are."

"I'm a real estate agent. I'm getting the house she rented ready to sell."

"Okay." I could practically hear him deciding if I was worth talking with. "Okay. I talked to her. She was interested in the permit for a house being built on Weller's Creek."

"Weller's Creek? You're sure?" A grunt. "Uh, thank you."

I hung up the phone before he could ask more questions. Lauren DeWitt had been inquiring into Vincent Darner's building permit? So, she hadn't called the Permit Application Center about the Rainey property. Interesting. And why hadn't I thought about doing that myself? I had a lot more to lose than she did.

I got in the car. The Jarvis house was silent and dark. Jimmy's dirt bike lay on the AstroTurf by the side entrance.

TWENTY-THREE

IT WAS APPROACHING five when I turned into the private road that led down to my cottage on Weller's Creek. Though it felt later. The adrenaline that had kept me going all day had evaporated as soon as I left Knapp's Point. But if my body felt saggy and drained, my mind still galloped full tilt, my focus back on Vincent Darner. What was there about his building permit that had interested Lauren DeWitt? And why did he need money so badly that he was trying to intimidate Lillian into cancelling the contract with Weber Realty? After the illegal tow last night, these were questions that needed answering. And then there was Lauren's missing gun. And the marks on her throat. Marks I couldn't tell anyone about. Then I remembered the blue smudge on Josie's neck.

By the time I'd pulled into the clearing in front of the cottage, my brain was overheating with possibilities. And I'd come to the regrettable conclusion that there were only two avenues of action. Or nonaction, since one choice was to do nothing. Or I could call Simmons and tell him about the bruise on Josie's neck. Let him decide what it meant and what to do, if anything. Telling him seemed the better of the choices.

My pager pulsed against my waist as I let the dogs out of the house for a run. I looked down at the number. Gaylin Realty, Mitch's Annapolis office. Good. I was sure Mitch knew about Vince Darner's business dealings, why he needed money so badly. And if he didn't, he could find out. And if he just didn't want to tell me, I'd keep asking until he told me to shut up.

Both Zeke and Lance headed off to the cove at a full gallop. I followed them. Was the heat diminishing a little? Maybe. Or maybe I just wanted it to. The sun was still strong as it slid across the water. Hard to believe that only just over fifteen hours ago, Mitch and I had sat talking in Lillian's driveway, the moon shining through the windshield. I yawned, my eyes watering I was so tired. I looked down at the old dock. I was going to have to have it repaired soon. Maybe Duck Jarvis would rebuild it, an irony at best. But, I reminded myself, it still wasn't my dock. And it wouldn't be unless I remembered to make an appointment with Weller to sign the settlement papers.

Suppressing a second yawn, I pulled my cell phone out of my pocket and punched in some numbers, then waited for Weller Church's elderly secretary to answer. Across the creek stood the site where the Darner's house would soon materialize. There were no sounds of bulldozers, no graders, or backhoes and chainsaws this late in the day, but the dense old-growth forest of oaks and pines and poplars seemed more airy, as if the interior of the woods had been thinned. Maybe I was imagining it. I hoped so. But in case I wasn't, tomorrow I'd make a trip to the Permit Application Center. To talk with Tim Clayson. It wasn't just Lauren who was interested in Vince Darner's building activities. This was personal.

Weller's secretary croaked hello, then apologized for the frog in her throat. We agreed I would stop by his law office in Annapolis tomorrow afternoon. I thanked her and hung up.

"Hey, no swimming." Lancelot had been testing the waters, standing on the beach, turning around to dare me to say something as he edged nearer. "No." He backed up, disappointed. Zeke slumped beside me on the dock, innocent dog eyes looking up at me. I would never do such a thing, they said. I leaned down to scratch black ears and reassure myself that the damp nose was cold. My reward was a wriggle of barely contained dog love, culminating in a sloppy kiss.

Wiping my face, I returned Mitch's call. We got through the initial courtesies pretty well, but then he felt obligated to remind me yet again that in no way was I obligated to him for fetching us last night. But he really wanted to get together again soon. How about dinner? Tonight? Crabs at Cantler's? We could eat outside, since the heat seemed to be moderating. Had I noticed it was a few degrees cooler? Still, there was no obligation. But, after all, I did have to eat, didn't I? He would meet me there—seven or so if that were okay? Okay.

Feeling like I'd been run over by a train, I agreed. It meant there was time for a nap and a shower. And the runover feeling wasn't Mitch's fault. It was nobody's fault. Well, maybe somebody's, I just didn't know whose. As for the crabs, maybe I could stave off a starvation death by having a snack ahead of time.

"How do I get to...what's the name of this place again?"

"Cantler's Riverside Inn." After complicated directions I only half heard, I hung up and called the dogs, then headed for the bungalow. Inside, the steady red light from my answering machine told me that business hadn't picked up any at Weber Realty. One more thing to worry about.

But first things first. I sat down at the desk, pawed through my Rolodex until I found Simmons's card. It had his private number penciled in.

"Simmons."

"Uh, Simmons?"

"Who do you want?"

"Uh, you, I think. This is Eve, uh, Eve Elliott."

"I know your last name."

"Yes, yes, I'm sure you do. I was just surprised that you answered, that's all."

"Well, I do answer my phone sometimes, you know."

I was suddenly weary. "Simmons, can we stop the dancing, please? I've got something to tell you. I don't know if I should and maybe you know already."

A short silence, while he apparently considered the unlikeliness of my volunteering information. "What?" His voice was a little hoarse, a voice not very good at conversations with people he knew, people who could even remotely be called friends.

As succinctly as I could, without emotion, I described some of my conversation with Jenny. From the other end of the phone a sigh told me how hard he was trying to be patient, not to interrupt and demand I get to the point. Sooner not later.

"Look, what I want to tell you is this. When I was in Lyle's

Market the other day—you know Lyle's, don't you, now that you live here?'' A grunt. ''Well, Josie Jarvis had a bruise on her neck. It was pretty well covered by hair and makeup, but it was definitely a bruise.''

A throat clear. ''Eve.''

''What?''

''Let me lay it out for you all nice and clear. I think you are telling me that Duck Jarvis hits his wife and that you somehow think it's related to Lauren DeWitt's death. You with me so far?'' I sputtered but before I could interrupt, he went on. ''Well, here's the deal with situations like this: You can do nothing or you can do nothing.''

''Two equally crappy choices.''

''Yup.''

''Simmons?''

''What?''

I hesitated. ''The bruise on her neck? You saw it? And still you can't do anything?'' I hoped he wouldn't feel my words demanded a sarcastic response.

To my surprise, what came from the other end of the phone was the deepest sigh I'd ever heard. ''This is off the record, you know. You know?''

''I know.''

''Yes.'' I heard papers rustling.

''Yes? Yes, you saw the bruise? Or yes, you can't do anything?''

''Both.''

''That's truly shitty.''

''Yes, again. It's also the law.'' A pause. ''For you, too, it's the law. You can't rush in and break up a family, just because you suspect something. And that's all this is, suspicion.''

''Jenny says you think that her father killed Lauren.'' I was fishing, but I didn't care. ''She won't talk to you, Simmons. She told me that.'' A rasping noise on the other end. I decided to take pity on him. ''But I gave the girl my phone numbers. What if she phones me?''

''Well, what if she does?'' But he didn't sound antagonistic, as if for once, I'd done the right thing. "And if she tells you something, you will call me up and tell me? Right?"

Depending on what she says, I thought. "Yes, I'll tell you."

"Eve?"

"What?"

"Look, you did what you could do." His voice was quiet, unprovocative. "You did. So let it go. The child sounds smart. Maybe she'll call you if she needs to. Now I got to go."

I could feel Simmons's supply of benevolence—never deep and wide—about gone. I thanked him and hung up, then realized that his kindness had caught me off guard. I again had forgotten to tell him about last night's illegal tow and about Vince Darner's buried oil tank and subsequent threats.

I fed the dogs, then lay down on the couch, trying hard not to think about anything for a few minutes. From the kitchen came the sounds of crunching. Lance chased his empty dish around the linoleum, unhappy that dinner was all gone and so fast. Light softened at the windows and I could feel myself falling, helplessly crumpling into a deep and calm and dreamless place where body and bones and mind and spirit would be restored.

I awoke to the pager on my belt buzzing a hole in my side. Where was I? How long had I slept? I yanked off the pager and glanced at the digital display. It wasn't a number I recognized, but getting to my feet, I stumbled over to the desk, picked up the phone on the desk, and dialed.

"Hello? Who is this?"

"Eve? You okay?"

Mitch. I glanced at my watch. Oh, God, almost eight. "Sorry. I fell asleep. On the couch. I was...oh, never mind. I'm very sorry." He mumbled something. "You still want me to meet you tonight? It'll be at least an hour—probably more—before I can get there."

"That's okay," he said. "Take your time. Dick Hubbard's here and I wouldn't mind talking to him for a bit."

"Mitch?"

"What?"

"You don't need any sleep?"

"Nap. In the office. An hour at lunch, if you can believe that?" I had a picture of the long squashy sofa in his office, the kind it's impossible to get up from, so comfortable you didn't care. Had his black office cat tucked himself into the curve of his knees and purred? "You have the directions?"

I repeated what I could remember, got it all wrong and was forced to find paper and pencil and write down in minute detail how to get there.

"Mitch. I'm really sorry about this."

"Don't worry about it."

TWENTY-FOUR

No one had ever stumbled across Jimmy Cantler's Riverside Inn. Keeping one eye on the road, I was forced to pay close attention to Mitch's directions. Then a final turn and the crab house squatted big and lumpy on the water, between waterfront properties, some newly renovated and enlarged. Only a few shabby houses were left on this stretch of waterfront. I gave them five years to be gentrified. It was the same story throughout Anne Arundel County.

The restaurant's parking lot was full. A bored kid sitting on a kitchen chair at the entrance held up his hand, then pointed at a sports car that was gingerly backing out.

Summer in Maryland assaulted my senses. Heat and water and the delicious and unmistakable smell of seafood hit me squarely, tainted only by an undercurrent of fishiness, of dirt and metal and gasoline. A hum slapped at my ears—air-conditioning and kitchen noises mixed with the low conversations of folks relaxed from beer and food and sitting companionably in the night air. There were a few lights on the other side of the water. Someone cut the engine of an outboard motor as the boat glided the last yards toward the restaurant's dock below. It was still hot.

"Eve? Over here." Mitch stood on the railed open deck above the dock and the holding tanks. "You have to go through the restaurant. Meet you inside."

He pointed at the side door, then turned back to the table. Dick Hubbard was cleaning his hands with one paper napkin after another. In front of him on the long picnic table was a pile of crab wreckage. I wondered if Mitch had eaten.

He was waiting at the entrance door to the deck, impeding it. "Sorry," he said to a waitress, moving. "Gwenda, can we get a couple of beers? Over there?" He pointed to a table in the far corner overlooking the water. On my right, I could see

Dick Hubbard signing a credit card slip that another waitress had handed him. He put his arm around on her waist, pulled her in close, then released her and moved toward us. I got out of the way of a waiter with a full tray.

"Think about it," Dick Hubbard said to Mitch. "The land's buildable if we handle it carefully. There'll be mitigation, but I think the county will go for a little trade on this one. They're more interested in that wetlands area in South County I told you about."

"Maybe."

"Well, you're gonna lose out if you wait. Better think about it. Not much left, you know, not as good as this." He moved closer. "I already got something on the table. I don't much like it, but I don't know how much longer I can wait."

Mitch stared at him, unsmiling. Then he touched my shoulder, pulled me into their circle, and made introductions.

Dick Hubbard's smile careened to the edges of his tanned face. "We've met," he said. "Yes, of course, we've met. Though not formally and not under the happiest of circumstances, I'm afraid."

"Happier for my aunt than for Carl Rainey."

"Ain't that the truth?" He shook his head. "The zoning guy really dropped the ball on that one. Still, better that we do it right. I keep telling Carl that. Better to do it right now than to have it come back to haunt us all ten years from now." He shook his head.

Did he know just how strongly Carl Rainey disagreed with him? Another waitress passed us and he noticed and stopped her, pulling some money off a wad from the pocket of his pants. I didn't see how much but I did see the smile on her face. I also noticed that nobody seemed to mind that we were impeding traffic, further evidence of lavish-tipping regular customers.

"I told..." Then he stopped himself, shaking his head. "No, not tonight." He smiled, allowing it to fade. "I heard about your aunt's dock. I'm sorry." I nodded. "Dreadful to find somebody dying like that on your own place. And the dock gone, too. How's she handling it?"

"Amazingly well," I said.

"Glad to hear it. Heard it was pretty grim."

Hadn't he been there? He'd been talking with Vince Darner in the parking lot before the fireworks began. I saw he was older than Mitch by a few years, but his hair had no gray and his body looked like he spent hours on a squash or tennis court. Maybe swimming laps. I wondered if he were married. Suddenly I realized that both Mitch and he were staring at me.

"Sorry, did you say something?"

"No. No," he said. "This isn't the time and place to talk about the other night. I'm sure the police will find whoever killed that girl. That red-haired guy seems like a good man."

I started to say I'd tell the red-haired guy, then bit my tongue.

"Well, you let me know if there's anything I can do for your aunt. Mitch here knows where to find me."

Social niceties out of the way, he turned to Mitch and after another hushed conversation, he winked at me and left. I could see him inside Cantler's going from table to table, joking and laughing.

"Dicky Hubbard, get your friggin' self over here," someone yelled.

A FEW MINUTES LATER, we sat overlooking the water.

"Beer okay, I hope?"

"Fine. What was that about? With Dick Hubbard?"

"A heads-up on some waterfront." Mitch was opposite me. "I think he's driving off the cliff with this one. The EPA's going to get involved. As well as the state. Still, it's a great spot and if he manages to pull it off, somebody's going to get rich."

"And that person will be Dick Hubbard? Or will it be you?"

"Not me." He shrugged. "If the EPA or the Department of the Environment decide they don't like what they find, the developer may find himself with nothing to develop."

I thought a bit, between sips of beer. "I don't get it. Does Dick Hubbard sell real estate?"

"No, not technically. Let's just say that whatever real estate agency the seller lists his property with doesn't have to do much after he's involved."

"He finds the buyer? The developer?"

"And then lends them money to buy and develop the land. And handles the legal work."

"So he's an investor? With a law practice?"

"Basically. Though—how shall I put this? I think that otherwise some of this land might not get sold or built."

"Because it's got environmental issues?"

He nodded. "Virtually all of it is either waterfront or tidal wetlands."

"But why would you or any other developer take the chance on buying something that could have environmental problems?"

"Two reasons. One, because there's hardly any sizeable waterfront left. And two, because Hubbard has a way of making environmental issues go away."

I thought of Eli Claggett's words, how Dick Hubbard had friends. "Where does he get his capital? To lend to developers?"

"Now that's an interesting question. Some of it's probably his, but the lion's share…"

"What?"

"Nothing actually. I expect he has some investors. Or maybe a silent partner. Hubbard works very close to the edge of what's legal sometimes, jumping back over the line when he thinks someone's watching. Still, he's good at what he does and as far as I know, he's never been accused of anything illegal. He's just aggressive about things. Plus he gets to know people, spends a little money." He stretched, then settled down to stare at me. "You know how much I would like to talk about something else? I just had an hour of Dick Hubbard and his deals." He drank deeply. "Which is about all anybody could be expected to handle in one evening."

The smell of crab was stronger here, the suggestion of rawness gone.

"Why don't you sit over here," Mitch said. "You'll be able to see the water." He got up and let me in next to him. "Most of these people will clear out soon. So, you find the place okay?"

"Fine."

"Good." He glanced around for the waitress and gestured when she turned around. "Crabs?"

I hesitated. The time of reckoning. I couldn't live in Maryland for much longer and not eat crabs. But maybe tonight I was just too hungry. Mitch watched my waffling with interest, swigging his beer.

"So?"

"Okay. But be warned that I will embarrass you."

The people at a nearby table got up, leaving a mountain of shells, dead bodies, and slimy gunk on the brown paper. Corn cobs. Cold onion rings and cole slaw containers spilling over with uneaten mayonnaisie strands of raw cabbage. A waiter came by and efficiently sorted out wooden mallets and paring knives, sweeping up the paper and crab remains into a messy and leaking ball. Mitch was watching me, the half sunbursts giving away his amusement.

"You can embarrass me all you want."

Why hadn't I practiced my dismembering skills with Lillian? Why hadn't I just stopped some evening at Arundel Seafood, ordered a dozen, and taken them home to make a mess on the kitchen table, with only the dogs to watch? Too late. And now, it was going to be this pleased-with-himself man who showed me the ropes. Who watched as crab bits flew across the table and dribbled down my shirt, as I spit shells and green slime. Not some uninterested party. Not some unamused party.

"If you laugh," I said, "just one small laugh, I am out of here. Got that?"

"Got it." Then he laughed. Hard enough that the waitress stopped by to see if everything was okay. "A dozen extra large and another round." He held up his beer bottle to remind her what we were drinking. "Oh, and, Gwenda, crab dip with extra bread. Fries and a couple of ears of corn." Then he began to laugh again.

The waitress reappeared with a length of brown paper and knives and mallets, then the rest of the order. Finally a big tray arrived. The crabs, hot and pungent, were dumped in a drift of red-brown bodies. I looked around and wished a few more people had felt the need to escape to their air-conditioned homes. Mitch finished his beer.

"Look, I'll show you how. It's easy. You'll be good at it in no time." I resisted the temptation to respond. Instead I watched what his hands were doing.

What they were doing was snapping off the creature's legs and arms, then putting the big, fat, serious middle aside. Picking up the thick mallet and each leg in turn, he pounded, gently crushing the long leg shells. Then—very carefully with a knife—he teased out a lovely piece of meat. For half a second, time stopped, as the crab meat dangled between us over the table, uneaten. Then grinning, he stuck it in his mouth.

"See. Like that." Quickly, he did a second leg joint. The meat was smaller and he sucked it out. "Okay. Now you."

Ground zero. I looked around. People were watching, smiling. No place to hide. Feeling like Attila the Hun, I broke off legs until I had a pile of limbs on my right and a hideous and legless corpse on my left. I tried not to look at it. Mitch stopped eating to watch what my hands were doing, his face intense, no smile visible. I snapped the limbs in half at the jointed cartilage. Then with mallet in my right hand, a crab forearm in my left, I applied a little pressure. A bad noise. Small but bad. I held up my work. Nothing. I tried again a little harder. And I found myself holding a crushed shell, hard parts mixed with soft parts.

"Too hard. You gotta relax, take your time. Eating crabs takes time." This from the next table behind me, a powerful older man, his buzz cut giving away his career choice. "And you gotta go easy."

I put the pulpy, shelly mess in a growing garbage pile. Next to me, Mitch was cracking and sucking and discarding. When he was done with the legs, he waited for me to catch up. I turned to him, nearly colliding with the marine who had decided apparently that I needed his full attention.

"Your friend," I said, in a low voice, "seems to take quite an interest."

"Ignore him."

"It's a little hard."

"Now look, don't get discouraged," the marine said. "Try this one." The bench behind me scraped over the deck as he moved closer. Then he reached around me and handed me another crab leg. "You try that again. Not so much pressure this time." His big flat head was near mine. I pounded. "Easy...easy...that's it." I held up the leg. Still nothing. Grabbing the thing, I pounded hard, causing the crab leg to fly out of my hands and across the table. The marine sat back. I could practically feel his disappointment.

Mitch was suddenly very interested in a particularly difficult extraction job.

"I hope you're happy."

He looked over at me, his mouth full. "You have absolutely no idea."

I wanted to put my head in my hands, but they were far too covered with crab goo. So, instead I brushed my bangs out of my eyes with what I hoped was a clean forearm, and went back to work. I ate the pieces I had liberated so far, suffering the tiny bits of shells that lodged among the soft flesh, too exhausted to spit them out. I would probably die of some sort of intestinal obstruction. If I didn't die of hunger first.

Mitch had returned to earth. "Here's what you do next." He had picked up a wide flat body and turned it over. "See this?" He pointed to what looked like a pop top on the underside of the crab. "That's the apron. You put your thumb or your knife under it and pry it off." He pried and then added the little hinge to the growing pile of remains in front of us. "Then you have to pull the crab apart." He did this with ease. The marine was back, watching and grunting with satisfaction when the shell released its grip on the crab's torso. "There."

I looked down at a tangle of tiny white flopping fingers with dots of blackish fingernails—one on each side of the crab, as if to hold it together. Worse, in the far corners of the crab torso were small globs of some yellowish green stuff.

"Caviar," said the marine. "You eat it on crackers."

"No," I said. "I don't."

"Pardon me." He half turned around again, then unable to stand the suspense, returned to breathe hot air along my neck.

"You don't have to eat it. A lot of people don't," Mitch said. "But you do have to get rid of these gills." He pointed at the little white hands.

"Called dead man's fingers," the marine said. I looked at Mitch.

"Yeah, they are. Parents around here tell their kids not to eat the dead man."

"Or devil's fingers," said someone at another table.

Mitch nodded. "That too. Okay, now you want to take it like this." He held the crab away from himself and snapped it in half, then in half again. "There. Now you just use your fingers to get at the meat." He showed how, offering me the largest lumps. My pride gone, I took them. And would have been perfectly happy to sit there while he snapped and pounded and cracked and rooted, then handed over the loot. Instead, I found a napkin, cleaned up my hands, finished one beer and started a second, ate fries and corn and crab dip, then finished the second beer.

Fortified, the first level of hunger and all self-consciousness wiped out, I attacked the crab pile in front of me, trying to remember what I'd just learned. The marine disappeared, but not for good. I was soon up and running, snapping and cracking and pounding away. Beside me, Mitch ate steadily, not watching. Shards of crab flew across the table, and in one particularly wicked explosion, covered my face and hair and lodged inside the open neck of my sleeveless shirt. The waitress brought more napkins and another round of beer. I mopped up. My edges felt fuzzy, my mouth slightly numb from the Old Bay and beer. Finally, I pushed the mess away.

Behind me, the marine apparently thought compliments were in order. "Good girl," he said. "Good job."

TWENTY-FIVE

WITH THE CRABS GONE, the marine lost interest, turning back to chew on ancient tales of victory and plunder with his two pals. Or maybe they were just discussing their digestion or their pension plans. They left soon.

Behind us a family was getting ready to go, the parents fed up with their antsy kids. I watched as a teenage boy splattered his younger sister with crab parts. She remained dignified and righteous, ten times more grown-up than the boy. They, too, left, the boy slinging insults. I thought again of Jenny Jarvis, her thin legs and short shorts. But my conversation with her this afternoon seemed unreal and distant.

The mountain of garbage had been removed from our table, the brown paper gone, the flat surface swept clean.

"After last night," Mitch said, "I'm half afraid to ask what you were up to today."

"You want to know, I'll tell you. First, I liberated Lillian's car from the clutches of the towing company. Then I returned to the office and had lunch. You want to know what?" He didn't answer, so I gave in and told him about Lauren's house.

"Why do I think that this is the expurgated version?"

Below us, I could hear the brother and sister chasing each other between the crab tanks, the boy still yelling taunts. Their parents were talking with friends near the door.

"Okay," I said, "there are a couple of other things. For one, I talked with Carl Rainey." Mitch drew closer. "He's still furious with Lillian. Dick Hubbard may think he's convinced him to do the right thing, but he hasn't. The guy's got a grudge a mile wide."

"And you think he's responsible for those flyers?"

"Well, don't you?" Mitch shrugged. "Okay, I've got no proof but he certainly didn't deny it when I confronted him. He also got pretty upset when I asked if he set Lillian's dock on fire.'' Mitch's eyes opened up. ''In fact, he was so scandalized about it that I think maybe he didn't do it. Besides, who knows if the fire was purposely set anyway. You hear anything about that?''

He shook his head. ''You just asked Carl Rainey outright if he set Lillian's dock on fire?''

''Took him by surprise. He's just a bully. Spineless and mean, even to his mother. Maybe someone's using him.''

''And you think this why?''

''Don't know really. You'll laugh at me if I say intuition.''

''No, I won't. Usually something underlies intuition. Even yours.''

''No, really. It's just a guess. I saw him at the hearing last Monday and then a day later at the debate at the community center. He blusters a lot, but that's all it seems to be. He gets drunk and rants and raves, but doesn't have a clue beyond that. He spit on Lauren, for God's sakes. Spit. How stupid and boorish is that? And that was after he'd punched Will for utterly no reason other than he was with her. But you know, underneath everything, I feel this anxiety coming off him.''

''Oh.''

I laughed. ''See. I told you intuition was going to give you trouble.'' He propped one foot onto a nearby bench. ''Mitch, where do most people go to crab around here? I know that sounds crazy, but where are the most popular public spots?''

''You liked the crabs so much, you plan on doing a little crabbing on your own?'' I didn't dignify this with an answer. ''Okay, okay, but there are hundreds of places.'' He named some bridges and piers in and around Annapolis.

''No, not a bridge or in a town or city. Someplace in the woods, near a little wooded area.'' A small woods, the woman at the towing company had said. ''Near a small woods? What public place could you go to crab near a small woods?''

''I don't suppose you'd like to tell me what this is about?'' I shook my head. Then I saw something dawn on him.

''What? What did you just think of?''

He hesitated, as if he were calculating how sorry he'd be if he told me. Then he relented. "A small woods? Fort Small-wood?"

I couldn't believe how dense I'd been. I'd shown houses in the new developments along Fort Smallwood Road in north Anne Arundel County. Fort Smallwood Park itself edged the Patapsco River, which ran into the Chesapeake Bay.

"That's it, I'm sure of it. Have you ever actually been there?"

"When I was a kid."

"Is it still there?"

"What, the fort? I guess so." He was looking at me. "You are up to something and I'd like to know what."

I was saved by the waitress, who wanted to know if we'd like another round. Mitch smiled at her, then turned to me, running his hand down my back by way of asking.

"Yes?"

I nodded, wondering at the volley of sparks his hand had unleashed. The waitress left. I glanced at him and saw he knew about the sparks. And that he was trying hard not to laugh, though the eye crinkles were pretty much beyond his control for the moment.

"What were we talking about?"

"Fort Smallwood. You were just about to tell me why you are so interested."

"No, I wasn't."

"Okay, don't tell me. Please just don't do anything really stupid."

I changed the subject before he could think of more questions. "You know Vince Darner's house, the one he's going to build across from me?"

"Yes."

"I think Lauren DeWitt had some interest in it." I described my conversation with Tim Clayson at the Permit Application Center.

He whistled. "I knew it. You *have* been busy."

"Speaking of Vince Darner..." I stopped. There seemed to be a lot to talk about. And then there was Lauren's missing gun. Which I couldn't talk about. Unless he, like Will, guessed. But why would he?

"What about Darner?"

"Mitch, why does he need money?"

"You're not thinking of confronting him for some reason, are you?" A muscle near his mouth had begun to tick.

"Of course not. I'm not that dumb."

"I didn't say that. But I do think that you have some cockamamie idea that he's in the middle of all that's happened lately and that you're determined to find out how."

"I believe that's the first time I've ever heard anyone use 'cockamamie' in a sentence."

"Don't change the subject."

"Okay. But Darner may have been behind Lillian's car being towed last night."

To my surprise, he didn't deny it. "I don't know if I should tell you this," he said, slowly.

"Well, you either trust me or you don't."

"That's blackmail."

"Yes."

"Okay," he said. "I'll probably be sorry, but here goes. It's not yet common knowledge since the company's private, but Darner's lumber and hardware stores are in trouble. Too many national chains moving in. He's traditionally sold to contractors, but now they're getting better prices and better service elsewhere." I didn't ask him how he knew this. "He needs to computerize and centralize his administrative functions and retrain his personnel, all of which will take millions. Otherwise, he's out of business in a year. He just can't compete."

I took this in. "Does he have other businesses? Like the towing company?"

"I don't really know, but if he does, it's small potatoes."

No wonder the underground oil tank was such a problem. The stakes were higher for Vince Darner than either Lillian or I could have known. A prickle of fear crept through me. I had to tell Simmons about Darner's threats. I also had to persuade Lillian that she might need to take some precautions.

I looked over at Mitch, suddenly glad he was here, solid and safe. "You know, I'm a bit afraid for Lillian. I'd almost like to get someone to stay with her or something. Is that overreacting?"

He took a long, deep breath. "I don't know. But how are you going to get Lillian to accept a nanny?"

"Maybe I'll begin by taking Lance over there tomorrow. As a temporary measure, but it'll buy some time." My thoughts tumbled and spun. "There's another thing."

"What?"

"Not about Darner. Well, not directly anyway. It's something Eli Claggett said the other day that's been bothering me ever since. It was after the variance hearing. Something about how Carl Rainey shouldn't worry too much about getting a building permit since Dick Hubbard has friends in all the right places. I take that to mean political friends. You think that it's something to do with Darner?" An old abandoned work boat was drifting in the creek below us. "I told Lillian about it and she just sniffed. But I can't help but wonder."

I had a picture of Vince Darner and Dick Hubbard huddled together on July Fourth, oblivious to the carnival and the crowd all around them. If Hubbard were to be believed, he must have left just after that. And where was Vince Darner during the fireworks?

I sat back and tried to enjoy the hot night air, the glitter off the water below us. Maybe I was just seeing stuff where there wasn't anything to see. I needed to give it a rest, to stop trying to make sense of what was probably an incredible string of coincidences. But the thoughts just wouldn't go.

"It does make you wonder," I said again, this time more to myself than to Mitch. "And where does Lauren's murder fit in?"

The question hung there, unresolved and repugnant. I shrugged, then pointed to the dark creek.

"Where are we anyway? There were so many turns and it was half-dark driving here."

"Mill Creek. It opens out to the Bay." He swung one leg over the bench, straddling it. "That direction." He pointed to where the creek faded away in the dark. I turned to see where he was pointing, my back to him.

Across the deck, another party of crab-eaters got to their feet, shoving benches aside and lurching toward the door. One jumped the railing. Their laughter drained away. The kid from the parking lot carried food and drink to a corner table. And Mitch's arms circled my shoulders and pulled me back to him. I could feel him breathing with me, exhaling into my hair.

The boy was eating now, not crabs, something easier. He was starved, chewing fast, drinking down something in long gulps, looking passively out to the water. The tension drained from my shoulders. And Mitch's arms tightened a little. I could smell him, feel the hair on his arms. In the parking lot, a car was started, a good-bye shouted. The boy had finished eating and was inspecting the remains to see if he'd missed anything.

I turned to find Mitch watching me. His body was relaxed. I could see his pager clinging to a loop on his jeans. On his feet were rubber-soled deck shoes, worn, like generations before him, without socks. Someday I'd find out where he came from, who he was. Tonight it was easier not to. He moved closer, the air around us itchy and electric. Ground zero again.

From the dock below us, a large outboard motor sped off into the night sending up a wave of gasoline-saturated air. A pool of sweat formed at my throat, reached critical mass, and ran down into the front of my shirt. Across the water, there was a whoop, then an echo. The boy gathered up his garbage and went inside.

"Will you please just let things be whatever they are going to be?" he said.

I nodded, watching the pupils of his eyes expanding in the darkness.

The day's heat was beginning to drain away as the waitress put the round of beers on the table. I excused myself and went inside to find the ladies' room. What I found was that the long, brown paper-covered tables were still occupied. The bar was doing a good business. And Dick Hubbard was still here, laughing with someone at the far end.

The ladies' room was empty and surprisingly cold. I snagged

bits of crab off my shirt and out of my hair and contemplated the graffiti on the side of the stall. A beery buzz fogged my brain. I fished out two aspirin and swallowed them with water held in cupped hands, then shivered. Maybe there was a sweater in my car.

The parking lot had thinned out and no cars were waiting for spaces. Slipping into an old sweatshirt I found in the BMW's cluttered trunk, I looked up just as Dick Hubbard came out of the restaurant. He hesitated, looked around, then nodded as a woman stepped out of her car. She stood there—somehow familiar—with the door open. I saw the lawyer smile, check the parking lot once more, and head towards her. He got in her car and the door closed. But it didn't move.

With a glance around me, I latched the trunk and zigzagged carefully between cars. The light went from dim to nearly nonexistent as I neared the one into which Dick Hubbard had disappeared. I stumbled once, righting myself by groping the tail fin of some classic sedan. Who was he meeting in a dark car late at night in the parking lot?

Suddenly, from behind me an engine turned over, its lights illuminating the surrounding houses and trees. A car began to back out slowly, the lights sweeping over the car with Dick Hubbard and the woman. Then over me. For a long moment, my shadow loomed absurdly tall and narrow over their car. I ducked down behind a van, hoping that they were too busy talking or whatever they were doing to notice me. But it was too late. I saw the woman sitting up in the driver's seat, peering into the rearview mirror.

Holding my breath and still crouching, I heard the car door open. Dick Hubbard got out, then wandered up and down the row of parked cars. Lights now swept through from the other direction as the departing car swung around. The driver honked and Dick Hubbard waved, then turned and got back in the car. I muffled a sneeze. He said something to the woman, his arms gesturing toward where I hunched, but he closed the door. I watched for a few minutes, considering the possibilities. Innocent or not, it was interesting. When I was satisfied that they were no longer concerned about shadows, I ducked back to the BMW, then stood up straight and walked to the restaurant.

TWENTY-SIX

"YOU OKAY?" Mitch stood up to make room for me to squeeze by him. "I nearly went looking for you."

I slid onto the bench. "Yes. No. You wouldn't believe what I just saw."

"I'm afraid to ask."

"I went to my car to get a sweatshirt and saw your pal Dick Hubbard come out of the restaurant. He just stood there, like he was waiting for someone. Then a woman gets out of her car and she just stands there, too, with the car door open. As if she's waiting for him to notice her. And he does. And he goes over and gets in the car."

"That's it? Hubbard had a date? Who was it?"

"I couldn't see. But don't you think that it's a little strange that Hubbard's sneaking around in the dark?"

"Did he see you?"

"No, I don't think so."

He nodded. Then he started to laugh. "This is good. But I don't think it would be the first time that Dick Hubbard has been discovered doing somebody's wife in the back seat of her car. That's what his divorce was about a couple of years ago." He laughed, coughed, gulped beer. "But best of all, he has no idea that you're tiptoeing around the parking lot, peering into windows, seeing what you can see. All that's missing is a camera."

He put his head down, his shoulders shaking with laughter.

"It's not *that* funny."

"Yes," he said. "It is."

He recovered finally. Enough to squeeze closer. This closeness might have gone on a whole lot longer had the pager at my waist not buzzed. He felt it, too, jerking back as if stung. I looked down at the number. Lillian. It was almost eleven. I found my phone. Simmons picked up on the first ring.

Five minutes later I was standing on the deck at Cantler's still bellowing into my phone. Simmons *had* managed to tell me that someone had thrown a large rock through one of the sliding glass doors that led to Lillian's deck, shattering it. It had scared her to death. She'd called 911 and the operator on duty had relayed the incident to him. No one was found lurking outside. But my relief that Lillian was okay had been replaced by a large, marauding wave of anger.

"Simmons, how could you answer the phone like that? You scared the shit out of me. It never occurred to you that I'd nearly have a heart attack thinking something happened to Lillian if you answered the phone?" I didn't care if everyone in Anne Arundel County heard me. "How could you?" Mitch, to his credit, wasn't trying to pretend he didn't know me. "I mean, thank God that Lillian's okay, but you could have let her answer the phone. What were you thinking?"

"You done?"

"Yeah. I'm done. For now. We'll be there in..." I held my hand over the receiver and looked at Mitch. "How long does it take to get to Lillian's?"

"Half hour, maybe less."

"Half hour, maybe less," I said into the phone.

LILLIAN OPENED the front door as soon as we pulled in the drive, first my BMW and then Mitch's Jeep right behind me. She threw her arms around me, then seeing Mitch, widened her embrace.

I finally held her at arms length. "You okay?" She was in a brushed acrylic robe and matching pink mules. One side of her hair was flattened from her pillow.

"I'm okay now. But it scared me. Sounded just like an explosion. I was in the bedroom watching TV and then there was this terrible noise. So I ran in and slammed the door shut between the hallway and the kitchen." She realized we were still standing in the doorway. "Sorry. Come in. And then I called 911. Detective Simmons, thank goodness, was here almost immediately."

"Do they know what happened?" Mitch asked.

"The stone came through one of the sliding doors. Probably from the lawn below the deck." Lillian pointed to overstuffed chairs in the living room. "They're in the kitchen and on the deck. Dusting for prints or whatever they do." I could hear voices and the crunch of broken glass.

I sat down with Lillian. Mitch went to find Simmons. He returned two minutes later with the detective, who, amazingly, wasn't going to be awful about my little outburst on the phone. Then I saw why. In his gloved hand was a stone, the size of a baked potato. On it was a dark brown stain. He showed me, he showed Lillian, and then he took it back into the kitchen to dump into a plastic evidence bag. The gloves were gone when he returned. Lillian was shaking her head.

"I'm sorry I was, er, that I yelled on the phone," I said. He nodded. "You'll test that rock for blood?"

"And prints."

My nice beery buzz was long gone and in its place was apprehension and adrenaline. Was the bloody stone a kind of message from Lauren's killer to Lillian? She's dead, it seemed to say, and you're next. But why? And who?

Clearly, questions Simmons wanted answers for, too. He pulled out his notebook and I steeled myself for a long night. The detective listened carefully as Lillian, then I, talked, making notes when I told him about Vince Darner's threats the night of the debate.

Across the room Lillian sat up in her chair and looked over at me. "You didn't tell me Vince threatened you."

"I didn't want to worry you."

"Thanks, but maybe I *should* be worried."

I was surprised. "Sorry. You're right." I turned back to Simmons to tell him about the car towing incident in Baltimore last night. Lillian listened quietly, then started to get up to find the Baltimore cop's badge number. He told her not to bother for now.

Simmons seemed to be wrapping things up surprisingly efficiently. The evidence van had left twenty minutes after Mitch and I'd arrived and a patrol car had been assigned to the house overnight. He turned to Lillian.

"You need to take some steps, Mrs. Weber."

"What steps?"

"Well, the best thing to do would be to take a little vacation until we can find the...wrap up this investigation." Lillian shook her head. I knew what she was thinking: If she left, they won. Simmons must have known it, too. "Okay, but tomorrow you need to find someone to stay here with you. Tonight there will be a patrol car outside, but we don't have the resources to..."

"I'll stay," I said. "I just need to go home first."

"No, you don't," said Lillian. "That young man outside is plenty for tonight." She glanced then at Mitch. "Tell her she can't stay."

"Lillian," I said, "bad things are happening. Think about it. Lauren is dead and now someone has lobbed a big rock through your door. And that certainly looks like blood on it. Like someone is trying to send you a message."

I saw Lillian frown and I was sorry I said it.

Simmons got up. "I think your aunt is taking this very seriously. She'll get someone here tomorrow. Right, Mrs. Weber?" Lillian nodded.

I walked him to the door. "How long will it take to test that rock?"

"Tomorrow."

"Will you call me? Please?"

He agreed, then left. Mitch had found some plywood in Lillian's garage. With the help of the cop, he nailed it quickly in place. It wasn't pretty and it wasn't waterproof, but it would do for tonight. I swept up the worst of the glass.

Lillian was exhausted, I could see, trying hard not to shove us out of the house. "Tomorrow we'll talk."

"Why don't I bring Lance over tomorrow morning?"

"Okay. If that makes you feel better, but I'm also going to call Weller. Maybe he'll have some ideas."

"Promise?" She nodded. "Good." I kissed her good night, told her I'd call first thing tomorrow, and got into my car. Suddenly, Simmons's words came back to me. Lillian needed to get away, he had said, until he found the—he had stopped then—perhaps to spare Lillian—and rephrased his statement. Wrap up the investigation, he'd finally said. I let out a breath. No question now that he, too, thought everything that had happened this last week was connected with Lauren's murder.

MITCH FOLLOWED me home. He hadn't said anything, but I wasn't surprised. My house, unlike Lillian's, was undisturbed, peaceful in the moonlight. But the lightness of the evening had fled, replaced by something darker. I let the dogs run a bit and then without much talking, we went upstairs. The sex was edgy, fueled by nerves. Passionate but not tender. Afterwards, I fell almost immediately into thick sleep.

I awoke hours later to find him sleeping facedown beside me, his hand between my legs, a gesture so possessive it took my breath away. Then I remembered the bloody stone. The broken glass. My undiluted fear when Simmons had answered Lillian's phone. I saw that the moon was gone. I shuddered and pinched my eyes shut, aware of tumbling thoughts, of vivid oily colors, like the lovely spreading stain of kerosine on dark water.

Mitch moved. I felt the air change, his breathing become more shallow. He turned over and pulled me close. Carefully, gently, the distance between every vertebra a lifetime, his fingers found their way down my back. Until they reached the tiny last bone, where they lingered.

When we were through, our bodies drifting among foggy sheets, he kissed me, then turned away to sleep what was left of the night. I stared at his back in the dark and couldn't begin to fathom what he meant to me, only that the sheets were warm where he had been.

TWENTY-SEVEN

MITCH WAS DRESSING when I awoke. He noticed, then sat down on the edge of the bed. Outside, it was still dark.

"Go back to sleep. I'll call you later."

"If you let the dogs out," I said, "you have to let them back in."

He nodded, then pulled the fallen sheets onto the bed and over me. After sitting for a few seconds more, he touched my hair and left. I thought I heard the front door close.

I awoke an hour later to find myself clinging to the edge of the bed, kicked there by dog feet. Too whipped to argue with sixty pounds of sleeping dog, I stayed where I was, eyes shut.

The events of last night seemed unreal, diluted, their meaning twisted. If the scene at Lillian's house had happened at all, maybe it wasn't all that serious. The darkness and the hour had undoubtedly distorted the gravity of it. Besides, Simmons would find who threw the rock. Kids maybe.

These thoughts lasted for about ten seconds, fleeing as soon as I was fully awake. I barely thought about Mitch, shoving the night with him to a warm, safe place in my mind. I'd let myself think about it later. I got up and looked out the window. Nothing had changed. The sun was coming up hot. The ground looked hard and dry. I turned on the fan and went downstairs. The dogs padded after me, heavy-eyed and indignant at the hour.

By seven I'd showered, found fresh clothes, and settled onto the porch with my laptop and coffee. I started to type. Out came unintelligible garbage, the downloading of an overheated mind. I pissed and moaned and bitched and complained and the machine duly processed it. And after five minutes, I got to the good stuff.

It never failed, this stream of consciousness method. Out gushed hidden fears, passions, sadness. Twenty years of writing ads told me it was here that I would eventually find answers. That deep in the unexpected, often peculiar sinkhole of my own emotions there would be fresh thoughts. Solutions for problems. If not now, later, and only if I dared to go deep enough, to look without flinching.

Out came stuff about Lillian and my concerns for her safety, my fears that I would never be any better at helping her run her office. How could I live up to her standards? How could I protect her? There was pain watching her weather the recent storm of hatred at the hands of her neighbors. And now her fear. I found anger at my own helplessness.

Out came stuff about Will, whose truck hadn't been by his bungalow last night when we'd driven by. Prickles of something—jealousy?—surprised me as I wrote about him. He never lacked for women. Not looking the way he did. Not smelling of salt and water and work.

Mitch, then. My fingers hesitated. Last night with him was a blur of images, colored by laughter and desire and gladness and anxiety. With some effort, I continued writing, trying to stay honest, my emotions lighting up the small screen as fast as I could type. What I read made me bewildered, uneasy, shocked all over again by how little I was in control.

Then I was done. I leaned back in the wicker chair, tired, but also lighter, unburdened and okay. The power of confession, even when the confessor was a machine.

I got up for more coffee. The dogs followed me, cadging for dog biscuits. I sat back down, calm now, and newly energized from dumping everything onto the laptop's strong circuits. I knew now I'd be able to think more clearly about Lillian's predicament and Lauren's death. About Vincent Darner and Carl Rainey. About Dick Hubbard's late-night, secret rendezvous in the restaurant parking lot. About the Jarvis family and the sense I'd had yesterday afternoon that Jenny knew something she wouldn't—maybe couldn't—tell Simmons. With luck, I'd be able to figure out what I could do, couldn't do, shouldn't do. For after last night, there was no question that I had to do something.

What started to appear now on the laptop's screen were the

events of the last week. How they related to each other and how they didn't. Theories. Conjecture. Connections between people. Downright guesses. Intuition. No solutions came yet. But a half hour later, I had a plan. I didn't know if it would solve anything, but it was a start.

It was eight-fifteen. The phone rang. Simmons. Blood on the rock, he said. The victim's. Fingerprints that hadn't yet found a match. The connection was broken before I could do more than mutter thank you. Lauren's blood.

The phone rang again. Mitch. My insides did a small sexual pirouette. I told him about the blood. He murmured something. I heard another voice with him. He couldn't talk now, but maybe we could get together. For dinner or whatever. He'd call. Or I would.

A third ring. Lillian. Telling me not to bring Lance. Weller had arranged for a nice young Anne Arundel police officer to moonlight until the danger was past. I didn't say anything about the stone and she didn't ask. Instead, I breathed a sigh of relief and hung up. Then I could have kicked myself. Why was it so easy to forget to tell people you love what they mean to you?

I WAS WAITING at the Permit Application Center in Annapolis's Heritage Center office complex when the doors opened at nine. At my request, a woman behind a semicircle of a desk provided me with a booklet titled "Building Permits for Critical Area and Waterfront Properties."

I sat down in a nearby chair to read. Someone had done the best he could to make the permit process less burdensome, adding charts and graphs and lists and little drawings. It didn't matter. The complexity of it all nearly made my head explode. I forced myself to read about land use classifications and legal lots and the building permit process. I read about impervious coverage, buffers, habitat protection areas, and reforestation. I studied little pictures of shore erosion measures: marshes and riprap and bulkheads. I now knew why you needed a consultant, preferably one who specialized in environmental law with a doctorate in ecology on the side.

Feeling overwhelmed, I went back to join the line growing

in front of the semicircular desk, then requested the paperwork for Vince Darner's building permit. The clerk shoved a request form my way. After a short wait, someone handed me a file and ushered me into a small conference room with a long table and no windows. Reading was hardly worth the effort. If the pamphlet had been too much, this was worse. It included copies of the building permit, the application sheet, and the construction and site plans. There was a grading permit, a topography map, and information about the lots on either side of the Darner site.

I leaned back in my chair, everything spread out in front of me. If I had thought that I would be able to find what had interested Lauren, I was more than a little wrong. I got up and went back to the clerk.

"Can I have copies of these made?"

She added up the charges, handed me a receipt, and sent me scurrying to the cashier in another office. After ten minutes of tap dancing in front of another desk, I returned. The clerk suggested I might want to call later to see if the copies were ready.

"I can't get them now?"

"Now? All those?" She laughed.

"Is Tim Clayson here? I spoke with him about this yesterday."

"Tim Clayson is a summer intern."

Oh. Low man on the totem pole. Still, even interns—however much they usually try to pretend otherwise—know how to use the copy machine. The clerk was waiting, as was the line behind me. I could feel the anxiety here, all those people wanting new fences, new sunrooms, new decks. There were contractors and subcontractors waiting for permits. And there were those in escalating disputes with neighbors—disputes that had turned serious enough to warrant research. Just to make sure there was a legal leg to stand on. In a tiny room nearby, I saw a man poring over huge maps of the county.

"So you want me to get Tim Clayson?" the clerk asked.

"Please." She called. I tried not to be intimidated by the growing impatience of the line behind me. Interesting what the tedious subject of land use regulation could do to people. Nor-

mally Marylanders were patient and polite, sometimes to the
point of total paralysis. I still despaired of four-way stop signs.
But land use regulation was different. It made people nervous.

"He'll be here in a minute."

"Thank you." The people behind me gave a collective sigh
of relief as I stepped aside. In about thirty seconds a very young
man appeared. He was wearing a loud tie and no jacket. He
glanced at the clerk, who pointed at me.

"Her."

"Hi. I'm Tim Clayson."

"Eve Elliott."

"You called yesterday."

"Yes."

He looked all too interested. "Get what you need?"

"Not really. What I need is to have some copies made right
now."

"And I come into this where?"

"I was hoping you could do it." He sized me up and I knew
there was going to be a price. This was a young man who knew
the value of information. One undoubtedly well on his way to
a prosperous career, probably in the law. "It's important."

He pulled me further away from the others. "Okay, here's
the deal." I listened, trying not to slap him. "Promise you'll
tell me what you're looking for and why, and I'll go do it right
now, including the oversize stuff. Deal?"

I thought about it, staring at him. He stared right back. Maybe
I could tell him the truth, but only enough of it that Simmons
wouldn't launch me to the moon or some place worse if he
found out. "Okay. Deal."

I sat back down. Half an hour later, he was back. There were
papers in his hand and a strange look on his face.

"You want to come in here?" He pointed to the airless conference room, then shut the door behind us and draped not one
or two but four large site plans over the table.

"I don't know who you really are and why you are looking
into this, but there's something wrong here." The smartass was
gone and in its place was a young man intent upon showing
me what he had found. He glanced down again at the plans of

the Weller's Creek site, looking back and forth, reassuring himself that he wasn't seeing things. "I think Vince Darner was issued a building permit based on fake site and topographical plans." He looked up at me. "Are you really a real estate agent?"

"Yes. Are you really a law student?"

He looked surprised. "Huh? What? No. I'm in college. Sophomore. A journalism major."

It figured. "You want to tell me why you think these are fake."

"Okay, first, look at this." He pointed. "And now this. I compared it to the original plans—these here—and things have been altered."

"How do you mean, altered?"

"Someone has taken the time to have new plans made. Maybe took it to a place that does architectural blueprint work or can do oversize sheets, then copied it a few times to make it look genuine. People know that the original plans are old and that we have to use copies. But these copies aren't really copies of what we provided. They are copies of a new site plan and a new topo map. Both have altered elements."

"Like what?"

"Well the most noticeable is the geography. It affects the distance of the house from the water. That's the buffer and it's a big deal in getting a permit." He rattled off the acceptable distances, stuff I'd read earlier in the pamphlet. "You see here." He pointed and I leaned closer. "This looks like the geography of the site has actually been changed. On this new one there seems to be plenty of room to build the house right there on the water." He looked up. "But look over here." I walked around the table to look where he pointed. "On the original site plan, it isn't that way. The grade is much steeper. See those lines close together? The house would be far too close to the water."

"How did you know to look at the originals?"

"Because I am one smart boy." He grinned. "Sorry. I just saw that this road here seemed to be in kind of the wrong place." He pointed again. "I grew up in Anne Arundel County near there and I knew that couldn't be right."

"Forgive me if I'm dense, but I'm not sure I get this."

He took a deep breath, trying to be patient. "In reality this is an almost unbuildable site, if you consider the geography and topography. At least from a legal and environmental point of view. The house—if it should be built at all—should be built way back here, with no waterview. And that is not what owners of waterfront property want, is it?"

We were both silent, looking down, considering the implications. No, Vincent Darner wouldn't be satisfied looking at trees. He'd want the creek. My creek.

"So you think that someone created new plans, altering the actual site, in order to be granted a waterfront building permit?"

"Yup. That's what I think. But they had to adjust this road to make it fit. Oh, look, this one isn't right either. It's been fixed, too." He was pointing to another thin line. He looked up. "This is what Lauren DeWitt was looking for, wasn't it? Probably got her killed."

"I don't know."

"Well, how come you are so interested?"

"I live on the property across from the house Vince Darner is building. On Weller's Creek."

He nodded. "But I don't think that's all. I think it's to do with her murder."

I took a deep breath. "Okay, okay, it may be. Look, Tim, all I can say is that she may have found out what you just discovered. Forgive me but I can't tell you more. I really intended to, but now I don't think I can. I think it may be a police matter and I can't get you involved. Please understand."

"What do you plan to do?" He was glum but he didn't press further.

"I'm going to take this to my attorney and dump it in his lap. Let him take it to the police." I stopped. "Actually, I should ask the same for you."

"What do you want me to do?"

I considered. "Nothing. Not just yet." I sized him up. "Tim, do you ever do any...how shall I put this? Investigative journalism?''

He stared, then nodded. "I could.''

"Then maybe...'' He took the business card I fished out. "Don't do anything yet. And call me if you think of anything else? Or hear or see anything? I also may need you to do some research for me. I'll call you.''

His eyes were glittering when I left, not a good sign. With luck, he'd keep his mouth shut. At least for a while.

I left the building, passing John Battles, the zoning analyst from Monday's hearing, in the entranceway. He looked fatigued, a bit older than I remembered. He didn't see me, and I turned to watch him disappear down an interior hallway. What on earth could he and the upwardly mobile Doreen possibly have to talk about? I shrugged to myself. You just can't tell about other people's marriages. If nothing else, my own marriage to Ben Elliott, which had looked perfect to everyone else, had proved that.

I settled into the BMW and considered what I'd just learned: Lauren had suspected, apparently correctly, that Vince Darner was building under an illegal permit. If that got out, it would be enough to ruin his chances for election. People might be furious at what they thought was overregulation and support his call for a less intrusive government, but they wouldn't like him getting perks that they couldn't have.

But did Darner know the permit was bogus? Or did Dick Hubbard quietly get a new site plan made without telling Darner? What would that get him? Two distinct scenarios came to mind: Vince Darner, grateful for the favor after his election to the Maryland Senate, would reward him with legislation favorable to his business. Or Vince Darner, fearful of being found out, even under threat of blackmail, would do the same. Dick Hubbard couldn't lose. And maybe Darner's need for money extended beyond his failing lumber business.

But what *did* a bogus building permit have to do with Lauren's death? Had she been throttled and shoved onto the riprap by someone who hadn't wanted Darner's secret to get out? By someone who saw her public battles with Duck Jarvis and Carl Rainey as good cover for murder?

TWENTY-EIGHT

IF IT HAD TAKEN ME almost a year to decide to buy Ray Tilghman's property, it took me ten minutes to do it. I signed the papers and it was over. Then, the copies sorted, I sat back in Weller Church's leather armchair.

We'd already talked about Lillian's predicament. And I'd confirmed that indeed the brown splotch on the rock that had come through the sliding glass door was Lauren's blood. Suddenly, Lillian's words the morning after Lauren's death came back to me. Half the community, she'd said, had been there to watch the fire marshall work. But one of them had stayed when the authorities left. One of them had picked up the bloody rock that everyone else—including Simmons—had missed.

Weller was red this morning, sunburned unevenly in patches on his face and neck. The burned spots overlapped the brown age marks. He also smelled a little musty, odd in a summer when rain was nearly nonexistent.

"There's something else," I said. Weller grunted, leaned forward to listen. I told him what I'd found out about Vince Darner's building permit. His eyebrows shot up half an inch, but otherwise, he didn't react.

"You have copies of the site plan and topographical map?" I shoved them across the desk. "Okay. Do nothing. I want to go over these." He put them neatly on a window table.

"You think I should tell Simmons about this?"

"I'll see that Detective Simmons is informed. You want to tell me how you knew to look into this?" I told him. "All right. Here's what we'll do. I'll look these over now, then give that detective a call. That's appropriate since I'm handling Ms. DeWitt's legal affairs at the request of her mother."

"What about Vince Darner?"

"What about him?"

"Well, if he knew that his building permit was based on a

bogus site plan and people find that out, he could lose the election.'' The lawyer was quiet. ''And what about Dick Hubbard? Wouldn't that also make him a suspect in Lauren's murder? After all, we know now that she knew something was wrong with the permit. And we also know she never had a problem going public with things. If Dick Hubbard had a phony site plan made up, he would have every reason to want to keep it quiet.''

Weller was searching for something in his desk drawer. He didn't find it, so he shut the drawer with a bang and looked up.

''There's something you should know,'' he said. His voice put me on notice. ''Vince Darner and his wife were sitting in front of us throughout the fireworks display. And for some time before the first round went up. Lillian saw them. And Dixie.'' He scooted his chair around. ''Everyone will remember. You see, before you got there, they, er, had words.''

I stared. Vince Darner had an alibi. And all because he had a fight with his wife. Nuts. It seemed so anticlimactic, so, well, disappointing. It blew the theory that he was somehow at the center of everything that had happened, including Lauren's death.

I took a deep breath. Vince Darner was apparently just another middle-aged man, with political ambitions, yes, but with money problems and a marriage that wasn't going well. I looked over at the old lawyer.

''Weller, I hear what you just said, but suppose Lauren had proof that Vince Darner asked Dick Hubbard to create a new site plan? So he could build where he wanted? What if she confronted Darner?''

''I think,'' he said, ''we'd better take this one step at a time. But let me assure you that I've known Vince Darner for many years and although I really don't like the direction his campaign is...''

''Weller,'' I said, ''Darner had to know that the Weller's Creek property is not legally buildable. At least not a big house at the water's edge.''

''Maybe. Maybe not. I don't know that people really understand buffers and the like. Or even think about them. That's why people hire consultants." He stood up, refusing to say what we both knew: that people also hired consultants to find creative ways around environmental regulations. Consultants like Dick Hubbard. "So, we'll let Detective Simmons have a go at it. Better that way."

I thought how different everything was from what I'd imagined. Just a day ago, it seemed obvious that Simmons should be talking to Duck Jarvis and Carl Rainey about Lauren's death. Now, there were all these twists and turns. Dick Hubbard's mysterious date. And Vince Darner himself with his bogus permit and ruptured marriage. And then there was the matter of the buried and unreported oil tank on the Knapp's Point land. His failing lumber and hardware business. His threats to Lillian. The blood on the stone.

"Let me handle Simmons," Weller said. "He can talk to Messieurs Darner and Hubbard." I stood up, suddenly wishing that I could just turn the rest of the mess in my mind over to him. "About Lillian."

"What about her?"

"Well, I know you're worried about her, but you've just given her the thing she wanted most." He nodded toward the envelope of papers in my hand.

ONCE IN THE CAR, I glanced again at the envelope on the passenger's seat, letting the full meaning of what I had just done sink in. As always, Weller had been right: It had been the one thing I could do for Lillian. And she wasn't the only one. It was also the one clear thing I could do for myself.

Pulling out my cell phone, I called her. Lillian's voice went a bit soft when I told her, but she recovered and announced she was preparing a relocation packet for people moving to the western edge of the Chesapeake. If her neighbors wouldn't use Weber Realty to buy and sell houses, then she'd market herself to outsiders who hadn't been poisoned against her. She didn't mention last night. And I didn't bring it up.

"By the way, I'm closing early today. Shirley's got some appointment and there's no one around anyway."

"Okay." I'd tried to keep the surprise out of my voice. I'd

never known Lillian to close early on a summer afternoon. So she *wasn't* quite as unafraid as she pretended to be. She didn't want to be alone in the office.

"One other thing," she said. "The fire marshall called. The dock burned because someone accidentally dropped a cigarette butt."

"The kids on the riprap?"

"Probably. Makes me feel a little better, though the dock is just as burned." I heard her other phone ring. She said goodbye.

I sat thinking about Vince Darner. He had an alibi before and during the fireworks. Well, it changed things, certainly. Nevertheless, I decided to follow through with the rest of the plan I'd made this morning. Largely because I couldn't think of anything else to do.

Rummaging around in the back seat, I found a map of Maryland and studied the web of roads, then headed north. As the strip malls and gas stations drifted by, I tried to think of what it was I wanted to find out from the Chesapeake Towing night clerk. If she was, as she had promised her friend on the phone, crabbing at Fort Smallwood.

I also wondered if Lauren had been in the habit of looking over permits whenever she saw building in the Magothy area. But that was crazy. Far too many houses. Through the side windows, I could even now see a new development of townhouses going up in a field.

But maybe, when a property interested her—the Rainey's land, for example—she made a trip to the Permit Application Center. But...oh, why hadn't I thought of this before? With one hand, I reached for my cell phone, then dialed the number for the Permit Application Center and asked for Tim Clayson.

"Hi Tim, it's Eve Elliott. I need you to find out something." I didn't wait for an answer. "Check that log—you know, that request you make people fill out so they can look at the paperwork for a specific property. See if you have proof that Lauren DeWitt actually came to your office and looked at Vince Darner's permit."

He made a few halfhearted squawks, but did as I asked, and called me back three minutes later.

"She did." He named the date. It was the Friday before her death. "I don't suppose you're planning on telling me anytime soon what this is about?"

"I can't yet."

I listened to another recital of how much I owed him, then surprised him by asking for a bigger favor. I could hear a sort of choking gulp on the other end.

"Are you kidding? How am I going to find that out?"

"No, I'm not kidding. And I don't know because I don't work there, but here's what I would do if I were you." I told him.

Silence. So I added a little cash to my request. Which got him talking again.

"Do you know how long that will take me? Forever. If I can do it at all. I mean I'll have to think of some excuse to stay late."

"You're good. I'm sure you'll think of something."

Another sputtery noise. "Well, it sounds like a wild goose chase." Then he shut up and agreed to do it. I thanked him and hung up.

I took a deep breath. There was proof that Lauren had known about the Darner's bogus permit. She had probably discovered something was wrong the same way Tim Clayson had—from simple mistakes in the way the roads were drawn. I could picture the detailed maps over her desk, the Magothy area ringed in red ink. She must have studied the map, then the plan, then realized that the roads and elevations and geography were inaccurate.

Now what? I didn't know. Maybe Tim Clayson's wild goose chase would produce something interesting. Vince Darner and Dick Hubbard, one or the other or both, seemed to be up to something. Whether it involved murdering Lauren—either directly or by hiring someone else—remained to be seen.

I tried to remember where I'd seen Vince Darner on the Fourth of July. He'd been talking to supporters, then Dick Hubbard. Charlotte had gone for ice cream, then rejoined them.

Based on what Weller had told me, the Darners had watched the fireworks, arguing loudly. And Dick Hubbard had left before they began. Or so he said. I wondered again what Simmons knew about that. Maybe I should ask him the next time I saw him. And knowing Simmons that wouldn't be long.

TWENTY-NINE

FORT SMALLWOOD burned white in the sun. A lovely truncated ruin, it was built in low flat levels, like some of the palaces of the classical Maya. It was also badly damaged and in need of the strong convictions of a historical preservation committee. A rough wooden stairway offered access to the main level and the round, hollow gun turrets a few steps up from that.

I parked the car and climbed up, admiring the vistas of water. Sunbathers and lovers had scaled rusting ladders to sit on the flat top. Beneath them a sign read: Danger: No One Allowed on the Top of the Fort. I watched as teenagers fumbled with panicky fingers to pass a joint back and forth. The sweet warm smell of marijuana rose up around me. Nearby, in a hollow turret where the fort's armor must have once stood, someone had painted a red swastika. The relentless noonday sun beat down. Monotonous music flowed from a car radio. I looked around, then climbed down past the concrete-filled windows on the ground level. One had been left open for storage.

What was I doing here? Discouraged, I walked along the water, the heat sucking the oxygen out of the air, the small of my back sopping with sweat. There were more fishermen and a motorbike rally, then a few campsites dotting the baking lawns. As the hottest part of the day took hold, I could see campers prostrate in darkened tents beside rows of sleeping children. From one came the unmistakable sounds of lovemaking. I looked away from the flashes of damp, inflamed skin. At the seawall, a fisherman fought to bring in something. And in the distance, where the Patapsco River met a smaller creek, a long pier stretched into the water. An Arundel Marine van passed me, headed in the same direction.

THE NIGHT CLERK was a little drunk and as red as the shirt she was wearing. And if the stretch pants of the other night had

been an unhappy choice, today's knit shorts weren't any better.
At her feet was the inevitable package of chicken parts, necks
and backs, to be used for bait. On the water, boats and Jet Skis
sped past stone outcroppings, past the smokestacks of an electric plant on the far shore. At the end of the pier, a wide barrier
blocked a section that had been damaged to the point of falling
into the water. Two men from Arundel Marine were inspecting
the damage, one with a clipboard, the second going over the
side to judge the extent of the repairs. Another chickennecker
tended her lines not far from them.

She hadn't recognized me at first. Partly because I was wearing sunglasses. Partly because I was out of context. But I decided that pretending to shoot the breeze on this breezeless,
scorching day, was a waste of time, hers and mine. So as she
popped open another beer and squinted at me, I told her who I
was and reminded her of the scene at Chesapeake Towing a
couple of nights ago. From time to time, she glanced at the
ranks of parallel lines marching down the pier. The smell of
raw chicken flesh drifted our way. Despite park regulations, no
one confiscated her beer.

"Why you telling me all this?"

"My aunt and I need your help."

A tiny flicker of something—maybe people didn't ask her
for help very often—glanced off her eyes. She sat down hard
in a beach chair, its bright plastic webbing slack and low from
heavy use. I followed, my legs stretched on from the rough and
baking planks. I wished I'd thought to apply sunscreen.

"Look, I don't know if you remember hearing about this,
but on July Fourth, a woman named Lauren DeWitt was killed
in Pines on Magothy. After the fireworks, down on the riprap.
Right before she was found, a fire destroyed a nearby dock.
The fire was an accident, caused by a cigarette, but her death
wasn't. And the police don't know who killed her."

I waited while she thought about this. "So, how's that my
business?"

"It's kind of a long story, but the dock belonged to my
aunt," I said. "The woman you met the other night. It was her

Cadillac that was towed. Illegally towed." She finished her beer and lit a cigarette. "A cop in Baltimore confirmed that. Now maybe business was slow, but there is something else you should know. And that is that your boss, Mr. Darner, is very angry with my aunt. He lied about something in a real estate deal and he's furious that she found out. So, I think that he had her car towed to harass her." The sun scorched my face. "Another thing. Last night someone threw a bloody stone into my aunt's kitchen. Broke a lot of glass and scared her half to death."

There was a shout from the end of the pier.

"Hey, Estelle," the other woman yelled. The night clerk waved and together we watched as her friend reached for a broken ruler, then measured the flailing crab to see if it was big enough to take. The woman then dumped it into her basket, gave Estelle and me a thumb's up, and went back to her lines. By Maryland law, crabs not five inches tip to tip had to be thrown back. In a world of everyday rape and murder, people actually measured their crabs. As if they understood the consequences of depleting the crab population and in a burst of environmental self-interest, did the right thing.

Estelle flipped her lighted cigarette toward the water. It grazed the pier, then fell harmlessly into the river.

"Wasn't Vince had the Caddy towed," she said. "It was Carl."

"Carl? Carl Rainey? He works for Vince Darner?"

"I feel real sorry about your aunt's car," she said. "Carl, he knows I drink a little maybe sometimes, so, you see, I was drinking a little the other night at work. Carl, he..."

I stared at her, not comprehending, not even listening. My mind had instead returned to Bolton Hill, to the car creeping behind us, street after street. Lillian had slowed to let it around but it had stayed with us. It had been the same car that later wanted the parking place we'd found. Not suspecting anything, we hadn't noticed Carl Rainey. Out of context again. The sun burned my nose and arms and ear lobes. Carl had known about the concert, since Lillian had called his mother. How had I not guessed?

"Carl, he's got some grudge with your aunt. Ain't got nothing to do with Vince."

"But why wouldn't you even let us use the office phone?" I asked.

"You been listening to me?" she asked. "I didn't wanna do that. I told him that." She shook her head. "But Carl, he told me he'd tell Vince about my drinking if I didn't make you wait some." I looked at her now, her victim status oozing out of every pore. "I woulda let you use the phone later."

"Okay, I'm sure," I said. "But, Estelle, Vince Darner is in financial trouble. You know that?"

If she were grateful I'd moved on, she didn't give any sign. "Yeah. I hear his lumber stores ain't doing all that good since that big chain of Home Depots moved in."

"What about his other businesses?"

"Ain't none."

Oh. I wondered what else to ask. "How long have you worked for him?"

"Near fifteen years now. About the time Vince, he married Charlotte."

"Charlotte? You know her?"

She nodded. "Got her job." Vince Darner had married his night clerk? I had a flash of the scene at Knapp's Point last Sunday. Of Darner, prosperous and overbearing, berating his wife, then leaning in the window of his expensive car to look at her as she sat staring straight ahead. "Vince, he got his troubles for sure."

"With his marriage? With Charlotte?"

She nodded, settling in for some good gossip. "Between you and me, he don't think Charlotte's good enough for him no more. Now that he's a big politician and all, he don't like her old friends. Like me and Dorrie." She leaned over and plucked another beer from her cooler. "But Charlotte, she got her inheritance. And Vince, he needs it."

"So she's got him over a barrel?"

"Yes, ma'am, over a barrel."

I suddenly realized she was deeply enjoying our conversation. It *was* a kind of morality tale, reassuring evidence that the boss who appeared to have everything had as many problems as she did. Even if they weren't the same ones. I suddenly wondered if she was in touch with Charlotte.

"Do you see Charlotte sometimes?"

She lit another cigarette, looked around, and scooted her battered chair a little closer to me. "She calls, you know. At night sometimes. She's lonely, she is." I nodded. "Vince, he's out all hours, so Charlotte, she's alone most times."

"So she calls you to talk?"

"She says..." The woman drank deeply.

"She says what?" I could picture her, sitting in Chesapeake Towing's hot ugly office, talking to the boss's wife on the phone, glad for a call to help her make it through the long and boring night.

"Charlotte, she says she and Vince, they're building themselves a big new house. It ain't going so good, either. Costs more than he's got." She leaned toward me, her breath foggy. "Charlotte says Vince, he wants to keep things quiet about that house with the election and all." She squinted from the cigarette smoke, then tossed the butt. It landed on a wet spot on the pier and fizzled. "I ain't seen it myself, the house, that is."

I decided to do a little fishing. "Estelle, do you know about a man named Dick Hubbard?"

Her eyes flashed. Bingo. She recognized the name. Charlotte *had* told her something.

Suddenly she was up, propelled by some movement too small and subtle for my New York eyes. I also scrambled to my feet, scraping the rough boards and barely getting out of her way as she hauled in a huge thrashing crab with the long-handled net and flung it into the bushel basket. My slacks were wet where I'd been sprayed. Estelle was smiling. No need to measure this one.

"Big jimmy."

"Huh? What?"

"Jimmy." She lit another cigarette and looked at me with exasperation. "You know. A jimmy. A male." She looked over at me. "Charlotte, she's gonna kill me if you tell her I told you about that guy Dick Hubbard.'' She slapped the scrabbling crab back into the bushel basket.

"You didn't tell me anything.''

"Charlotte, she thinks he and Vince are doing some business deal.'' Her voice lowered. "If you ask me, I think Dick Hubbard, he got something on Vince. The guy, he screwed Carl, too.''

Not surprising that with Carl Rainey as her information source, she hadn't heard that the county zoning analyst had made a mistake and that Dick Hubbard had less to do with his variance being denied than Carl wanted to believe.

"Carl tell you that? About Dick Hubbard screwing up the building permit?''

She nodded, then lit another cigarette and returned to her crab lines, newly encouraged by success.

"Are you camping here?''

She pointed to a campsite I couldn't see. For ten bucks, you couldn't beat it as a vacation value. For a minute I envied her the hot night, the water lapping gently, even the fresh crabs.

I tried to think of what else she might know, but I could see she was beyond listening to questions. She was on her knees inspecting her supper, which was climbing up the side of the bushel basket. I could see the rolls of unevenly sunburned flesh on her neck, the inner parts whitish and vulnerable. I thanked her, then I turned and walked back the length of the pier.

Dick Hubbard and Vince Darner and Carl Rainey. My mind was a tangle of theories and impressions as I neared a shuttered Chatauqua-era concession stand. In its heyday, customers would have stood under the wide round eaves, shielded from the sun and rain. To my right, on the water, was another building, this one overgrown with weeds and unrecognizable. I was reminded of the Maya again, of temples and palaces taken back by the jungle. Here in Fort Smallwood Park, the jungle had taken over, too, but a different kind: one brought on by reduced tax revenues, by the changes of the late twentieth century.

I headed for the car. The Arundel Marine van passed me going the opposite direction, then parked on the grass. The two men got out. I put on my sunglasses. A few yards along, compelled by something, I looked back.

Duck Jarvis stood staring at me. I could feel my heart quicken. I glanced once more at the pier. Estelle was checking her lines. I'd probably made trouble for someone who didn't need more. It was unintentional, but it was there. A shiver flowed down my spine, cutting through the sweat.

Half running, half walking, aware that my uneasiness wasn't logical, I got in the BMW and locked the door. What was I afraid of? That Duck would tell his pal Carl Rainey that I was asking questions of Estelle? That I'd found out that Carl worked for Vincent Darner? Or that I was getting too close to something Duck himself wanted kept secret? Jenny's small, intelligent face flitted across my mind's eye.

Simmons. I needed to talk with him. Let him wrestle with these questions. I fumbled for my cell phone.

"It's Eve. We need to talk."

"We do?"

"We do."

He agreed to meet me at around five at the Lido Beach Inn. I hung up, wondering if perhaps this time I wasn't half-grateful for his growly persistence. Still, it meant hours to kill.

Suddenly, the heat was unbearable. I yanked off my sunglasses and glanced in the rearview mirror at my sun-scorched face. Why wasn't the air-conditioning working harder?

I drove slowly out of the park, past the fishermen, past the pier. I could see Duck Jarvis interrogating the night clerk. Estelle looked weary, battered by all the attention she hadn't asked for. I drove through the gates. The attendant was nowhere to be seen.

THIRTY

I LOOKED AT my watch. Two and half hours to kill. Driving was often useful for thinking, but two and a half hours? Still, it wasn't worth going home. I calmed and cooled down and headed south. I wanted to know more about Vince Darner's relationship with Dick Hubbard. And where Dick had been during the fireworks.

In no hurry, I took Mountain Road east, staying in the right lane. A plan began to form in my mind.

A convenience store appeared on the left, and my rumbling stomach sent me scurrying inside for a prepackaged sandwich and a bottle of water. Heading to the counter, I got a glimpse of my sunburned face in the concave security mirror over the milk section. Sunblock. Heading down another aisle, I found a brown plastic bottle of SPF 30. The better-late-than-never school of skin care.

"Looks like you're a little late with that." I looked up, wondering how to respond to the large smiling uniformed firefighter in front of me. Why did everyone in Maryland comment on everything you did? Unlike New York, here you couldn't even get out of the supermarket without answering questions regarding your diet. "My wife's got me using that stuff every morning," he said, "though the guys at the station think it's pretty funny."

"Fire station?" He nodded. "Around here?"

He named a firehouse on Mountain Road. "Why?"

"I heard that investigators found out that that dock fire on July Fourth was caused by a cigarette." I felt only moderately guilty to be fishing for information.

"Looks like it. Probably kids. They're careless and then there's a disaster." He accepted change from the clerk. I slid my purchases toward her, then fished out a twenty. "We were pretty lucky that the fire didn't spread to the woods and the nearby houses.''

"What happened to that firefighter who fell onto the riprap? The one who found the body? Is he okay?"

"Jarvis? Sure. Got a thick skull." He shook his head. "Old Duck is still auditioning for a career job, I guess."

"Career job? He's applied to be a full-time firefighter?"

"Yeah. He's got the education requirements and all but..."

"But what?"

His laughter faded. "Well, between you and me, he had some trouble with the background check. Too much boozing and—" He stopped for a second time.

"And what?"

"Nothing. Nah, I can't say. I've already said more than I should've." He was peering into his bag to see if everything was there. "You gotta feel sorry for him, though, with his little brother making the police department."

Behind me the clerk made an impatient noise. I turned to find her holding out my change. "You want a bag?" she asked. I nodded, then turned back to ask more questions, but the man was gone.

My overworked brain cells leaped into action. So the uniformed cop I'd seen Duck Jarvis with at the community center was his brother? Another interesting fragment of information. And Duck had wanted to be a career firefighter. But where did these pieces fit in the events of the last week? If they fit anywhere at all. I suddenly wondered if Simmons knew about the cop.

Sitting in the car, I thought a minute, then got out my cell phone and made a call. Then I unwrapped the sandwich and devoured it in six bites. When I was done, I pulled the rearview mirror toward me. The fireman had been right: too little, too late in the sunblock department. Nevertheless, I patted some on, trying to avoid gunking up my overgrown bangs. I again checked the mirror. My face was now not just red and hot, but greasy-looking as well. I drank the water, then turned back onto Mountain Road. Nearby, rising over a patch of gravel, a large billboard said Blood Drive Cancelled, Jesus Already Gave.

DAMIEN'S WAS LOCATED on a stretch of low-lying waterfront on a stubby creek. Clusters of tall bay grasses shielded wetlands that hadn't seen water in weeks. I parked in a neglected lot, the grass growing brown and dry between the squares of broken concrete. The sound of hammering came from somewhere, metal on wood, rhythmic and solid and echoing in my chest.

My earlier call to Dick Hubbard's office had been answered by a frothy young woman. I'd dropped Mitch's name squarely into the conversation, then told her what I wanted. Of course, Dick would be happy to see me this afternoon, she said. Not to worry about an appointment. And besides, he was in my neck of the woods, all the better. She'd just call Damien's and let him know I was coming. I'd thanked her and hung up.

Damien's wasn't a restaurant in the sense that just anyone with money in their pocket could expect to get a drink or a meal here. A semiprivate club, it did parties and weddings. Mostly the management catered to the whims of Maryland's ruling class: legislators and political appointees, moneymen and moguls, developers and lawyers and sports tycoons who needed a place, their private place, to eat, drink, dance, and make deals. All the while steering the Ship of State for the rest of us. That the restaurant looked out over a hidden creek was all to the good. Maryland's power brokers needed their waterfront.

I headed to the bar entrance at the back, past a blue striped tent covering a garden pavilion with a central serving area and a bandstand. A couple of waiters, still in their civilian clothes, were humping roasts of beef and whole hams onto carving blocks.

"Watch your back."

I jerked around, half colliding with a waiter backing out of the kitchen.

"Oh, God, I'm sorry," I said. We danced for a split second, while he balanced his load of tableware. "You surprised me."

"My fault," he said. But he didn't look like he thought so.

Dick Hubbard was standing outside on the bar's patio waiting for me. He smiled and held out his hand, then stared past me to the pavilion for a second.

"Fund raiser for Vince Darner," he said. I saw him motion

a waiter, before turning back to me. "When I said last night I hoped to see you again, I didn't know I'd have the pleasure so soon."

I wondered what he'd say if he knew I'd already seen more of him than he might have wanted me to. "I hope this is a good time."

"Of course, it's a good time. For a friend of Mitch's, anytime is a good time." The waiter came up to him. "Why don't you just go in and order a drink. I've got something to attend to here. Just take me a minute."

The bar was surrounded on three sides by glass, commanding a great waterview. It was empty except for a female bartender in a short red cutaway jacket. She was carving up limes for the evening trade.

I slid onto a bar stool and was soon gazing at a glass of white wine. Outside, Dick Hubbard was talking with the waiter. He motioned with his hand, then slid some money out of his pocket. Seconds later, he pulled up the stool next to mine.

"Been here before?" I shook my head. "Nice view, huh? Great place to watch the fireworks. Next July Fourth, you and your aunt should come as my guests." He glanced out over the water. "There is where they go up." He pointed to an empty spot in the sky, then something struck him funny. "Have to tell you, poor old Vince didn't appreciate sitting on the beach getting sand in his pants the other night. I don't think he realized that running for elected office means fraternizing with the peasants sometimes."

I smiled politely, wondering if it were possible to dislike him more than I did.

"How on earth," I said, my voice as full of admiration as I could manage, "how on earth did you get out of the Pines with that traffic and the accident? And all those parked cars?"

That made him laugh harder. "Helps to have a police escort. Never underestimate the value of a gumball on top of your car." He leaned closer. "Of course, you gotta ask real nice."

Ask nice and just happen to have a handful of money. But that was that. Hubbard apparently had an alibi for the time of Lauren's death. Again, disappointment hit hard, even as a small prickle of conscience seeped through me. Did I want him to be Lauren's murderer? Yes, I decided, if someone had to be, he was as good as any. Then I decided I must have suffered heat stroke at Fort Smallwood.

Behind him a stern middle-aged woman from the restaurant approached, her eyes scanning the papers in her hands. She looked up over her glasses, then quickly backed off when she saw me. He turned around.

"No, no, Gloria. You're not interrupting. Just let me sign that. Then we're all set for tonight." He signed something, she evaporated, and he was all mine again.

"Now, Eve, what can I do for you?"

I launched into my speech, the one I'd rehearsed on the way over. How I was thinking of enlarging Ray Tilghman's cottage. How it really needed to be completely renovated—maybe even demolished—to be liveable. Well, at least I didn't have to lie about owning the property. I had owned it for all of about three hours.

Dick Hubbard listened hard.

"You know the property?" I asked. "Ray Tilghman's place?"

"Of course. Didn't know you'd closed on it yet."

I merely nodded, then swiveled toward him and leaned in. "I have to confess to you, I did go over to the Permit Application Center in Annapolis to see about doing things myself." I studied him as I said it, hoping a shadow would slip across his eyes. Nothing. I shook my head sadly. "Everyone there was just as nice and helpful as they could be. They spent a long time with me. Went way out of their way. Everybody, from the front desk clerks right up through the supervisor. But the regulations and the process…" I threw up my hands.

If he had inwardly flinched at my new friendship with the entire staff of the Permit Application Center, he didn't show it.

"Well, you wouldn't be the first to think that. What exactly were you thinking of doing to Ray's cottage?"

For the next few minutes, I described a multimillion dollar Chesapeake Bay estate I'd seen a month ago, right down to the kitchen fixtures and the choice of stone for the fireplace. That, I said, was what I wanted. It seemed to satisfy him.

"Well, that's quite a change from the way old Ray lived. Can't say I blame you. The place sounds pretty primitive the way it is. Now, it's hard to say conclusively what wiggle room we'll have, but I can probably help you get what you need." He finished whatever he was drinking. "You know, of course, there are going to be regulations to overcome?" He leaned back a little, studied the creek, which blazed white, then looked at me. "You don't want to build right on the water?"

"Well, that would be nice, but after the Rainey hearing, I didn't think I could. There is that little creek on one side of the property. And what about that 1952 law that prevents...well, you know. The one that the zoning analyst made a mistake about?"

"Yes, I know." He laughed tightly. "And I'm sure he won't make the same mistake anytime soon. So, yes, to answer your question, we'd have to look into it. It may be that the same problem exists for you. But it may not. I don't doubt if you were willing to take Ray's cottage down, you could get the permits. Or you could enlarge Ray's house so that it extended far enough that you could have water vistas." He drew his barstool closer. "There's another way, too. We could get a permit to alter the interior. Then if somehow the project got a bit bigger, who's to say. And if it got bigger than the original house, well, so it did. And if you had to pull the original house out the front door, walls and all..." He winked. "Happens all the time."

"That's legal?"

"Well, let me put it this way. It's not illegal." The bartender came over to tell him he had a phone call. "See, Eve, we have a lot of choices. But we're getting ahead of ourselves, aren't we?" I nodded. He excused himself and went to the phone at the end of the bar, returning in two minutes.

"I'm afraid I have to go put out a fire. But you stay here and finish your wine. In fact, take your time. Have another one. Enjoy the view and the air-conditioning. Donna there will take good care of you.'' He motioned to the bartender again, then gave her instructions to put anything I'd like on his tab.

I scrambled to think of a way to ask the rest of the questions I wanted to ask. Questions about his dealings with Vince Darner. But he held out his hand. I promised to make an appointment to discuss my house plans in further detail. Thirty seconds after leaving, he was back. ''You tell Mitch I owe him one.''

I watched him leave a second time, pause at the striped tent, then keep on walking. He may have had an alibi for July Fourth, but something was strange. Problem was I couldn't have said what. The one thing not in question was that he went all the way out to the edge of the law for his clients. I wondered how Tim Clayson was doing.

''Can I get you another glass of wine?'' The bartender's accent was slightly British.

''Thanks, but I'm fine.''

She nodded, then went back to cutting limes on a small plastic board. ''You certainly turned his mood around.''

''Why?''

''Well before you came, he was mad as blazes. Some woman drops in he's not expecting and Mr. Hubbard isn't happy to see her.''

''What did she want?'' I aimed for a just-between-us-girls tone.

She shrugged. ''Hard to say. Jittery, but at the same time, real angry. Real angry.''

The middle-aged manager chose that moment to walk past us to a table near the window. The bartender made a face at her back.

''Wicked Witch of the West, that one. She'd just as soon throw you out as look at you.''

''Was this woman bothering Mr. Hubbard?''

''Actually, I sort of think she was. And they definitely knew each other.''

The bartender showed no curiosity at my curiosity and I decided it was to spite the manager that she was answering my questions. ''You never saw her before?''

"No. But they talked for a while and she seemed to calm down a little. But then she got mad all over again."

"You didn't hear any of their conversation?"

"No, not really. Mr. Hubbard just kept talking to her in this low voice." She thought for a few seconds. "It was almost like the voice I use when I'm trying to get my kid to calm down about something. You know the voice?" I nodded. "Sort of promising and comforting and fudging all at the same time. Though from the looks of her, this one wasn't about to be..."

She suddenly looked down. I turned. The manager was scowling at us from a table near the window. When I turned back, the bartender had finished with her limes. I watched her dump them into a compartment of a fishing-tackle box, right next to the lemons and cocktail onions. Then she reached under the counter and pulled out a bottle of maraschino cherries and emptied them in another compartment. But not before stuffing one in her mouth.

She looked up. "Want one?" I did. And in an instant I was six years old and my parents were giving a party in our Fifth Avenue apartment. A party I was too young to attend. As consolation, I was always allowed a ration of maraschino cherries, never mind that I'd made myself sick more than once.

"Reminds me of when I was a kid," I said. She smiled and I leaned over the bar, feigning interest in my cocktail napkin. "So she just left? The woman who came to see Dick Hubbard?"

She nodded. I started to ask what the woman looked like, but the air had changed and I looked up to find myself staring into the reproachful face of the manager. She'd apparently had enough of our tête-à-tête. The bartender was standing behind her, her laughter barely under control. I looked back at the manager, half expecting her to count the maraschino cherries in the fishing tackle box.

"Excuse me. Where's the ladies' room?" Both of them pointed. Maybe, if I were lucky, the manager would be distracted and I could ask the bartender a few more questions on my way out.

In the meantime, I wanted to fix my face enough so that

Simmons wouldn't feel obligated to comment. The cold water felt good, though the maroon and gray lounge reeked of perfume or air freshener. I sneezed a couple of times, probably from the air-conditioning, then patted my face with paper towels. There was some soothing lotion near the sink.

After a couple of minutes, I looked in the mirror and decided things weren't going to get much better. I threw some money in the jar for the absent attendant. Out in the bar, I found that the female bartender was gone, in her place a sweet-looking Latino man.

Outside, the heat hit me hard. I cranked up the BMW's air conditioning. Down the street, an Arundel Marine van was parked in the driveway of a new house. The hammering, however, had stopped.

THIRTY-ONE

THE LIDO BEACH INN was doing a tidy business if the crowded parking lot was any measure. I had just slipped the BMW into the last parking spot when a familiar truck pulled up behind me. Eli Claggett leered at me through an open window.

"Hey, could you maybe take your time leaving?"

"I'm not leaving." I walked around to the window of the cab. His words of a few days ago were still running loose in my mind. And a few other thoughts had begun to run along beside them. "Got a minute, Eli? Beer isn't going to run out anytime soon in there."

"Oh, great, now you wanna have a little chat while I block traffic?"

"There's nothing behind you."

"There will be."

"Eli, just one minute. I want to know something." He gave up and put the truck in neutral. I could practically feel the emissions soaking into my hair. At least the muffler had been replaced. "It's important and I'm serious."

"Well, in that case."

"Eli, when Simmons interviewed you about what you saw on July Fourth, what did he want to know?"

"Not a thing." His eyes dared me to ask more, then relented. "Okay, okay, you're gonna know sooner or later. I asked to talk to him."

"Oh." He waited for me to ask why. "Why?"

"Because I knew that Carl Rainey was gonna distribute that lousy crap about Lil."

"You did?"

"Overheard him talking to that moron Duck Jarvis. Before the fireworks." So Carl had confided in his friend. "Well?"

"Well what?"

"Thought you wanted to hear all about it?"

I moved closer. "Eli, I guess I don't get this. You overheard Carl Rainey tell Duck Jarvis that he planned to distribute those flyers about Lillian and so you went to Detective Simmons?"

"Ah, yes, but before I did that, I had a little talk with Rainey." He grinned, an interesting collection of muscle contractions. "Made a few suggestions. Like how he should be mighty careful with his plans."

Had he been standing in front of me, I might have embarrassed both of us by hugging him, but he was still leering at me from the cab of his truck. "And did your suggestions, uh, how shall I put this, did they include some possible consequences, should he not be inclined to take you seriously?"

He grinned some more, his mouth practically swallowing the bottom half of his face. "You could say that." His elf face darkened. "But the pus-face creep did it anyway."

I decided not to tell him about the towing episode. Completely ruin his faith in his powers of persuasion, if they weren't ruined already. And the bloody stone. That was likely Carl's work as well. I reminded myself I didn't know for sure. Maybe Simmons would tell me. If he knew. Or maybe not.

"Eli, let me make sure I have this clear. You were, er, talking with Carl Rainey during the time the police think Lauren DeWitt was killed."

"Yeah. Florence was there, too, by that beach shed. But she had the good sense to stand back when it started to get ugly." Someone in a big car behind Eli's truck touched his horn. Eli's benevolence faded and he leaned out the window. "Put a sock in it, you fat idiot."

I didn't look to see which fat idiot was behind us. "Thanks, Eli. For more than you know."

He grumped something, then moved on to look for a parking spot. Carl Rainey was accounted for. He wasn't a killer, just a coward out to make Lillian's life miserable. Except I was missing something. It wasn't this simple. I headed into the bar to find Simmons.

THE LIDO BEACH INN was cold. And as the crowd—two or three or four deep around the horseshoe-shaped bar—kept reminding one another, the beer was colder.

Simmons wasn't here yet. I grabbed a booth at the back, as far from the bar and pool table as I could get. Marian Beall made no attempt to come over. Not surprising, since she had her hands full. Besides, there was the problem of my being Lillian's niece, a fact that didn't exactly endear me to many in the crowd. But so far nobody had noticed my arrival. For something to do, I called Mitch and left a message on his voice mail.

Simmons appeared looking unexpectedly refreshed this hot afternoon, as if he'd just had a nap, shower, and shave, then slipped into fresh clothes. He must have gotten settled in his new house. Or perhaps he was beginning to mellow and enjoy the hot Maryland summer. His greeting cleared up that notion.

He went to fetch coffee. Was he a potential friend just because we were both from New York? Probably not. Though someday, maybe, when there was nothing else to talk about, I'd ask him about his life in New York. He'd probably tell me to mind my own business. But today, there were more pressing things to discuss. Across the room, I got a glimpse of Carl Rainey. He hadn't seen me. I wondered what would happen when Eli appeared.

"Okay." Simmons put the coffee mugs down, then put a beer coaster over his to keep it warm. He shuffled through his pockets looking for something.

I sipped coffee. He was going to be unhappy that I'd been busy today, but so what else was new? This time I was going to hold nothing back. An hour from now, everything I knew, he would know. And the whole of it would—blessedly—be his problem. I could go back to living a life. Maybe actually try to sell some houses. And never ever get involved in police business again. Too nerve-wracking. Then I remembered my call to Tim Clayson.

There was more squirming around in the booth, as Simmons grubbed for something in his pockets. Out came his pen and notebook onto the table, and finally, a small brown plastic bottle. I watched as he struggled with the childproof cap. Pulling out a tiny pill, he dumped it into his mouth without benefit of water and swallowed, unceremoniously stashing the bottle back in a pocket. He put the coaster back under the coffee mug and looked up.

"Cholesterol, since you're dying to ask."

If I didn't know where to begin, Simmons did. We began with my sins against him and the Anne Arundel Police Department, my meddling, my inability—congenital, he thought—to leave things well enough alone. I let him have his harangue. Better to get it out of the way. Though after about five minutes, it was going on a bit longer than I thought absolutely necessary. He finally stopped.

"Aren't you forgetting I called you?" I asked.

"About time, given what Mr. Church told me. Let's start with your latest adventures. That phone number penciled on the supermarket bag, it inspired you, no? And you thought it necessary to follow up right off?"

"Simmons..." Should I tell him about Tim Clayson poring over plats and maps? Even as we spoke?

"What?"

"Nothing. I gather Weller told you that I found proof that Vince Darner's site plan was falsified? And that Lauren DeWitt knew about it?"

"And?"

"Well, it obviously gives both Darner and Dick Hubbard, who is his attorney, a motive for wanting her out of the way." Not so much as a flicker in his pale eyes. "Yes, yes, I know that a lot of people saw Vince Darner that night. Including my aunt and Weller himself. So even if he hadn't wanted Lauren around asking embarrassing questions, he didn't kill her himself. Nor did Dick Hubbard since he was at Damien's." I told him about my visit to the restaurant.

He stared, maybe trying to see into my head. "And your conclusion is?"

"My conclusion is...I don't know what my conclusion is. Look, Simmons, enough of this cat and mouse. If I've meddled, it was at least well meaning. I'm scared to death for my aunt. That bloody stone was the absolute last straw. Though I think it must be Carl Rainey again, it makes those flyers seem like a

bad joke by comparison. And now this false permit thing.
Which may or may not be relevant to Lauren's murder.'' He
drank, watching me over the top of his mug. "Look, all your
indignation about my part in this gets us nowhere at all.''

"Us?"

"Simmons, you are making this very hard.'' I got to my feet.

"Sit down.''

I sat. Thoughts careened through my head. "Everything
seems to go back to July Fourth.'' I looked at him across the
table. Jenny Jarvis's face unexpectedly washed up at the edges
of my mind. What did she have to do with Vince Darner and
Dick Hubbard? "Which means...I don't know what it means.
Or how you hold all the possibilities in your head. I...''

"You gonna move on anytime soon?''

I shut my eyes briefly, then opened them. He was still there.
"You remember our phone conversation yesterday? About the
Jarvis family?'' No response, so I plowed on. "Simmons, the
other night, July Fourth, Duck Jarvis and his wife had a bad
fight. Then he yelled at the girl.'' I stopped, aware that he was
waiting for me to talk about Vince Darner and Dick Hubbard.
"Yes, yes, I'll get to the others in a minute. But first, hear me
out about this.''

"Go on.''

"Duck Jarvis hated Lauren DeWitt. He tore up her dock last
Sunday with his Jet Ski and although it was an accident, she
called the cops. I was there. I saw it. And...''

"And what?''

Here it comes. I was going to end up talking about things
that I couldn't prove. Intuitive things. "I know that Jenny Jarvis
and her mother, and maybe other women in Knapp's Point,
admired Lauren and maybe even wanted to be like her. Certainly the girl did. Duck Jarvis knew that. And it pissed him
off because he couldn't control it. I also think that the girl may
know something.'' Seeing his face fight impatience, I steeled
myself. "Will says there were pitched battles between Duck
and Lauren. About the Jet Ski business. But I'll bet he...''

"We've talked with Donald Jarvis,'' he said, quietly. "He
reported your aunt's dock fire.''

I processed this. "Do you know Duck Jarvis applied for a job as a career firefighter? And that he was turned down?"

Simmons was shaking his head. "I swear to God. You ever get around to selling any houses?"

"Duck Jarvis's brother is a cop. Do you also know that?" He grunted, an unpleasant sound which I took to mean yes. "You do?"

"Yes. I do. How can I make that any clearer?" I stared. "The brother came forward."

"Came forward? What?" Simmons glanced at the ceiling. "No really, I don't know what you're talking about."

"Tony Jarvis was with his brother during the time that the victim would have been killed. He knew that we might like his brother for her murder, so he came forward. That clear enough for you?"

I looked around the bar, not seeing anything, my head filling with random and speeding thoughts. Duck Jarvis had an alibi. So why did he make me so nervous? I glanced at the detective. Did Duck Jarvis's brother have a reason to be less than candid?

"You're completely satisfied that Duck Jarvis didn't have anything to do with Lauren's death?"

"And you think he did? What happened to Mr. Darner as your prime candidate?"

"I don't have a prime candidate. I just said that Vince Darner..." I thought of something else. "You never said where Duck Jarvis went after he left the carnival."

Simmons fiddled with his empty mug. "Yeah. Well, you can forget whatever cockeyed theory you're on to. Like he went to meet the victim on your aunt's dock. Or maybe followed her." I waited. Nothing.

From the corner of my eye, as if this talk had caused him to materialize, I saw Duck Jarvis wade into the mob at the bar. My heart jumped a little, but he didn't see me. Simmons followed my glance, then slumped back in the red plastic booth. I glanced at my watch.

"Am I keeping you?" he asked.

I looked down at the chipped Formica. Again, I wondered if I should I tell him about Tim Clayson's renewed efforts.

"You got any idea at all I'm still here?" Simmons asked. "Or you think maybe I left already?"

"What? What did you say?" His eyes blinked once. "Okay, look. Here's a couple of things." I told him briefly about Fort Smallwood and Estelle's revelations about Carl Rainey's juvenile plan to harass Lillian by towing her car.

"Simmons, it must have been Carl who threw that stone into my aunt's house. He'd have had the most opportunity to find it on the riprap after the cops and fire marshall left."

"Carl Rainey is a moron, but he's not a criminal. At least so far. We don't have a record of his prints. Therefore, I can't match the prints on the stone. If indeed they are his. And they might not be." I tried to order my thoughts. "You got anything else to tell me?"

"Some, yes." No glimmer of surprise. "I know why Vince Darner needs cash. And it's not his political campaign. It's because his business is in trouble. He's got a local lumber and hardware chain. It's a private company so this isn't common knowledge." I decided to do a little fishing. "You know, Simmons, I'll bet it's not the only reason. Which has something to do with Dick Hubbard. And with the house Darner's building on Weller's Creek." I rolled to a stop. "There is something going on between Hubbard and Darner. Beyond the lawyer, client thing. I have no proof. I think there's some sort of development scam, one in which people are getting rich. And somebody's getting paid off." The detective didn't respond, so I continued. "Look, Dick Hubbard really wants Vince Darner elected to the Maryland Senate. I can think of a whole bunch of reasons how that would be useful to him. So much so that he is sponsoring a fund raiser for him tonight at Damien's."

If he found this interesting, I couldn't tell. He was too busy pulling out his pager and trying to read the digital display without glasses. He looked around at the public phone on the wall behind the bar. It was busy.

"You got a cell phone?" I fished it out and handed it to him. He listened, his face serious, then he grunted and hung up. "I gotta take this." He threw some money on the table. "You think you could manage not to do any more freelancing? Or maybe call me if you get the urge?'' I nodded, thought of Tim Clayson, crossed my fingers. "Good."

I watched him leave. He got as far as the door, then turned around and walked back. "By the way, you're gonna get cancer if you don't start using stuff on your face."

THIRTY-TWO

WITHOUT SIMMONS'S stolid presence, I wasn't sure I wanted to hang out at the Lido Beach Inn. Not with Duck Jarvis and Carl Rainey and half of their high school buddies standing twenty feet away. But nobody had noticed me, so, defeated by inertia and sunburn, I sat thinking. Somewhere in this clutter of facts— beyond alibis, beyond motives—there was something that tied Darner, Jarvis, Rainey, and Hubbard together. And when I knew what that was I would know the name of Lauren's killer.

Then I dropped back to earth. Yanked there by Simmons's voice. No more freelancing. He *was* right. Let him solve this thing. Or things.

But thoughts of my meeting with Dick Hubbard persisted. How had I let him slip through my fingers? Why hadn't I guided the conversation to his business dealings with Vince Darner? But I knew why. The lawyer was a man who understood one up and one down. If you weren't up, you were down. And I'd been down this time, on his turf, the supplicant for his services. Without Donna the bartender and her animus toward Damien's manager, I wouldn't even have known about the nervous and angry woman who had turned up this afternoon. Not that discovering that Dick Hubbard had women problems surprised me much. Not after last night.

One up. I needed to be one up. Since raw power was all Hubbard understood, it would be the only way he'd give up what he knew. And he knew something. I was sure of it. But how to get his attention? Maybe if I returned to Damien's, I could find Donna and ask her about... No more freelancing, said Simmons's voice.

My thoughts idled, then flew off again into outer space, way beyond my control. There was something I was forgetting. The gun. I'd nearly forgotten all about Lauren's missing gun. And Simmons hadn't mentioned it since that first time.

I took a deep breath of the bar's smoky air. It was probably forming some carcinogenic substance with the greasy lotion on my face. I didn't want to think about my lungs. Okay, no more freelancing. I'd go home, feed the dogs, then spend the evening with Lillian. And Tim Clayson? It was almost six o'clock. What had he discovered going through old records at the Permit Application Center? Probably nothing yet, not if he'd just started. And not if his search was as labor intensive as he wanted me to believe.

Glancing over, I saw Duck Jarvis had discovered I was here. He stood at the bar—big-bodied, sunburned, his brown hair lightened from outdoor work—watching me with the same icy stare of a few hours before at Fort Smallwood Park. Had Jenny confided to Lauren what I suspected was going on in her home? That her father sometimes hit her mother? Had Duck Jarvis found that out? Or even imagined he had? I shook off my anxiety. Then I put my money on top of Simmons's and left.

TWENTY MINUTES LATER, the dogs raced around the clearing in front of the cottage. There were no calls so I washed my face, then went upstairs to change into shorts and a T-shirt. On the floor beside the bed, a huge pile of laundry overflowed its basket. I was going to have to make the trip to Lillian's, basket in hand, very soon. Pathetic really, this showing up on her doorstep begging to use her washer and dryer. Not that she minded.

Will was foraging in the kitchen when I went back downstairs. I hadn't heard him come in.

"Hi."

"Hi. Want a beer?" I nodded, then fed the dogs as he opened bottles. We settled on the porch. Above us, the fan spun hard, successful only at moving hot air around. It hurt my face and I got up and flipped it off. "You look pretty much well done," he said.

"The sun."

"I couldn't tell." He eyed my red nose and cheeks with interest. We sat companionably, stroking the dogs after they ate their dinner. Finishing his first beer, he relaxed, then got up to get himself another.

It was nice to be comfortable with someone, not to have to explain every little thing. That he was twenty-six years old made it even more remarkable that we sometimes achieved this. I cleared my throat and described what had happened since we'd parted yesterday at Lauren's house. I left out only Mitch's visit last night. He whistled at the rest, then asked some questions, falling silent after we talked again about Lauren's missing gun. Dusk was settling over us now, the crickets warming up for their nightly party.

"And you?" I asked, finally. "What did you do today?"

"Not much. I'm afraid I don't have your particular talent for finding stuff out."

"If you could make that more sarcastic, you'd sound just like Simmons."

"Yeah, well, maybe you *should* take it easy."

"Then you'll be pleased to know that even as we sit here, I'm staying out of trouble. Going over to Lillian's." I finished my beer and put the bottle on the floor, where Lance promptly overturned it. We watched it roll toward the door. "What about you?"

"Movies. You want to come? Take your mind off all this. And you'd stay out of trouble at the same time." He paused. "Bring Lillian."

"What movie?"

"Whatever's playing."

"You didn't call to find out?"

"Nope."

"You're going to just any movie?"

"I'm going to sit in a dark theater and eat a bushel of popcorn and probably spill Coke on the floor. With luck, the good guy will get the bad guy. And the bad guy will get creamed." His eyes watched mine. "Wanna come?"

"Another time."

He got up and stretched, then hauled me out of my chair and wrapped his arms around me for a long, long time. "I miss you," he said. "You know that?"

I watched him leave, the dogs sitting one on either side of me as he backed the truck out of the clearing. With Will gone,

I tried to push away the inescapable fact that Tim Clayson still hadn't called. A little prickle of worry surfaced. I decided it was ridiculous. My brain was as overheated as my face.

I headed for the kitchen. There were cans of soup and an unopened box of sesame crackers. The refrigerator revealed some cheese, greenish along the edges. I cut off the moldy spots and stuffed it into my mouth as I searched for other possibilities. A modern TV dinner, lowfat and complete with chicken medallions and linguini was the best the freezer had to offer. I nuked it and it wasn't too bad. It just wasn't enough. I was eyeing a can of tomato soup for dessert when the phone rang.

Lillian was calling to report that a nice young man was camped in front of her house in an unmarked car. She'd tried to get him to come in, but he'd said no. I had a picture of the cop sitting in my aunt's living room, politely eating her snacks and trying not to get grease on her delicate brocade chair. No wonder he preferred his car. We chatted a bit. I offered to come over. Mentioned the laundry. She laughed, said okay. But she sounded tired, the way I felt. Maybe tomorrow, I said. Doesn't matter, she said. Tomorrow'd be better, I said. Okay, she said. Get some sleep. I love you. We hung up.

I returned to the porch and sat watching night fall. The dogs clumped to the floor beside me. Outside the crickets cranked up. After a few minutes, I got up for a magazine, turned on the light, and sat back down. It was glossy and smelly and insincere. Had I once really read these things? Odd, how they now so clearly had nothing to do with my life. Or maybe anybody's life. I slung it onto the table. A perfume sample fell out, its stench reaching through the plastic. I picked it up with two fingers and carried it to the garbage. Molecules of patchouli or ambergris or something sped through the air. I sneezed. Then again. The stuff was virulent.

Suddenly, I touched my belt. No pager. There'd been no pager when I'd changed clothes an hour ago. Racing upstairs, I pawed through the laundry to make sure. Not there. It probably fell off in the booth at the Lido Beach Inn. Back downstairs, I called the bar and got a busy signal. Tomorrow, I'd stop by to retrieve it.

Standing at the desk, I dialed Mitch's home number, listened to it ring three times, then hung up. I stared at the phone. Was I already awash in expectations? It rang.

"I have caller ID, you know."

"Figures. You also have voice mail. But that you don't check." God, had I said that? "Sorry, that was horribly snotty. I didn't mean to say that."

But he was laughing. "Things have been utterly crazy today."

"That comes of building a real estate empire," I said.

He hadn't heard me. That was because he was talking to someone in the room. Then he was back. "Eve? Dora's here, helping with a contract." Another ring. I heard his secretary talking again. "You okay?"

"Yes, fine."

"Lillian?"

"She's home and she's tired. Doesn't want me there. Weller found an off-duty cop to sit in front of her house for a few nights."

"Good. Look, I have to finish this up. But it shouldn't take that much longer. Have you eaten?"

"Afraid so. It was frozen and came in a little box."

"Got another one?" I heard his secretary ask him something. "Hold on a sec," he said. Dead air.

I thought about last night, the newness of his body, the excitement, my disordered feelings. The safety of being with him. So much had happened since then. So much to catch him up on. Or not. Maybe we'd just go back to bed.

Then, as I waited, all of the random floating images that I'd been trying not to let creep back into my conscious mind flooded back. Front and center, jumping up and down. Demanding to be explained. Images and words and theories. The flames eating Lillian's dock, Lauren's missing gun, Jenny's long blond hair, blood on stones. The Arundel Marine van.

Why hadn't Tim Clayson called? It was nearly dark. I listened to a few more seconds of silence, then hung up. Cradling the phone between my shoulder and ear, I called the Permit Application Center. A recording told me the center's hours. I hung up and checked the phone directory, my finger roving down the columns. I found the number I'd just called. I dialed directory assistance.

"What name?" said a machine voice. "What city?"

"Annapolis. I know you're there listening to me, Operator. Please come on the line."

"What name?" said the machine again. "What city?"

I sat quietly. Then there was a click and a female voice, angry at being outed, asked through grated teeth what I wanted. A minute later I thanked her and hung up. She had one number— the same one I had. The phone rang.

"Sorry," Mitch said. "Give me an hour. Hour and a half outside. Maybe not even that."

"Mitch, one thing before you come."

"What?"

"Well, there's something that you..."

"That I should know?" I sucked in my breath. "This have anything to do with why Dick Hubbard called to thank me for suggesting you hire him to get permits to rebuild Ray's house?"

"He called you?"

"Yes." I couldn't think of anything to say that wouldn't get me in deeper. "Eve?"

"I promise to explain. Really."

More itchy silence. "Okay. Later."

I hung up and went out to sit on the porch steps. It was a wonderful hot night, a fat gibbous moon rising. The usual drone of civilization was absent. No planes or cars. The dogs scampered down the path to the beach. I whistled them back. Then the sound of the desk phone ringing cut through the night air. Tim Clayson. Zeke, happy for the game and determined to beat Lancelot inside, plowed past me. The ringing stopped.

I stumbled to the phone and hit *69, listening as Bell Atlantic informed me of the phone number and time and date. I wrote the number down. Not the Permit Application Center. Not Mitch. Not Lillian or Will or Simmons or anybody else I knew. Suddenly another thought swept through me. There was another possibility. My heart lurching, I pulled out the white pages. Oh, no. I sunk into the swivel chair. Then I dialed the number and listened to a busy signal. Twice more.

With a last glance at dejected dog eyes, I grabbed my handbag and headed for the car.

THIRTY-THREE

"JENNY? IT'S EVE." I rapped on the side door of the Jarvis house, then listened to a rustling sound. "Jenny? Are you there?"

The door opened and the girl stood silhouetted against the fluttering blue glow of the television, its sound turned low. Behind her, the mutt crept close, interested in me but not enough to make a big thing of it. She drew the door closed behind her. There were no cars parked behind the house.

"How come you knew to come?"

I explained, which took us off into the neutral land of telephone technology, giving us each time to get our bearings. For if I were surprised that there was no crisis in progress, she was apparently even more surprised to find me standing at her front door.

"Is Jimmy here?"

"He went to the mall with his friends."

"And your mother's at work?"

A nod. "My dad's out," she said. "He probably won't be home until way later."

I could picture Duck Jarvis glaring at me across the bar, his face reddened from beer and sun.

We were standing by the side door, the chain-link fence only feet away. Nearby, neighbor children were getting in their last few minutes of freedom before being called inside for the night. Somewhere, an outboard motor came to life, then cut out.

I looked around. "Why don't we go sit over there?" I pointed to the crumbling picnic table near the public beach. Halfway there, she turned, ran back to the house, and let out the dog. It followed at her heels, then found a place under the table.

"Jenny, why did you call me?"

"You told me to."

"I did and I'm glad you called, but did something happen that made you phone me tonight?"

She carefully crossed her arms and legs, four long sticks. At the end of each toe and finger was glimmery blue nail polish. I'd seen in the dim light near the house that she was wearing lipstick and a lurid shade of eyeshadow. I was dangerously close to sneezing from her perfume.

"Jenny?"

"You have a terrible sunburn," she said. "You're going to get wrinkles."

Not to mention cancer. "You are about the tenth person today to tell me that."

"How come you didn't put on sunblock? Like you're supposed to."

"I guess I just didn't think about it."

Clearly, there was no emergency here. I'd blown my fears for her family all out of proportion. Still, my nerve endings felt twitchy. The girl knew something. Maybe if I just took my time, let her trust me, maybe she'd tell me why she'd called.

We settled in to make small talk. Sounds came from the woods and the water as night folded its tent over us. I wondered about her relationship with Lauren. Had it been more about nail polish than marine biology? This conversation, like the one the other afternoon, was oddly companionable. Maybe, sick of trying on her mother's makeup, she'd just wanted company.

"Is Will your boyfriend now?" she asked.

"He's my friend."

"Lauren liked Will a lot," she said.

"What about you?"

She nodded. "Yes. Though my dad doesn't." She didn't explain and I didn't ask.

I let the silence ride, then glanced at the girl. She'd taken the first step by phoning and now she was waiting for me to ask her what I wanted to know.

"Jenny," I said, "Did Lauren ever call the police about anything other than the noise from your father's Jet Ski?" She kicked at the sand and the dog scuttled away in surprise. "Jenny?"

She took her time, then nodded. "She called because my dad hit my mom."

"Did the police come?"

"My uncle Tony came."

"What happened then?"

"My uncle Tony told my dad he'd better stop it or he'd have to tell." Her voice was matter-of-fact, just reporting the news.

"But he didn't report him?"

She shook her head. I shouldn't have been shocked, but I was. The problem was so common that there was a program to help abused women who were afraid to call the police—afraid because the police were often family or friends who covered up for the abuser. I thought about my conversation in the convenience store. The firefighter had known that Duck Jarvis hit his wife, but had been unwilling to say so. Alcohol was no longer the pink elephant in the living room. The abuse that went with it was.

"Jenny, is this why your dad hated Lauren? Because he was afraid that she would tell what he did to your mom?"

She nodded. "He only did it a couple of times."

"And this is why you would never talk to Detective Simmons?"

She looked at me strangely, then shook her head, vigorously back and forth. It wasn't? I made myself sit still, while she wiggled and kicked the legs of the table. Each kick went through me with a thud.

"My dad'll kill me if he finds out I'm talking to you," she said.

"Did he tell you not to?"

"Uh-huh."

"Well, he's not here now." I inhaled her perfume, saw her gunky blue eyelids. She was thinking, sizing me up, deciding if she could trust me.

"Okay," she said.

From the main road came the drone of a car engine. The girl stiffened. We listened as the hum faded some. She relaxed. I decided to press a little more. But there *was* a car was coming down the road. She heard it, too. She stood up.

"Jenny?" She turned back to me. For the first time, I saw that the firewall separating her feelings into dangerous and benign was in danger of cracking. "Jenny, a little while ago you called my home phone number?" She nodded. "And you got my answering machine and so you hung up? Is that right?" Second nod. "Did you then try calling my pager? Is that why your phone was busy when I tried to call you back?"

"Uh-huh. But I didn't know how to do it right at first. I mean, call your pager. So I did it a lot of times."

Suddenly, I could almost feel the rough boards of the Fort Smallwood pier as I scrambled to my feet and tried to get out of the way as Estelle hauled in the thrashing blue crab. My pager would have lain forgotten in the sun, baking on the pier, where it fell off my belt. Until someone picked it up. Someone who was now screening my calls. Someone who had seen his home number flash again and again on the pager. Duck Jarvis knew his daughter had called me. My heart hammered.

"Jenny, tell me quickly, did something happen on the Fourth of July?"

"I saw my dad go after Lauren."

"What? Why do you say that? Did you see them together?"

"No, but I saw him leave the carnival. In the same direction as Lauren. It was before the fireworks started. After he got mad and yelled at me. He was real mad that my mom and I both talked to her. After he told us not to. He was real mad at her, too."

I could feel the hairs on my arms rise. She was not just afraid that her father had followed Lauren, she was afraid he'd *killed* her.

"Jenny, listen to me." She didn't look up. I didn't know if she heard. "Your father didn't kill Lauren. Do you hear me?" A barely visible nod. "And the police know that. Jenny?" Now she was staring at the road. I couldn't see her face. "Jenny?"

"What?"

"Did you see something else that night? The night of the fireworks? Did you see someone have a fight with Lauren?"

She leaned down and patted the dog. "I followed my dad

but then it was so dark that he kind of got lost so I just kept going but I couldn't really see." I could hardly hear her.

"Where was your mother?"

She looked up, surprised. "At the fireworks. With my brother."

"Oh. You couldn't see...well, did you hear something in the dark? People talking maybe?"

She was shaking her head. "I didn't hear nothing. I just kept going and going. The path would light up when the fireworks exploded. But there wasn't anyone around. But I..."

I held my breath. Behind the house, Duck Jarvis's car pulled to a stop. She saw it, too. "What? Jenny?"

She straightened up. "I found a gun. It was in the grass."

"By my aunt's dock?" She nodded. "You have it?"

This time she shook her head. "But I know where it is."

DUCK JARVIS wasn't as drunk as he might have been. But his mood wasn't any too benevolent. He walked toward his house, but then he saw us. Before he reached the picnic table, the girl took off running along the water, the dog slogging along behind her in the darkness. I watched helplessly as he lumbered a few feet after her, bellowing for her to come back. Head down, she did.

"Look at me," he said. She lifted up her head. "You look like a little whore. With all that stuff on. Go wipe it off your face. And get rid of that stink, too."

She marched toward the house, small and defeated.

"That's what Lauren DeWitt did," Duck was saying. "Gave her all those stupid magazines and makeup stuff. Put ideas in her head."

"She thought you killed Lauren."

He froze. Around us, crickets were beginning the night's concert, oblivious to human problems.

"She just told me. The other night, she saw you leave the carnival before the fireworks began. She knew you were angry at Lauren and thought you followed her along the water."

"I didn't kill nobody. Cops know it."

"And I know it." This brought him up short in the dark, his

hostility momentarily forgotten. "I think you hit your wife sometimes, but so far you haven't killed anyone."

His face changed and I wished I'd left it alone. For the girl's sake. I glanced toward the small houses lining the waterfront. With luck someone in Knapp's Point had the TV off and was watching or listening.

"Look, you need to go in and straighten things out with her. Tell her where you were." I could hear my voice, both angry and pleading. "And tell her that Detective Simmons knows this. You also need to give me back my pager."

I wasn't prepared for what came next. This half-drunk bull of a man shook his head and backed off, his face changing from belligerent to puzzled. Pager? No, he didn't have my pager. What made me say that? For some reason only he knew, this accusation cut deeper than his daughter's fear that he was a murderer.

"At Fort Smallwood," I said. "I must have dropped it on the dock. You didn't pick it up?"

More violent head shaking. But if he didn't have it, who did? A piercing cold thought fluttered through my mind. Had Tim Clayson tried to page me? And if so, who knew this? I let my mind run down the places I'd been this afternoon.

Then I knew. I felt the bump as the waiter outside Damien's sideswiped me as he lurched under his heavy tray. I heard him apologize. I saw Dick Hubbard watching from the patio outside the bar, then motioning the waiter to him.

Dick Hubbard. With his wad of bills. His deals and charm. His airtight alibi.

A slight breeze came off the water, bringing with it the smell of summer, a fragrance so full of pleasure that it made me gasp. Instead I sneezed, chills tearing through my body despite the night's heat. And a buried truth, so primitive it wouldn't be denied, struggled into words. There *was* something else. I glanced at Duck Jarvis. No, he hadn't killed Lauren. But I knew who had. And because of me, someone was in danger.

THIRTY-FOUR

THE WOODS ON either side of the long drive down to my cottage at Weller's Creek crackled from plants and trees too long without water. It was momentarily dark, the moon having gone behind a hazy cloud. Did this mean rain? Probably not.

I'd turned off my headlights as soon as I'd left Lido Beach Road. Then I felt my right tire leave the road. I corrected, sending the car swerving off to the other side. Damn. Even if my insides hadn't been a stew of fear and dread, driving in the dark was impossible. Brake. Gas again. Just a little. Creep forward. Stop. The car window was down. I listened. Nothing. Just the cricket chorus in full symphonic production.

I crept along, trying not to amplify my fears. Once I thought I saw headlights in my rearview mirror, something turning off Lido Beach Road after me. I pulled over. Nothing. Careful. Creep forward. Brake slightly as the road curved a bit. On my right, a quarter mile along, Will's bungalow came into view. His truck wasn't there. Just the usual creepy glow from a grow lamp throwing purple light into the darkness.

I moved forward, my nerve endings ragged. The moon came out from behind the hazy cloud briefly, then disappeared again. My cottage took shape in front of me. And in the near dark, I could feel more than see the nearby cove, with its view of Weller's Creek. I drifted into the clearing, put the car in gear, and killed the engine. No one here. The dogs barked. I'd forgotten to turn on the porch light.

Once inside, I ran to the telephone. Twice the red light blinked. I pushed the play button.

"Eve, this is Tim. Tim Clayson. At the Permit Application Center." His voice was excited, breathless. "You are not going to believe what I've found. I'll try your pager. Here's my direct number if you get this." I pushed the button again. "Eve, Tim again, uh, since I can't reach you, I think, I'll uh, maybe I'll just come by your house.''

My heart pitched. Then a noise came from somewhere. An engine. I flipped off the answering machine. Again the noise. Then nothing. Quickly, I dialed the number Tim Clayson had left. No answer. I dialed 911. The engine noise was back and getting louder. I dropped the phone.

"Come on, Zeke. Lance. Come.''

The dogs ran out to play in the dry pine needles. I looked around the yard. Whatever I'd just heard was coming down the road. With luck it would be Tim Clayson. But maybe it wasn't. I ran by the outdoor shower Will had built for me and headed for the back of the house. Then I stopped, leaning against the cedar shakes, listening. Nothing for a second. I whistled. Both dogs came running. Silently, I got down on the ground with them, arms around both. Their panting pulsed through my body, as if I were panting myself. I waited. The car kept on coming.

With hand signals, I told both to stay down. Incredibly, they did, liquid dog eyes puzzled but not unhappy with this exciting new game. Above us the moon had fled its hazy cloud. The engine noise was closer now. I edged around the back of the house, trying to see the clearing without being seen. As I watched, a car pulled in alongside mine.

Thank God. I ran out to the clearing as Tim Clayson got out of his car. He started when he saw me.

"Tim, it's Eve, come on. I got your message. But there is no time now to talk. You'll just have to trust me.''

"You won't believe what I've found.''

"I would. But not now. Listen.'' We listened. Another engine droned in the distance, taking the gravel road faster than it should. "Come on. Just leave your car.'' He hesitated and I grabbed him and pulled him back around the house. The dogs got up. I put my hand on Zeke's collar and hoped like hell he liked this guy. Tim opened his mouth again. "Later,'' I said.

The car was moving fast. We needed to go somewhere. Otherwise, well, I didn't want to think. Once someone has killed...I again shook off the thought and looked around. If we ran for the cove and water, there was no way out. And the stinging nettles. My skin crawled. We'd have to go through the shadowy forest that lay behind my house. A forest full of vines and undergrowth, but it was the only way.

"Come on." I was whispering now. "Quickly. Follow me. We'll have to chance it."

We headed out in the near dark, stumbling and tripping. The dogs followed, crashing into the brush. The noise was going to give us away. We stopped. I put my hand on Tim Clayson's shoulder. We listened. The car was closer. Near Will's bungalow.

"Keep going. Keep going." We turned and ran deeper, the dogs ahead of us this time. I could feel twigs scratching my face and arms and legs. Then Tim was down. He groaned.

"You okay?"

"Uh. Yeah."

The dogs came back to see what had happened to us and their fine game. I pushed them down by us, behind a fallen and rotting tree. Dry leaves crackled.

"We're making too much noise. We'll have to stay here."

"Look," he said. "You've got to tell me..."

I shushed him. The car was getting closer. Zeke stuck his wet nose on my neck, his hunting instincts aroused, waiting for permission to get whatever was out there. Lights spun around the clearing and died.

"Keep down very low. And quiet."

Every twig made noise. And every noise scared me. I could feel the perspiration on the back of Tim Clayson's shirt, from heat and fear. Zeke leaned against me, making me warmer. As the moon shone, we could see the clearing.

From our bed of twigs and vines and dry leaves, we watched as Doreen and John Battles got out of their car. She towered over him. I'd forgotten how tall she was. Or maybe how small he was. Her face was steely. Beside me, Tim breathed in when he saw the zoning analyst.

"What's he doing here?" he whispered. "And his wife? How'd they know to come here? Are they after me?"

I squeezed his shoulder and whispered directly into his ear. "Us. After us. Long story. But they know you paged me. And

I think they know that you found proof that Lauren DeWitt had discovered that John Battles was falsifying documents.''

I heard him suck air. ''You mean...you think...'' His mind leaped the chasm and the full implication of what was happening settled over him. ''And you think they killed Lauren DeWitt? Because of what she knew?''

''Yes. One of them did, yes.'' I held on tight to him and the dogs, my muscles strained from not moving. ''I was afraid that if they didn't find you at your office, they'd look for you here next.''

Tim Clayson hardly breathed as he struggled to understand. How I knew all this no longer mattered. What mattered was how we were going to survive. We waited, sweating and afraid. I tried not to think, but it was impossible not to.

Doreen Battles and her husband were here just as surely as if I'd issued an invitation. Tim Clayson and I were the unhappy bait, cheese in the trap. And if the police didn't respond to my 911 call, cut short as it was, we were...well, I tried not to think what we were. It would take just a dry snap of a twig. A yip from a dog whose fur got accidentally pulled. I deepened my hold on both Zeke and Lance, praying that they'd remain calm enough to obey me. Tim moved slightly. I heard his intake of breath, then looked where he pointed.

John Battles was getting a tank of gasoline from the trunk of the car. Doreen was nowhere in sight. Then I heard the screen door slam shut. She came into view. In her hand was a gun.

''Gone. They're gone, but with the cars here they're not far,'' she said. ''Put that down, you moron. We have to find them first.'' She gestured at the oil can in his hand. ''Go down and check the cove.''

The zoning analyst set down the tank and pulled a flashlight out from somewhere and disappeared in the direction of the water. Doreen herself stood back in the clearing, looking up at the trees, then over the cottage. I remembered our first meeting at Thom's Landing Estates. She'd wanted to know what I'd paid for the Tilghman property.

I suddenly imagined her pouring gasoline over my precious cabin. So newly mine. But already filled with memories. First the cedar shakes, dry and old, would go. Then, as flames licked the rest to charcoal, the woods would catch. I felt rage flow over me, then fear that I could lose more than a house.

Doreen looked directly into the woods, as if she could see us. I felt Tim shiver. John Battles was back.

"Nothing down there."

"Then they're in the woods. In there." She pointed.

"This is a damn fool plan, Dorrie. A damn fool plan."

"Well, you got any better?" She stared at him. "No, I didn't think so. You never do have a plan, do you? Not when I married you and not now. So, you just leave it to me. I'll get us out of this." I saw him shake his head, as if he feared how many more lives that would cost. "Oh, you don't think so. Well, I've got some money."

"Dorrie, we need to give it up. We won't get away with this, too. Maybe they don't know. Maybe, if we just left and lay low for a while."

"You dummy, you said yourself that kid was snooping around at the office. And Dick Hubbard told me the Elliott woman knows something. That she made up some fool story in order to get information out of him earlier today."

Tim moved slightly, setting off a domino effect of crackling twigs. I hung tightly to the dogs, praying they'd stay still. Time expanded. My muscles ached. My heart hammered in my ears.

I couldn't hear John Battles's answer, but whatever it was, it surprised and angered her.

But what was her plan? To burn down the cottage with Tim Clayson and me in it, hoping that the woods would catch and obliterate everything? Then in the confusion, run for it? Probably something like that. It was desperate and it was crazy. And it wouldn't work. But before it didn't work, Tim and I might be dead or burned. I felt him breathing hard next to me.

John Battles was near the edge of the woods. He stood peering into the darkness. I could feel Zeke nervous under my touch. I wasn't going to be able to keep him here much longer.

"Get going," Doreen said. "They're definitely in there."

A car engine in the distance. John Battles turned to his wife.

"Come on, Dorrie. We've got to get out of here. Before it's too late."

"It's already too late. That girl is dead because of me, remember?"

The car came closer. Police, I prayed. Let it be the police. I listened harder. Oh, God, I knew that engine and it belonged to Will's truck. My fear turned me cold. Will was going to hear something and come down to investigate. Or he might just stop by for no reason, like he often did. Or go down to the water. One way or the other, he was going to walk right into this. There had to be a way to warn him. But if there was, I didn't know what it was. His truck stopped, the engine died. Please don't come down here. Please. I listened. Nothing. John Battles backed away. Where were the police?

"Go in there and roust them. Now." Doreen's voice was livid, hissing. "Or you'll end up like they're going to. I'm not giving up. You got that?"

Horrified, I watched as she focused the gun on her husband's back. He turned to her. Didn't he see? Then I realized he did. And that he no longer cared. He'd already given up. He walked toward her as she held the gun on him.

"No, Dorrie," he said. "Kill me if you like. But no, I've done enough. I've harmed enough people. I've stood by so..." She backed up as he walked toward her. Then they were out of our range of vision. A shot. John Battles' scream. The dogs panted, struggled. In the near distance, I heard sirens. And from the clearing, through the night air, came the lustrous, sick smell of gasoline.

The sirens came nearer, the dogs barked out of control as the police moved in. And in the woods, my nervous system was straining to keep it together. Tim Clayson, next to me, was sweaty and relieved.

The cruisers drew up, their lights burning the pine clearing into a dazzling milky stage set. I could see bulletproof vests, rifles drawn. Simmons, his face intense. I could see Doreen Battles, her tough glamour bizarre and out of place as she waited. Then her face collapsed, and she leaned over carefully to place the gun at her feet. Her hands flew up, and the fingers splayed, the fingernails polished, each tip shining black in the glare of lights.

I could hear the tires of the EMS van spitting gravel as it rushed into the clearing. Medics leaped out. I watched them stabilize John Battles and lash him to a stretcher to take him somewhere for doctors to repair the hole his wife had opened in his chest. The van left in a billow of dust. Would it ever rain? Would we swallow dust forever?

I slumped again on the forest floor, my hand holding Zeke's collar, watching through shocked eyes as things unfolded, my heartbeats crushing my chest. Nearby, Tim Clayson quivered, excited, his budding journalistic instincts on the prowl now that the danger was over.

THIRTY-FIVE

"I DON'T GET IT," said Will. "How did you know it was that woman?"

We were sitting in the living room of my cottage. The same cottage that just hours ago I feared might be gone forever. Taking Tim Clayson and me with it. Mitch slouched on the couch. Will sat upright, alert in Ray Tilghman's old chair by the fireplace. He was the one with the questions. But then, Lauren had been his friend. Glancing at him, I saw that tonight's events had been the epilogue he'd been waiting for.

"Eve?" I dragged myself out of my daze and looked at Will. "How did you know it was Doreen Battles?"

Were we still on that? I felt like I'd been explaining the unexplainable for hours. My mind suddenly twitched. What would have happened had the police not...I glanced at Mitch, who looked back at me. I knew he was thinking the same thing.

"I'd like to know that, too," he said. Odd, like an echo in my mind. Then I realized that he merely wanted an answer to Will's question. I rocked a bit, the gasoline fumes still potent. "How did you know it was Doreen? Why not her husband?"

"Perfume." It seemed so clear now, so utterly apparent I could hardly believe I'd missed it for so long. I stopped rocking. "The few times I met her she had practically bathed in it." I turned to face Mitch directly. "And last night..." Had it been only last night? "Last night, at Cantler's. When she was in the car with Dick Hubbard? The perfume was so strong I smelled it when she opened the car door." He stared, unblinking. "Then today, that same smell was in the bathroom at Damien's. You remember I told you that Dick Hubbard had just had a visit from some woman?"

"What? No. I don't remember. You didn't tell me."

Oh. I looked from one to the other, grateful for their presence. But it was getting harder and harder to remember what I'd told Simmons and what I'd told them.

I explained about the bartender. "The woman who came to see Hubbard was obviously Doreen Battles. She must have used the ladies' room, too. It reeked of her perfume. Except at the time, I didn't realize it was hers. Although it made me sneeze, I didn't really think about it." Will glanced at Mitch. "I saw that. And for what it's worth, Simmons looked at me the same way when I told him."

Zeke touched my hand with a cold nose, dog eyes saying he believed absolutely everything. Even if no one else much did.

"Let me see if I've got this straight," Simmons had said. "You think that Doreen Battles killed Lauren DeWitt because she wore perfume?"

"Come on, Simmons, that's not what I said. I said that there were a whole lot of things which sort of came together in my head. The perfume thing was just one of them."

As most police vehicles disappeared from the clearing, Simmons had led Tim Clayson and me inside to answer questions. I was vaguely aware that Will was hosing down the steps and the side of the porch where Doreen had thrown gasoline. If anything, it made the smell worse, dispersing it into the air. When Mitch had arrived I didn't know.

It had taken me a few minutes to tell the detective what had just happened. He'd taken a few notes, but mostly he listened, interrupting to ask questions that occurred to him. Then he returned to Lauren's murder. Tim Clayson looked like he wished he had a notebook himself.

"You want to tell me how you think the victim was killed?" Simmons said.

I tried to focus. "Okay. The little girl, Jenny Jarvis? Duck Jarvis's daughter?" He nodded. "She told me that she saw her father, who was angry at her and her mother for talking to Lauren, which Duck had forbidden..." Tim Clayson looked confused here but Simmons raised his hand as soon as the intern opened his mouth. "Jenny knew, of course, that her father and Lauren feuded all the time. And she'd seen her father be violent to her mother." Here I stopped, wondering if this were the time to bring up Tony Jarvis's part in this. His refusal to report his brother's abuse.

"Feuded all the time."

I looked up from my hands. Simmons was actually prompting me. Later I'd tell him about Tony Jarvis. First, there was Lauren's murder.

"Jenny knew her father could be violent, so she was afraid he might do something to Lauren. She went after him. I guess to try to stop him," I said. "But in the dark, she didn't see where he went. She told me she walked along the Magothy—it's mostly just grass and dirt. It was dark except for the moments when the fireworks went up."

"What did she see?"

"Nothing apparently. Nor did she hear anything. It's what she found." He leaned in. Tim Clayson stared. "She found Lauren's gun in the grass not far from my aunt's dock. And because she was afraid that her father might have done something to Lauren, she took it and hid it. And didn't tell you. Or anyone."

If he was interested to know why Jenny had decided to tell me, he kept to it himself. It was a question I didn't know the answer to anyway.

"She mention where she put it? The gun?"

"Someplace near that little shed at the entrance to the beach. You'll have to have her show you."

Silence. He had waited for me to continue. I studied the sisal rug under my feet, replaying the familiar scene on July Fourth. The players said their lines. Made their entrances and exits. This time, however, what took place offstage was revealed. I looked up.

"Simmons, here's what I think happened. After talking with Jenny and Josie Jarvis, Lauren left to meet Will—as they had planned—on Lillian's dock. Doreen Battles must have seen her leave and known she was meeting him since the night before she was standing right beside Will and Lauren at the community center." I remembered the detective had been there. "You saw them. I'll bet she overheard their plans." He nodded. "By July Fourth, was afraid that Lauren was closing in on John Battles's involvement in some scheme making false documents for Dick Hubbard. And so she must have been very nervous that Lauren would find out more.''

Tim Clayson looked totally confused. ''Who's Dick Hubbard?''

Simmons ignored him. ''And?''

''Well, she probably went to confront Lauren on Lillian's dock. Before Will could get there. Who knows what she planned to do. Maybe it wasn't premeditated. Or maybe it was. You'll have to ask her. But somehow things must have gone wrong and there must have been a fight. Since Lauren was carrying a gun for protection, she may have tried to use it. And it somehow got thrown into the grass where Jenny found it.''

He waited for as long as he could manage. Then impatience took over. ''And?''

''And nothing. You asked me what I think happened and I'm telling you. I think there was a fight. Doreen went for her throat. Lauren lost her balance, fell, and hit her head. Doreen went back to the carnival. Nobody saw her. And she was long gone by the time Will reached Lillian's dock where he was supposed to meet Lauren. He said he was probably half an hour late because of the traffic. He didn't see her body in the dark, since she'd fallen down below the dock. So he left to look for her. But nobody had seen her. And then somehow a cigarette butt that those kids dropped earlier must have ignited my aunt's dock.''

I stopped. He knew the rest. Tim Clayson opened and closed his mouth. Simmons turned to him.

''What is your part in this?''

The intern did a good job of explaining John Battles's manufacture of bogus documents. I listened as he gave Simmons the facts, simply and powerfully. He did a less impressive job of leaving me out of it. The detective, after a reproachful look in my direction, said nothing.

The smell of gasoline flowed over me again and I became aware of Will and Mitch both looking at me. Waiting.

''I think Dick Hubbard is somehow at the bottom of this. Probably paying John Battles for his work. Though I don't know all the details." I leaned over to brush my hand over Zeke's dark head. "It's pretty clear that Doreen and John Battles were living above their means. After all, she doesn't work and he's a bureaucrat and they're living in a half-million-dollar executive house in Thom's Landing Estates."

Outside, there were yells. Then it grew quiet.

"From what Tim said he found," I said, "John Battles had been tampering with plats and other documents for a couple of years. And lying in hearings. Tim found nearly a dozen instances in just a few hours of looking through records."

"Vince Darner's site on Weller's Creek?"

"Yes. Be interesting to know if Vince Darner knew what Hubbard and John Battles were up to. My guess is that he did."

Mitch nodded. "You probably don't know this yet, since you've been busy..." His eyes crinkled. "Someone from the Department of the Environment must have leaked something about the buried oil tank at Knapp's Point to the media. It was on tonight's news. Norma Sprague is calling for Darner to withdraw from the Senate race."

"The Department of the Environment?" I asked. Mitch shrugged.

"Oh, I see."

Will wasn't listening to any of this. The Chesapeake Bay retriever had wandered over and was standing next to his chair, waiting to be touched. Will stroked the broad red face gently, then got up.

"I'm going now," he said. A moment of discomfort, a moment of silence as he looked at me, then at Mitch, then back at me. "You'll be okay?"

"Yes."

THIRTY-SIX

SEVENTEEN DAYS without rain. Crops stunted in the fields. At the edge of the clearing in front of the house, a small pine tree was turning rusty from the inside out. A sure sign of not enough water. By summer's end it would be dead in front of my eyes. A slow, parched, inoffensive vegetable death. I looked away.

I had awakened a few hours before, forgetting what made me afraid. From downstairs, I could hear the low murmur of voices. Smell the delicate, unhealthy smell of gasoline. Then I remembered.

I found Lillian and Mitch and the dogs in the kitchen, Mitch making coffee. The dogs were eating. It was safe, domestic. I hugged Lillian, then touched Mitch's shoulder. He turned, his hands full, his eyes warm.

"Morning."

"Morning." I looked at my aunt. She was wearing her pink suit. "When did you get here?"

"A few minutes ago." She pulled out a chair at my worn kitchen table. Lance finished eating and sat down by her, a solid, curly red statue. She patted him and he turned around to beam dog love at her.

"Are you okay?"

"Yes. You?" She nodded. Mitch handed me a mug of coffee. He was hiding his tiredness. I watched him pour cream and sugar in Lillian's coffee.

"How do you know Lillian takes that much sugar?" Then I remembered July Fourth. "Forget I asked."

He was like family. Pitching in, staying over, taking care of things. Last night, after everyone had left, we'd fallen into bed and instantly drifted into deadened sleep. Once during the night, I'd awakened briefly, to find his shoulder inches from my face. I'd gone back to sleep.

"How bad does the porch smell? Too bad to sit out there?"

"Not great. But we'll probably get used to it."

Five minutes later, we were settled on wicker chairs. The smell was a bit stronger but not unbearable. I glanced at my watch. Nine-thirty. "Simmons call?" Mitch shook his head.

Lillian put her mug down carefully on the coffee table, then moved it out of reach of Zeke's fluttery tail.

"It was on the early news. Doreen Battles confessed," she said. "I've been telling Mitch."

I looked at him. "Lauren's death happened pretty much as you thought," he said.

"John Battles?"

"He's alive. At Shock Trauma in Baltimore. Listed as critical."

I nodded. "Did they find Lauren's gun?"

"Behind the beach shed."

"Jenny Jarvis." They both nodded. I hoped that Simmons had been nice to her. Duck Jarvis, well, I didn't much care.

"By the way," Lillian said. "Something else." I waited. "I got a call from Duck this morning."

"You did?"

"He called to tell me that his son wanted to apologize."

I drank the rest of the coffee, hoping my uncaffeinated state was the reason that I didn't understand. "Apologize? For what?"

My aunt poked one long manicured forefinger into a thin patch of puffed hair and scratched hard. "His son is the one who threw the stone the other night. Through my sliding glass door."

Jimmy Jarvis? The horrible thirteen-year-old boy who wanted to be like his father? "Why?"

"Who knows, really." She accepted a refill from Mitch. "But Duck said that the boy apparently overheard him say some unprintable things about me. And so the boy felt his father was threatened. Then, the night before last he was prowling down on the riprap with his buddies. You know, ghoulish teenage boys loving the idea that someone died down there." She sipped coffee. "So, he picked up a stone and slung the thing through the glass and ran away."

"What are you going to do?"

"Nothing. Or rather, let the boy apologize."

"What I don't get is why Duck Jarvis called you up and told you about it."

"I think he's trying to do the right thing. Set a better example for the boy." She put her hand on my knee. "At least give him the benefit of the doubt. It was hard for him to make that call. I could tell. And he offered to pay for the door."

I nodded. "It's the alcohol," she said. "All his problems. So let's hope...let's just hope."

Nobody said anything more. No need. Alcohol had poisoned Lillian's life, too before she stopped drinking. She respected and cursed its hold on people. I thought of Tony Jarvis and suddenly felt undecided. Should I tell Simmons? I didn't know. Maybe tomorrow I'd know.

We sat for a few minutes. Each thinking our own thoughts. I hoped that Josie and Jenny were also the recipients of Duck's newfound courage. Lillian spoke.

"They said on the early news that Dick Hubbard is being questioned by the police about some, er, irregularities in the permit process." She looked over at me.

"Not irregularities, Lillian. It looks like he paid John Battles to create false documents for his clients in order to get building permits for environmentally sensitive land. Hubbard's been having an affair with Doreen for a while. Maybe for that very reason. She probably arranged it when she learned there was money involved. But then Lauren found out." Lillian glanced at Mitch to make sure I wasn't hallucinating. He nodded agreement. "It looks like one of the people who benefited was Vince Darner."

"Oh, that's another thing," Lillian said. "I don't know if you know this, but apparently someone at the Department of the Environment told a reporter about the underground oil tank on the Knapp's Point land." She smiled at me, then looked at Mitch, who was staring at the floor. Department of the Environment? I looked from one to the other, then decided I'd never know. "Vince's pulled his bid for the Senate seat. Which means Norma is in good shape."

But I was thinking about Charlotte Darner. She was going to be stuck with an angry, thwarted, arrogant husband whose political career was over before it began. Whose main business would probably go bankrupt. Who was contemptuous of her cheerful, down-to-earth disposition. Well, at least her land couldn't be sold. And maybe she'd find a way out, a way back to her Knapp's Point life. I watched as Zeke got up for a drink of water, then padded back to the porch.

"What will happen to Doreen Battles?" I asked.

"I guess that'll be up to the prosecutor," Mitch said. "And whether her husband lives or dies." He was silent.

I turned to Lillian. "And Carl Rainey?"

"What about him?"

"I don't know. It's just that..."

"He's still furious with everything," she said. "That's what Florence told me." She saw my raised eyebrows. "Yes, I went over there. Florence and I have been friends and neighbors for forty years and I didn't want...well, you know. Carl, I can live with."

I could tell she didn't like it much, but some things were the way they were. She got up and looked around for her handbag.

"Well, Dearhearts, I'm going to have my hair done. Then to the office," she said. After kissing both of us, she looked at me. "Laundry? Call me."

We hugged, then Mitch and I watched her Cadillac pull away. I collected coffee cups to take to the kitchen.

Saturday morning. A busy day for real estate agents. The day when people wanted to see houses. When agents made lists of possibilities for their clients, then drove them to eight, ten, perhaps a dozen places. Hard on the agent, hard on the client. And as the day wore on, with each house seen, the details blurred. By late afternoon, the client might remember an unexpected skylight or a tiny convenience in a kitchen. But the smell of a diaper, a counter the wrong height, ugly cabbage rose wallpaper in a foyer—the negative details would loom larger. Then came Sunday. And it would begin all over again. Or agents would descend into the routine tedium of open houses, waiting for people to show up.

Mitch picked up the phone on my desk. He looked back at me, then suddenly reached down to grab a pencil and write something. A pause, then he responded. Writing again, he pulled over Ray Tilghman's old swivel chair with his foot, and sat down.

I was filled with a strange, vacant feeling. I took a shower and washed my hair. What would it take to erase the smell of gasoline? I changed into jeans, far too hot for July, but the only thing clean in the drawer. My eyes smarted from not enough sleep and my bangs hung in wet strands. Mitch was off the phone. His eyes showed the deep strain of the night, even if his voice hadn't.

"You have any plans?"

"Not yet, but I imagine Simmons will think of something. Maybe I'll go into the office. Keep Lillian company." I shrugged. "And you heard her. I've got laundry. You?"

"A couple of appointments this afternoon."

"Oh."

I went out to the porch. Melancholy lingered in every corner of the house, swirling around me, pulling me into its suffocating spell. Mitch followed me out.

He took a breath, looked up at the silent fan, released his breath. Moments toiled by. He got up, turned the fan on, and sat back down. I looked at him through damp hair.

"Wait here," I said. "I need you to do something." He was standing up when I got back. I held out a pair of scissors and a comb. "Here. I'm desperate."

"No, Eve, no, I really can't." He shook his head. "No, Uh-huh. No."

"If you want me to be able to see you," I said, "then you can. Besides, it's just hair."

Above me the ceiling fan whipped the air, its rhythm uneven and lumbering. I sat down. Zeke whined, then wedged himself under my legs and around the chair rungs, as if in response to an approaching storm.

I felt Mitch's hand take the scissors from mine. I felt the comb go through my hair, then carve a hot line where my part should be. I felt his careful hands begin to separate stray pieces back where they belonged on either side. A cut of the scissors. A flutter of hair slipping past my eyes, falling over my shirt. Another cut.

Outside, high above the house, the cicada chorus began its climb, a full-voiced treble crescendo reaching for that rumored place where ears run blood and dogs go mad.